A FURY LIKE THUNDER
Dragons of Introvertia Book Three

By

James and Bit Barringer

ASIN B08LG4YVWH
ISBN 9798555835529

Cover design by Marshall Daley
@onetruehazard on Instagram

www.DragonsOfIntrovertia.com

Table of Contents

ONE

Cammie Ravenwood took a deep breath of the spring morning that greeted her as she stepped outside, arm in arm with Eza, leaving his house on the way to the royal palace. These mornings weren't chilly anymore now that the equinox had passed; soon she would be comfortable in short sleeves and the kind of swishy sundresses that she loved to wear when it was warm outside. Eza's hand slipped around her waist, and she smiled at him as they synchronized steps. She knew Eza was more in tune with nature than she was, but even Cammie couldn't help admiring the brilliant sunlight that poured down out of a stunning blue sky. For some reason the mornings back in Exclaimovia had never seemed this *breathtaking*. Maybe that tingle in her fingertips was Cammie beginning to feel the magic of nature after all...or maybe it was the boy with the captivating smile who was walking next to her. She snuck a glance at Eza, at his sandy-brown hair and green eyes, and couldn't help but grinning. Two days before, he'd asked her to court him, and she still wasn't over it. She hoped she never was.

"The queen said she wanted to talk about my theater company," Cammie said. "I wonder what she has in mind."

1

"I'm sure she has a bunch of good advice to share," observed Eza. "She was in Tranquility's best company for...six years, I think, before she met the king."

"I can't wait," Cammie answered with a gleeful smile.

"Well...you have to," Eza teased.

The one thing Cammie hadn't been expecting was for King Jazan and Queen Annaya to be outside the palace. In fact, they were down by the Rapidly Flowing River, holding hands like they were teenagers in love, with half a dozen royal guards nearby trying to pretend they weren't snooping. As Cammie and Eza approached, the king planted a gentle kiss on the queen's nose and the queen giggled. "Do you see the way she looks up at him?" Cammie asked dreamily. "That's true love. I want to look up at you that way, but you have to get taller than me first."

Eza laughed so hard he wheezed. "That was *so close* to being really romantic."

Cammie giggled. "Thanks."

The loud sound got the queen's attention, and she turned toward Cammie and Eza with a wide smile still on her face. "Cammaina," she said by way of greeting. "Thank you so much for coming. Please, follow us into the throne room. We have business to discuss."

"Business?" Cammie mouthed to Eza, who shrugged and smiled.

The throne room was a familiar location to Cammie,

who had been there with Eza perhaps half a dozen times, although usually under far more serious circumstances. The polished stone floors and walls, and the king's and queen's thrones situated three steps up from the ground floor, spoke of a room that was useful and regal. King Jazan and Queen Annaya did not ascend to their thrones, but rather stood facing Cammie and Eza. King Jazan offered a handshake to Eza and a hug to Cammie. She knew Introvertians were very reserved when it came to physical contact, and it made her grateful that both the king and queen were going out of their way to make her feel welcomed. "The queen and I have been talking," King Jazan began. "We were extremely impressed with your play, Cammaina. You have incredible talent, and your presence here in Introvertia is a gift."

Cammie gave a curtsy. "Thank you, Your Highness."

Queen Annaya spoke up. "That's why we would like to make you the first royally sponsored playwright in the kingdom."

Cammie's mind seized up and she smiled blankly. "I'm sorry?"

The queen laughed, putting her arms around her husband. "I told you she'd do that."

"You were right," he conceded.

"We want you to travel around Introvertia performing a play for anyone who wants to watch it," the queen explained. "All your expenses will be paid, and you'll perform for free in public squares and wherever you can find space."

"These are uncertain times," King Jazan added. "There's a threat of war with Exclaimovia, as you know, and we are still legally at war with Claira and Esteria. Introvertians are not people who do well with uncertainty. Being able to watch a play would boost morale and help our people understand that life is continuing on. The fact that you're from Exclaimovia is even better; it reminds your audience that peace is possible."

Cammie blinked in shock. "Y – b –"

"You'll pardon my court-mate," Eza said. "It's not often she's speechless. In fact, she usually has the opposite problem."

Cammie giggled and elbowed him. "That sounds WONDERFUL!" she shouted, not worrying about making the wrong impression on the king and queen. They knew her well enough by now, and they knew she was Exclaimovian; they got what they got. "Can we perform *The Ranger's Dilemma*?"

"I don't think that play is exactly the right tone," answered King Jazan apologetically. "I loved it and thought it was masterfully done, but at a time when our people are at war, I don't think a play where the main character decides *not* to serve in the army is the message we want to be sending."

"That's okay," Cammie said quickly. "I'll write a new play. When do you want us to leave?"

"You have two weeks left before your next term begins at Carnazon," said Queen Annaya. "If you could be leaving within three days, that would allow you a week of performances before you had to begin heading back. And, of course, if you were several days late for classes, I'm sure your professors would sympathize. I understand you've done quite a lot of private study yourselves due to how much class you've missed while on royal business."

"Three days is fine," Cammie said. "I'm sure I can write a play in that time, and Eza can memorize his lines."

"Very well," King Jazan nodded approvingly. "The queen and I are very excited for this, and we look forward to hearing stories when you return."

Again Cammie gave a curtsy. "Yes, Your Highness."

"You will see the royal treasurer on your way out," said the king. "We've budgeted twenty nayen per day for your expenses. Anything left at the end of your tour is yours to keep. Please, treat yourselves well."

Cammie was still unfamiliar with Introvertian money, but she saw Eza's eyes get huge and assumed the king had just named a substantial figure. "Thank you for your generosity," she said smoothly.

King Jazan opened his mouth to reply but was

interrupted by someone bursting into the throne room. "I'm sorry, sire," one of the royal guards said, "but he said it was urgent."

"Colonel Ennazar," King Jazan said in recognition. "Welcome. Please, have a seat."

"I'm afraid there is no time," said Aric Ennazar, his chin-length hair imperfectly combed as if he'd left his house in a hurry. He had briefly been head of magical instruction at Carnazon, something of a mentor to Cammie and Eza, before becoming oddly enamored with Introvertia's magical allies in the kingdom of Telravia. His obsession with Telravia had caused him to be passed up for a promotion, and since then, if Cammie could be really honest, he'd kind of given her the creeps.

Colonel Ennazar nodded briefly to Cammie and Eza, seeming not to wonder what they were doing in the throne room, and then turned his attention back to King Jazan. "Your Highness, I apologize for the manner of my entry, as well as for several of the other interactions we've had in the latter days. I understand that my manner has been...unbecoming of an Introvertian officer. I'm sure you would agree. As a result, I think the most expedient course of action is for me...to no longer be an Introvertian officer."

"Explain," said the king, looking intently into Ennazar's eyes.

"I have been thinking," said Ennazar, "about magic

and the pursuit of it. I am about the same age you are, Your Highness, at thirty-five years old, but whereas you were groomed from childhood for the job you're doing now, I was stifled. My magical abilities were not welcomed in this kingdom; I had to train them in secret, far away from here. When I joined the army, my commanding officers kept my ability hidden, at risk to themselves."

He stared at King Jazan, then continued. "When the prohibition on magic was lifted, I thought that my moment had finally arrived. I could use my magic to make Introvertia great in the way it had been great in the past. But...something was hollow. Introvertia has fallen far from the heights of magical excellence we enjoyed centuries ago, and we have many decades of hard work ahead of us before we can approach that level again."

"All growth is a gradual process," the king said. "No one ever achieved excellence overnight."

"But that's precisely it," Ennazar said, intensity in his eyes. "At the Battle of Denneval Plain, I communicated with Arianna, the leader of Telravia's Council of Seven, and I *felt* greatness. I *felt* that I could be a leader in that nation. And so...that's the decision I've reached. Your Highness, I resign my commission in the Introvertian army, effective immediately. I'm going to Telravia to take a seat on the Council of Seven."

"Are you insane?" blurted Cammie. "You told us

7

yourself that the only way to get a seat on the Council is to kill one of the Seven..."

"I've considered all of that," Ennazar assured her. "My plan is secure. I know which of the Seven is most vulnerable, and I know precisely how to take that seat. Don't fear for me, Cadet Ravenwood. The next time we meet, I will be on to bigger and better things."

"In that case, I grant your resignation," King Jazan said. "May you find the success you so obviously desire."

"Thank you, Your Highness. I assure you that I will use my seat on the Council of the Seven to work toward the good of Introvertia. We remain allies with Telravia, after all, and that alliance is to the mutual benefit of both nations."

And just like that, Ennazar was gone.

"Well," said Cammie, "good riddance to that guy."

Queen Annaya gave a slight smile. "His magical expertise will be a significant loss to the kingdom. However, you'll find when you run a theater company is that talent is not the most important thing. A person could have all the talent in the world, but if they don't believe in your group and what you stand for and the way you want to do things, their presence will be harmful, not helpful."

"Yes, Your Highness."

King Jazan was shaking his head. "This is the whole

reason we gave up magic in the first place. What can be done about people who believe the pursuit of power is all that matters in life?"

"Stay the course, my love," Queen Annaya said gently. "We are a nation of good-hearted people, and for every Ennazar, there will be a thousand who use magic to help their fellow Introvertians."

"But could one Ennazar do more damage than a thousand with good hearts?"

"I think," said the queen, "that if there are other Ennazars, we encourage them to follow the example of this one. We tell them Introvertia is not the place for people like them, and we encourage them to go find those who think like them. Introvertia stands for something beautiful and bright, my love. We have to jealously guard that."

King Jazan smiled. "You're correct, my love, as you always are. And one way we will win is by encouraging art and beauty, just like we are with Cammaina and Ezalen here. But come now, we've kept them long enough with matters that aren't their burden to bear. You're dismissed, Cadets."

Eza led Cammie back out into the morning sunlight. Cammie still felt dazed. "I can't believe Colonel Ennazar just...left Introvertia like that."

"I wonder what's going to happen to him," Eza mused.

"Do you seriously think he can kill one of the Seven and take their place?"

"I think the one advantage he has is that they have no clue who he is. I bet everyone on the Council has a long list of enemies who they keep eyes on at all times. It's got to be really hard to kill them because they're always expecting it. They've never heard of Ennazar, though. He's just going to stroll his way up there, murder someone who never sees it coming, and pat himself on the back."

"Until the next person murders him."

"Yeah." Eza took Cammie's hand. "Now, if I'm not mistaken, you have a play to write."

"I can't write without my inspiration," Cammie told him.

"Aww," Eza said, turning red. "That's really sweet of you."

"Well, you *were* the one who gave me the idea for *The Ranger's Dilemma.*"

"I gave you one line," Eza protested with a smile. "On accident."

"That's all it takes," Cammie said with a flourish. "Inspiration is just having your eyes and ears open at the right moment."

"How about having your mouth open? I could really do with some breakfast. There's a place on Fallingwind Avenue that Shanna keeps raving about. If we're going to be in a traveling theater company, we're going to be eating in restaurants a lot."

"Hmm," Cammie told him playfully. "I think I could get used to that. Lead the way."

Cammie had to admit that the Cherry Blossom Restaurant was pretty good – at least for Introvertian food. She didn't want to tell Eza, but she was slowly getting used to the more nuanced flavors and delicate textures of Introvertian cuisine, just the way she was slowly getting used to the quieter volume of Tranquility. That reminded her of a talk she'd had a long time ago with old Mr. Cappel, the owner of Eza's favorite bookstore, before she and Eza had first gone off on their adventure to Exclaimovia.

Mr. Cappel had asked whether she liked loud noises and interrupting people because they truly made her happy or whether because, as an Exclaimovian, she'd been raised to think those things were *supposed* to make her happy. Since then, she'd wrestled with that question: *Who is Cammie Ravenwood?* How much of her personality – what she thought of as *her* – was just sixteen years of habit from growing up in a loud place, and how much was authentically Cammie? Underneath it all, was she Exclaimovian or Introvertian – or some kind of hybrid?

Cammie wasn't the only one puzzling through those questions. So was Denavi Kiresti. Denavi had grown up in the nation of Claira, to Introvertia's northeast, and had been the lone survivor of a battle between her military company and an Introvertian expedition. Denavi had been brought back to Introvertia, questioned, and then released to go live with Eza, his father, and Cammie, free to start her life completely over and live however she wanted. The fascinating thing about Denavi, Cammie thought, was that Denavi totally rejected the Noble Enlightened Warrior culture of Claira – she'd turned her back on the entire way she'd been brought up. She didn't want to be a fighter, and she welcomed the chance to eject all her cultural habits and start a brand new life. She was discovering, day by day, who she was and who she wanted to be.

Cammie had the same choice, of course, but for some reason it felt more complicated to her. Eza loved her just the way she was – but what if she ended up becoming the wrong kind of person for him? Denavi could choose to be *anybody* – but if Cammie made the wrong choice, she might lose Eza forever...

"You're quiet," Eza said, his voice breaking into her thoughts.

"Maybe I'm just practicing," Cammie answered unconvincingly. "Fitting in as an Introvertian, I mean."

"Yeah...that's not a thing you do."

Cammie heaved a sigh. "How do you know me so well?"

"I study you," Eza said, his smile reaching all the way

to his green eyes. "I love watching you. I love the faces you make and the things you say. I watch what happens when you're happy and when you're upset. And I love all of it."

"Would you love me if I was different?" she asked.

"What do you mean?" Eza replied.

Sometimes Cammie felt like all the thoughts in her head were one big jumble, and she couldn't possibly get them out one word at a time. Eza must have seen the discomfort on her face, because he slid his chair next to hers and put his arm on her back. Cammie leaned her head on his shoulder. "It sounds really stupid."

"Anything that worries you isn't stupid," Eza assured her. "Now out with it."

"I just...I'm figuring out what it means for me to live here in Introvertia, right? And what if I change in a way that you don't like? You like me loud, so what if I get too quiet, or what if I stop doing the other things you like?"

Eza gently scratched her back with his fingertips. "You're worried I'll wake up one day and decide I don't love you anymore?"

"Yeah," Cammie said softly. "I never thought of it like that, but yeah."

"I worry about the same thing, about you deciding you don't want to be with me anymore," Eza told her. "I'll tell you what I tell myself. When we agreed to court, we made a promise to each other, and I don't break my

13

promises. Both of us are going to change a lot. We're young, and people change as they get older. Maybe we'll change in ways that make it easier for us to get along with each other. Maybe we'll go the other direction. But my promise to you is that I'm going to love you with everything inside me no matter what. If it's fun and easy, I'm going to enjoy it. If it's hard, I'm going to work at it, because Ezalen Skywing doesn't know how to be defeated." He squeezed Cammie's shoulder. "Either way you're going to get cherished, because nothing makes me happier than seeing you smile."

Cammie wriggled out of his grip. "I have to write all that down. I think you just gave me the ending to our next play."

She leaned down to grab her notebook from her pack and Eza tickled her sides. "So that's how it's going to be?" he teased. "Everything I say could end up in a script?"

Cammie finally squirmed away from him, desperately trying to hold in her giggles so she didn't disrupt the other diners. "It's a good thing," she reasoned. "Once we get married, I'll need to be writing new plays regularly to help support us. If you keep giving me ideas...I mean, that's just you doing your part, right?"

"Hmmm," Eza said, pretending to be deep in thought. "You make an excellent point."

For the next minute, the only sound was the scribble of Cammie's pencil on paper and the quiet conversations of the other patrons, until at last Cammie looked up. "Do you think we can go home so I can write there?" Eza smirked. "Why? Is there too much background noise here?"

Cammie tried to glare back at him, but the glare dissolved into a smile.

"For the love of loud noises," Eza said, mystified. "There's too much sound. You can't concentrate and you need it quiet."

"Don't you dare rub this in," Cammie warned him. "If you even open your mouth I swear I will tickle you until you can't breathe to beg for mercy."

Eza smiled mischievously at her.

"STOP RUBBING IT IN WITH YOUR EYES," Cammie hissed in the loudest whisper she could manage. "I'M WARNING YOU, EZA."

"I'm not rubbing anything in," he said unconvincingly. "I just finished saying I would love you no matter what happened. I'm just...surprised that the loudest person I know suddenly needs silence."

Very calmly Cammie placed her notebook and pencil back in her pack. "I would recommend you start running right now."

Eza was already gone.

15

A Fury Like Thunder

TWO

A few hours later Cammie was seated on one end of the couch with her bare feet in Eza's lap, receiving one of his customary massages, which was his apology for teasing her about wanting silence. He knew that was a really insensitive thing for him to say – he'd even kept going after she'd asked him to stop – and he'd felt bad about it as soon as the words had gone out of his mouth. He had only been joking, and he knew that Cammie knew it, and she'd reassured him repeatedly that she was only teasing him back and not really upset, but he was disappointed with himself anyway. The more he massaged her, and the more she smiled, the worse he felt – he should have known better than to say something so stupid and rude when she was already struggling with how best to fit in with her new home, when she was already obviously insecure about her personality changing. Why had he opened his mouth and tried to be funny? Why hadn't he just supported her and...

Those thoughts bounced around his head, seemingly unstoppable, feeding off each other. Eza's head was down, his attention on Cammie's feet, but at one point she shifted position and Eza met her gaze – her one brown and one blue eye behind the frame of her glasses.

17

"Eza, are you alright?" she asked, sounding concerned. "I still feel really awful for teasing you."

"It's okay," she insisted.

"It's not okay. I made you feel bad." Saying that out loud made Eza even more upset, and he looked down again.

"Listen," Cammie told him. "It's *okay*. It probably won't be the last time you make me feel bad. You can't do this to yourself every time you accidentally say something dumb. I say dumb stuff all the time and you've never gotten mad at me about it, have you?"

"No..."

"So go easy on yourself, okay?"

"Okay. I love you."

"I love you too, you goof. Always will."

That made Eza feel better. It was as if putting his fears out into the air had stripped them of their power. As long as the thoughts were inside his own head, they could do anything they wanted to him, but as soon as he told them to Cammie, she was able to stab them to death.

An odd muffled *fwoosh* sound came from outside, and before Eza could realize what had just happened, someone was knocking on his door. Eza slithered out from under Cammie's legs and went to the front door, with the odd feeling he knew who he was going to see.

"Gar," Eza said, smiling in spite of himself. "Come inside, please."

"I think I will," Gar the Artomancer said, stepping into Eza's house. "I have to say, Tranquility is beautiful this time of year. It's a shame you folks don't allow magic here. I'd like to visit more often." He spotted Cammie and waved a greeting. "Hello, Cammaina. It's a pleasure to see you again."

Cammie had never liked Gar, and thought (correctly, in Eza's opinion) that the Artomancer was too full of himself. Nonetheless, she waved back politely, immediately returning her attention to her notebook.

"I guess you haven't heard, then," Eza said. "The king and queen reversed the ban on magic. We're learning spellcasting at the Academy now."

"What?" Gar asked in astonishment. "When was this?"

"About a month ago. Have you been living in a cave or something?"

Gar laughed heartily at Eza's joke; the Artomancers' main settlement, the Prismatic City, was indeed completely underground. Eza and Cammie had passed through the place nearly two months before on their journey to Exclaimovia to free Introvertia's stolen dragons, and Eza had gotten his first taste of learning Artomancy magic. "We don't get many visitors from your kingdom," Gar told him. "And it's not as if you all are known for generating important news. You're usually happy to just mind your own business and hope other people ignore you."

"I think that's our royal motto," Eza agreed with a smile.

"This is great news," Gar said. "I came today to talk to you about continuing your studies. I know you're still a student at your dragon school thing..."

"The Dragon Academy," Eza said helpfully.

"Yes, that. But I was hoping I might get the opportunity to teach you some more. You have a lot of potential, Ezalen. The way you were able to empty your mind and receive what I was teaching you...I've hardly stopped thinking about it."

"Did Gar the Artomancer just compliment someone other than himself?" asked Cammie from the couch.

"Don't tell anyone," Gar warned. "I have a reputation to uphold, you know. Besides, I could train you at the Dragon Academy. If memory serves me correctly, it's a four-line nexus node, is it not?"

Confused, Eza shook his head. Lines of magical energy criscrossed the land, forming powerful locations called nexus nodes at the places where they intersected. The Prismatic City was the only known location where five lines came together, and the node there was extremely strong. But Eza only knew of a few nexus nodes within Introvertia; one was just two lines and one was most likely three. Carnazon Fortress, the campus of the Dragon Academy, wasn't a nexus node at all. "I'm sure I would have felt that," Eza told Gar. "You know how it feels when you're on one. I'll take you to Carnazon myself if you want, but I've never felt that...buzzing sensation I've gotten on the other nodes I've visited."

"Strange," Gar said. "I'm positive Carnazon Fortress was a four-line node in the old histories."

Now Eza was thoroughly perplexed. If Carnazon was really sitting on a nexus node, he was *sure* he would have noticed it by now. Yet Gar the Artomancer was many things – vain and arrogant, among others – but he was not stupid or forgetful. If he said Carnazon used to be a nexus node, then he was probably right.

That spawned an entirely new host of questions in Eza's mind. What did it mean that Carnazon *used to be* a nexus node? How did something *stop* being a node? Was it somehow possible to turn it back into a nexus node again? That would be incredibly useful to all the Dragon Academy students learning elemental magic, physical magic, defensive magic, and Artomancy within those walls. He suddenly realized he was staring at Gar, who was patiently waiting for him to come to his senses.

"Anyway," Gar said, "you seem like the kind of person who prefers reading over human contact, so I brought you a textbook I found in a box in the Prismatic City. You and I covered six terms worth of magic together, so if you can do some things from terms seven through ten the next time I pop by...well, I might not be entirely disappointed."

Cammie made a gagging sound, peeking over the top of the couch and grinning at Eza.

"It would be easier," conceded Gar, "if you were still in the Prismatic City and benefiting from the nexus node it sits on, which is why the offer to come train with me still stands."

"I really do want to learn more Artomancy, but Cammie and I have a very important mission from the king and queen, and after that it's back to class at the Dragon Academy."

"Very well. If the Prismatic City has need of you in the future, though, I hope you'll do all within your power to answer the summons."

"Why would the Artomancers need *me*?"

"It's been a long time since we *needed* anyone," Gar said. "But these are uncertain times, and one never knows what will happen. I don't like some of the things I've been hearing out of Esteria lately. They seem to have reacted...quite poorly to their recent defeat at Denneval Plain, and especially to the fact that Exclaimovia, after instigating the whole situation, declined to participate in the battle."

That had gotten Cammie's attention, and she peered over the top of the couch again.

"But you have your mission thingy from the king,"

Gar continued. "That's important. Just read the book and learn what you can, okay? That way when you show back up, everyone will be impressed." He paused. "With me, of course."

"For someone who's supposedly one of the greatest Artomancers alive, you sure are obsessed with people's opinion of you," Cammie observed.

"Magic is easy," countered Gar. "You do the spell the same way every time, and it never changes. Holding people's attention, that's hard. They're always going off after the new shiny thing. Things that impressed them six months ago don't impress them anymore. So being the best sorcerer in the room, that's pretty easy. Being the most interesting thing in people's lives, so interesting they can't ignore you, is the real challenge. That's what I live for."

Cammie gagged again, seeming to regret that she'd said anything and given Gar a chance to grandstand.

"And if that one ever says a kind word about me," Gar said, pointing at Cammie, "I'll really know I've made it."

"Don't hold your breath," cautioned Cammie.

Gar smiled, and then *fwoosh*, he was gone.

Denavi Kiresti chose that moment to come padding down the stairs from her bedroom on the house's second floor. "Hey, Eza. Hey, Cammie."

"Good morning, Denavi," Eza told her. "Are you just

waking up?"

"Mmhmm. I stayed up late reading *Heroes of Introvertia*. I should have realized something was up when I had to light a third reading candle, but I couldn't put the book down." Denavi peeked into the kitchen. "Is there anything left from breakfast?"

"Cammie and I ate out, but I think there's some bread from last night."

Denavi vanished into the kitchen, then reappeared a few moments later, holding a piece of flatbread in one hand and running her fingers through her black hair with the other hand. "What have you two been up to this morning?"

Cammie's eyes lit up. "Since you asked," she said with a flourish, "King Jazan and Queen Annaya commissioned us to travel around the kingdom performing a play for people."

"Exciting!" Denavi exclaimed. "The same one you performed at the Academy last week?"

"No, not that one. Since there's still a war on, the king doesn't want us performing a play where the main character decides not to be soldier."

"That makes sense," agreed Denavi, and Eza knew why; Denavi's father had been killed in a pointless war when she was eight, and growing up without a dad had been very hard on her. Denavi was, if not an actual pacifist who totally rejected warfare, at least something very close to that. She had seen what war and violence could do to a family, and she'd turned her back on it – knowing she'd never again be welcome in her old home kingdom of Claira, which worshiped the ideal of the Noble Enlightened Warrior. To Denavi, a play where the protagonist decided to get married instead of going to battle was probably the most natural thing in the world, but she was intelligent enough to see why the king of a nation at war might think otherwise.

"And I was thinking," Cammie continued, "that we could really use someone smart and responsible to help us out with organizing venues and making sure the stage is set up every night. Do you want to come?"

A huge smile spread over Denavi's face. "Yes!" she said immediately. "I'd love to, Cammie. This makes me so happy."

"Then it's settled," Cammie declared. "Eza and I will act the leads, and Denavi will be our stage manager. This is going to be great!"

The rest of the day was spent with Cammie furiously writing down ideas, blurting them out loud the way she always did when she got excited about things, and cheering whenever Denavi or Eza would take something she'd said and build on it. When dinnertime rolled around, all three of their stomachs were audibly growling, but before anyone had a chance to complain, Cammie triumphantly held her notebook in the air. "We

25

did it!" she announced. "*Love or Potatoes* is finished. I have to say, Eza, I wasn't sure it was going to work as a comedy, but it does. People are going to laugh and cry at the same time."

"I bet no one has ever seen a play where the main character wants to be the world's most famous traveling potato merchant," said Denavi.

"It'll be unforgettable," agreed Cammie. "And I never knew there were so many potato-related puns out there."

"That's what makes the play so..." Eza paused. "A-peel-ing."

Denavi covered her mouth to hide a giggle while Cammie put her hands on her hips and pretended to be furious.

Eza smiled. "Potato puns are easy. You just have to have an *eye* for them."

Denavi threw herself back on the sofa, not even trying to hide her laughter anymore. Cammie flung her hands in the air and acted like she was going to storm out of the room. Eza felt very pleased with himself.

Ezarra happened to come in the front door at that moment, and Eza saw Cammie and Denavi glance at each other and nod. Eza leaped up to hug his dad, as he always did, but immediately Cammie crashed into him, tackling him to the floor while Denavi ran to Ezarra to get the first hug instead.

"Sneaky," Eza grinned, looking up at Cammie, who

26

winked at him.

With a single quick motion, Eza slid out from under Cammie and sprinted to his dad, who lifted him into the air. "I love you, dad."

"I love you too, Eza."

And then Cammie and Denavi and Eza were chattering all at once, in a very un-Introvertian manner, telling Ezarra about the day's exciting news, about the king and queen's sponsorship, about Cammie's new play, about Denavi becoming the stage manager. "That sounds really exciting!" Ezarra said enthusiastically. "When do I get to see the new play?"

"We just finished it ten minutes ago," Cammie said. "We haven't started memorizing the lines or working on blocking yet. Maybe tomorrow?"

"Tomorrow would be great," Ezarra said. "But I've heard about thirty stomach grumbles since I walked in the door. How about we all go get some dinner together?"

"Sounds great, dad," Eza told him.

"Sounds great, dad," Denavi echoed.

"Sounds great, Mr. Skywing," Cammie said.

Eza thought he saw a flicker of something cross Cammie's face when she said it. Eza loved his father, and Denavi, who'd lived more than half her life without one, had sort of adopted Ezarra as her own. But Cammie's father was alive and well, an influential general in

Exclaimovia, and Eza knew that Cammie must miss him terribly. Seeing Ezarra lavish his fatherly affection on Eza and Denavi had to be reminding her of what she couldn't get from her own father – at least not right at the moment.

Eza went up behind Cammie and put his arms around her waist. "You'll see your dad again," he said. "There will be peace. And just like the king and queen told us once, maybe your artistic gifts will be the bridge between our people."

"I hope so," Cammie said, but Eza could tell from her tone that she didn't really believe it. "I'm hungry, though. Let's go eat."

Cammie was obviously feeling better by the time they got done with dinner, and on the walk back to the house she was leaning her head against Eza's shoulder and smiling at him. "We're going to have a late night tonight," Cammie said. "We have to get to work memorizing our lines. There are only a few days before we have to leave, and I assume the king and queen will want to see the finished product before we go, so..." She smiled. "Back in Exclaimovia, we called the week before a play opened Oil Week, because we were in the theater late every night and had to keep filling the lamps back up."

"We don't use oil lamps very much, but this can be Candle Week for us," Eza suggested.

Cammie laughed. "Perfect. Candle Week starts now!"

THREE

Razan Enara wore a huge smile as he reported to Mazaren Fortress on Monday morning for his two-week intensive, with his purple dragon Oreaza perched on his shoulders. During the breaks between classes when the school didn't already have something planned for the students – such as the survival practicum they'd been doing when Eza Skywing had met that Exclaimovian – there was usually an intensive offered in which the students could accompany an army unit on maneuvers, or on a scouting mission, or something along those lines. For the next two weeks, Razan would be an actual soldier, sleeping in a tent and taking orders from the company captain. He'd always wanted to be a front-line fighter, and ever since the first day of his first year at Carnazon, he'd been sure the intake test had made a mistake when it assigned him to Harmony Company – Harmony, of all places! – instead of Victory Company where most of the soldiers came from. Yes, Eza and Shanna had told him repeatedly that anybody from any company could sign up for front-line duty, but...it wasn't the same.

Anneka Azoana, the third-year Harmony student Razan had been spending a lot of time with lately, was originally enrolled in the intensive, but her parents were taking her to visit some relatives in Rushwind and she'd had to pull out. Razan hadn't yet seen anyone he knew at the mustering point, which wasn't a problem; he was good at keeping to himself and it didn't matter to him if he had anyone to talk to. That was what a *true* Introvertian should be, he thought to himself, not like that ridiculous Exclaimovian, Cammie, who wanted to talk to everybody. There was a place where she could do that if she wanted. It was called Exclaimovia.

Razan's smile faded a bit as he glanced up at the front gate of Mazaren Fortress and saw Shanna Cazaran, another of his Harmony classmates, entering with her own dragon. Shanna and Eza and Razan had been best friends for their first two years at Carnazon, but after Eza got Cammie into the Dragon Academy and people started fawning all over her – even though she would never be able to talk to dragons! Why was she even at the *Dragon Academy* if she couldn't talk to dragons? – Razan had pulled away from Eza and everyone else who was friends with Cammie.

After Shanna had called him out in front of hundreds of people in the courtyard one day, shouting at him like she'd been granted Exclaimovian citizenship herself, Razan had done some quiet self-exploration to figure out *why* he disliked Cammie. Eza thought it was jealousy. Cammie was popular and beloved despite being

Exclaimovian, getting audiences with the king and queen while Razan went unnoticed. That was part of it, Razan admitted to himself. He could be honest enough to see the truth, even when it was unpleasant.

But the bigger part, the realization that had really floored him, was that he didn't dislike Cammie *as a person*. He disliked what she represented – the outside world intruding into Introvertia, loud people coming to the one place that was supposed to be a refuge for those who didn't want to make small talk or be barraged by noise. Now – because of Cammie, or at least because of the way her people had reacted to her helping Introvertia – the outside world was *literally* intruding on Introvertia. If the kingdom had lost the Battle of Denneval Plain, Clairan and Esterian armies might be occupying Tranquility *at this very moment*. Everything was fine before Cammie came. Maybe, just maybe, if she left again, things would go back to being okay, and everyone could stop fighting and start getting along and just study dragon warfare together...

Ah, there it is, Razan thought to himself. *That's why I'm in Harmony Company.*

Shanna waved to him from across the courtyard but didn't come closer, dropping her pack and digging through it. Razan let his eyes drift over the other soldiers who had mustered there in the fortress. It looked like about five companies; the general were making a bit of a gamble sending five hundred soldiers off on maneuvers, out of around thirty-five thousand left in the whole army, when there was still a war on and the kingdom could be attacked again at any time. Razan smiled wryly. Well, maybe not at *any* time. It sounded like the Introvertian and Telravian armies had delivered a savage beating to the Clairans and Esterians, who would probably not have the ability or desire to attack again anytime soon.

But there were still the Exclaimovians, who hadn't been present at the battle – and no one knew why not...

Someone was ascending the podium in the corner of the courtyard, and the massed soldiers grew even more quiet than a gathering of Introvertians already was, pressing in closer so they could hear whatever was about to be said. "Attention, soldiers!" the woman began. "I am Colonel Ezora. You'll note there are elements of five different companies here, as well as a handful of students from the Dragon Academy, as is our custom on these occasions."

Razan had only seen himself and Shanna, but as the crowd moved toward Colonel Ezora, he did indeed spot a dozen or so people his own age in the crowd closer toward the podium.

"Our mission for these two weeks is quite simple," the colonel continued. "We'll be conducting maneuvers and coordinating between all five companies while we're in the field. Our army does not have much experience operating at a larger scale than company-level. That weakness was exposed at Denneval Plain. We struggled to respond rapidly to orders which required companies to coordinate their movements with each other. Over the next fourteen days we'll be crossing the Rapidly Flowing River to the Nether Reach, and operating in the woods between the river and the Great Sea. Most Introvertians have never seen the Great Sea, so this will be an enlightening diversion for you. For now, gather with your companies and prepare to march out in thirty minutes."

Razan had been assigned to 527 Company, which was collecting itself in the southeast corner of the courtyard under the supervision of Captain Eriazan. Razan had just finished registering himself with the captain when he heard a familiar voice next to him.

"Shanna Cazaran, third year student," his classmate was telling the captain.

"What company?" Captain Eriazan asked.

"Harmony, sir."

"Interesting. Do you know Cadet Enara here?"

"Yes, sir. We're friends," Shanna said, turning to acknowledge Razan.

We're friends. The phrase wouldn't have surprised Razan a few months ago, but with everything that had happened since, it took him off guard and he forced a smile. "Hello, Shanna."

"Good to see you, Razan."

He turned away to hide his shock. Unless that Exclaimovian was *really* rubbing off on her, she really believed what she'd said, since Introvertians didn't lie and didn't engage in social pleasantries. If she didn't think it was good to see him, she'd simply have said nothing at all. He'd been ready for her to be frosty with him, ready for her to hold a grudge. This was unexpected.

Razan solved the problem by positioning himself on the opposite end of the company from Shanna, buying himself some time to think what he'd say the next time they talked. Soon he had no time to think about it; the company was marching from Mazaren Fortress, through Aurion Park and south through the Music Square, to the Rapidly Flowing River. On the south side of the river, ten miles of rich and fertile forest separated Introvertia from the coast. The kingdom could easily have settled that land, could have built permanent bridges over the river and enjoyed fishing from the Great Sea, but the land had been left empty on purpose, as a buffer. If Introvertia bordered the sea, then any nation with a boat could sail up and make contact. Razan didn't know exactly how many other nations there might be along the Great Sea; he'd heard Exclaimovia had a trading fleet, but nobody in Introvertia was quite sure if there were other people in the opposite direction who also sailed the sea. That meant the Nether Reach was doing its job.

Crossing the Rapidly Flowing River was an interesting problem; the current was so strong that any boat would be swept halfway to Exclaimovia before it reached the other side. To get around that, a few of the more experienced dragon-companions had their dragons take ropes with grappling hooks to the other side, wrapping each rope around a tree and using the hook to secure the rope to itself. Razan watched in awe. His own dragon, Oreaza, barely understood anything he said; it was incredible that these companions could give such precise instructions to their dragons. Razan wondered how long it would be before he got to that point.

With ropes secured, the companies began filling rowboats, which worked their way along the ropes to keep from being pulled downstream. Any nation who wanted to invade Introvertia through the Nether Reach would have to do this same maneuver, or something similar, while dragons and Introvertian archers were pelting them the whole time from the other side. Razan hadn't realized until that moment what a great defense the river was.

Once they were finally across, the rest of the morning was filled with maneuvers; the companies kept pivoting to face imaginary attacking forces. After a break from lunch, the focus shifted slightly; three of the companies were designated attackers while the other two were defenders, forcing the defending companies to retreat toward favorable terrain while the attackers tried to flank them or force them into a bad defensive shape. Razan and Shanna were on defense, and he could feel his heart thudding as he watched the attackers working their way around the terrain, eventually splitting their force and attempting to overwhelm one side of the defenders' formation. It was exhilaration like Razan had never felt before, and if he'd ever doubted he was born to be a front-line soldier, those doubts evaporated like dew in the morning sun.

Hours passed, with the defenders growing more and more exhausted as the attacking companies mercilessly pressed their manpower advantage. Razan's company was pushed to the top of a hill, then to the far side of a valley, then, at last, to the Great Sea, where they made a final stand with their backs to the boulders that edged the beach. Razan had expected his first sight of the Great Sea to be more...romantic, perhaps, holding hands with Anneka, but this was what he got, exhausted physically and mentally as waves crashed fifty yards behind him. In that hopeless position, his company's captain finally signaled surrender, and Colonel Ezora ordered all five companies to stand down for dinner on the beach.

Razan made his way over the boulders and then collapsed on the sand. This rhythmic whooshing of the waves was...*relaxing*. Why didn't Introvertians come here more?

A shadow fell over his ration pack and he squinted up into the blue sky. Shanna was standing over him. "Mind if I join you?" she asked.

"I'd rather you didn't, but if you were going to anyway, then go ahead."

Shanna seated herself, obviously taking no offense at the comment. Maybe people from a different kingdom would have taken it as rude, but Introvertians spoke their minds and valued when other people spoke their minds, so Razan knew Shanna wouldn't hold it against him. "How are your classes going?" she inquired, her green eyes on his as she pushed brown hair out of her eyes.

"Great." Razan began to spear dried meat out of his ration pack. "Why are you here?"

"Here on the intensive, or here next to you?"

"Obviously the second."

Shanna gazed out at the ocean. "Because we're friends, Razan. Or at least we used to be."

Her dragon was peeking out from behind her, and made eye contact with Oreaza. The two dragons hopped around each other, then went dancing off along the sand, chittering at each other. Razan opened his mind link to Oreaza, trying to ask what she was doing, but she wasn't paying attention to him. Obviously he still had more work to do with her.

"Our dragons like each other, anyway," Shanna observed.

"I think you had it right," agreed Razan. "We used to be friends. Then you made a new friend, and we stopped spending time together."

"Why?"

"Because I don't like your new friend."

"Why?" Shanna repeated.

"I'm allowed to like certain people and dislike certain people."

Shanna nodded. "Of course you are. But Introvertians don't usually do things for no reason. We think through our options before settling on one. We make careful decisions. So you probably know exactly why you don't like Cammie."

"I do," agreed Razan. "I dislike what she represents. You know why Introvertia was founded: because Exclaimovia didn't understand the way we do things. The Exclaimovians kept insisting we be more like them. They kept wanting us to be loud, to be social. They don't understand that we like quiet, and we like solitude, and we like having deep conversations with friends rather than making small talk with strangers. We literally made our own kingdom because we broke away from Exclaimovia in order to have the kind of life we wanted for ourselves." He shook his head. "And we've had our

39

own way of doing things for thousands of years. But now there's an Exclaimovian *living here*, and we're at war because she's living here. And we're allied with the Telravians, who are literally vampires, and we're being attacked by kingdoms from hundreds of miles away."

Shanna had kept her eyes locked on Razan the whole time, and he could tell she was watching his face and his body language. "That makes sense," she said.

"It does?" Razan asked, bewildered. "But...then..." He was trying to form his thoughts into a question, but nothing came, so he trailed off.

"I said it makes sense," Shanna said gently. "I understand why you feel the way you feel. But I didn't say it was correct. We're not at war because Cammie is living here. We're at war because Exclaimovia stole our dragons. That had nothing to do with Cammie. That was a decision someone else made and it's not fair of you to blame Cammie for it."

"I don't *blame* Cammie for it," argued Razan defensively. "But Introvertia is supposed to be a safe place for people like us. It's a place where no one comes up to us on the street and tries to make small talk. Yet every morning, Anneka wakes up in a room with Cammie, who starts blathering to someone about something. That's not fair to Anneka, is it?"

"No," agreed Shanna. "It's not."

Again Razan hadn't been expecting Shanna to agree

with him, and he hesitated. "So why is it wrong for me to dislike Cammie? Why is it wrong for me to wish she wasn't here?"

"You can *wish* she wasn't here all you want to, but she's here, and she's here because of *that*," Shanna said, pointing at Oreaza. "She's here because she helped Eza steal *your* dragon, and hundreds of others, at an incredible cost to herself. She was banned from her country, torn away from her family. She may never see her mother and father again. Is that fair to Cammie?"

Razan was silent.

"Is that fair to Cammie?" Shanna pressed.

"No," Razan said, just like Shanna had. "It's not."

"So you may not want Cammie here, but she's here, because she sacrificed everything to help *you*, and you've repaid her kindness with hostility. Can she be annoying sometimes? Sure. Is she rude and inconsiderate sometimes? Sure. But don't you think we owe her a little grace because of everything she's done for us? Don't you think she deserves a little time to get settled in her new home?"

Razan didn't answer right away because he was still thinking.

"At the very least," Shanna added, "you have to admit the whole passive-aggressive thing you're doing with Anneka isn't working. The more you pick on Cammie, the more people love her."

"I'll think about what you've said," Razan told her.

"I know you will, Razan. You have a good heart, and you're better than this."

Shanna left before eating with him, and Razan spent the evening by himself, trying to communicate with Oreaza. Sometimes he was successful and sometimes he just wasn't. The dragon seemed to have a mind of her own, like a young child who was easily distracted. Eventually Captain Eriazan to make camp, and Razan pulled his tent out of his pack, pitching it right there on the beach where the sound of the waves lulled him to sleep.

But he awoke an hour after dawn with strong winds whipping at his tent. A storm was blowing in from the south, which was strange for this time of year; normally spring was dry and summer was the rainy season. Razan had an incredibly hard time collapsing his tent; it kept wanting to fly away every time the wind caught it a certain way. The morning's maneuvers were even harder, as the howling gales made it hard to move and also drowned out any shouted orders before Razan could even hear them.

As afternoon turned to evening and the gray sky began to darken, though, one of the soldiers near the beach raised a shout of alarm. A ship was blowing steadily toward the shore, coming in sideways as if out of control. Razan's stomach tightened. Whoever was on that ship, they weren't Introvertians, because Introvertians didn't sail.

The entire length of the Nether Reach coast was protected by wide rocky barrier shoals, which kept any ships from getting too close. The shoal here was about fifty yards from the coast, and if that ship kept drifting in the way it was doing now, it would be smashed to pieces on those rocks in short order. "Companies, form!" came the order from Colonel Ezora, and all five companies plus the Academy students made a line on the beach facing the ocean.

Razan's heart was pounding. What was the colonel going to do?

FOUR

Strong gusts blew sand and salt water into Razan's face as he squinted through the dusk. The company captains were in an intense conference with Colonel Ezora, and it was plain from their body language that none of them liked any of their options. Oreaza was tucked behind Razan's legs, using him as a shield from the wind. Even despite the weakness of their mind link, Razan could still tell that his dragon was scared and wanted to be somewhere else.

"It's okay, girl," he murmured out loud.

What was there to do? Most Introvertians didn't know how to swim, and certainly not well enough to cover fifty yards through massive waves and winds blowing right into their faces. And even if they made it out to the shoal, then what?

Captain Eriazan approached Razan and the others. "There's no way we can stop the ship from running aground and breaking up. But we can build fires on the beach and let the survivors know we're here. If necessary we can use our dragons to guide them in or to tow whatever pieces of wood they're clinging to. For now...all we can do is wait."

But it didn't look like they'd have to wait much

longer. Far out to sea, lightning split the sky, and a distant rumble of thunder eventually rolled to Razan's ears. The ship was closer to the shoals now, foundering wildly, and then it crashed against the rocks so hard it nearly split in half instantly. Some of the soldiers from 527 Company were rushing into the woods, trying to find fallen branches or chop down thin trees in order to build a bonfire. The ship was breaking into pieces now. Razan wondered how many other ships over the centuries had tried to approach the pristine coast only to be smashed to bits on the unforgiving rocks. Something in the water caught his eye: several other Introvertian soldiers were running toward the shipwreck. What were they doing? It wasn't possible to swim through seas like that...

But they didn't seem to be swimming at all, just running, or at least as best they could run through the water. The sea eventually came up to their necks, with the waves submerging them every few seconds, but they were about to reach the shoal. The water was shallow enough to wade through.

Captain Eriazan had been watching the scene, too, and she shouted, "Everybody into the water!" Razan dropped his pack on the beach, not wanting his rations or tools to get wet, and went sprinting into the ocean immediately. He wasn't prepared for the chill of the water and nearly screamed. The salt stung his eyes and the wind kept blowing water into his mouth, leaving a sour taste. He tried to wipe his face, but his hands were salty too, and that just made his eyes burn more. Blinking away tears, he searched for the ship, or what was left of it. Shanna was next to him, struggling through the water just like he was, and for some reason it reassured him to know she was there.

Razan's legs churned; he felt soft sand beneath his boots, and it felt like every step he took moved him forward only a few inches against the wind and waves. Lightning brightened the sky again and Razan could barely see the top part of the ship. The rest must have broken up or sunk already. He tried again to go faster, determined at least to beat Shanna there.

He couldn't tell how long it took him to reach the ship, only that he was chilled to the bone, shivering and soaked as the wind whipped through his clothes like they weren't even there. The ship's survivors were making their way onto the rocks, some screaming in pain, some moaning, some dazed.

"We're here to help," Razan heard one of the other dragon-companions saying. "Where are you from?"

"Exclaimovia," a wounded woman gasped.

Razan's blood ran even colder than it already was. They were helping the enemy.

The ship was creaking, and suddenly it split in half, with the rear immediately sinking below the waves and the front stuck on the rocks. Razan could hear cries of terror from inside the ship's front half. Shanna was next to him again. For a moment they looked at each other, then they both sprinted toward the ship.

Wooden timbers were howling their protest at being beaten against the rocks by a relentless wind. The ship's cargo hold was open to the elements, and Razan climbed inside, offering his hand to Shanna and pulling her up next to him. Several sailors and passengers were lying on the floor. Razan couldn't tell who was alive and who was dead. "Hey!" he shouted. "If you want to live, speak up!"

A few groans greeted this comment, and Razan rushed to one of them, a man whose body had been crushed between two heavy boxes. Razan leaned his shoulder into one of the boxes, trying to push it away, but his wet boots kept slipping on the wooden floor. Shanna appeared by his side, lifting the box with her physical magic and sliding it a few feet to the side. Razan gasped when he saw how mangled the man's legs were. "How are we supposed to..."

"Bring any survivors over here!" someone shouted from the open part of the hull.

Razan knew it could be dangerous to move someone who was injured, but none of these people would stand a chance unless they were moved to safety. Waves were still hammering the ship, and every few moments Razan had to catch his balance as he was rocked forward and back. "Take his other arm," he told Shanna. The man screamed as soon as they started dragging him. Razan gritted his teeth against the horrible noise.

He didn't see how the other Introvertian soldiers helped the man to the ground and had no idea how they were going to get him to shore, but there was no time to think about it. Lightning crashed again and then rain was falling – in fact, rain was almost all he could see. Even the bonfires on the shore, just fifty yards away, were barely visible through the downpour.

Shanna was ahead this time, and Razan followed her back into the cargo hold. Suddenly the ship pitched sideways and he was falling, hitting the side hull so hard the wind was knocked out of him.

"Razan!" Shanna called, doubling back to him.

"I'm fine," Razan insisted, holding his shoulder and wincing. "Come on."

Together they dragged back a woman with a head injury, a man with a broken arm dangling crazily at the elbow, and another man with a wooden post sticking clear through his stomach, in the front and out his back. They hadn't even finished clearing out the cargo hold yet, and there was still a level above this, and then the upper deck – if anyone was left alive there.

But suddenly a deafening screech filled the cargo hold, and the ceiling above Razan was yawning apart, revealing the gray sky overhead. Rain slammed down on

Razan as if there were a waterfall above him, and just then another wave hit the ship and the left side broke off the right, tumbling down toward the rocks below. Razan was in free fall, crates and boxes and supplies from the cargo hold tumbling around him, and then the hull hit the rocks and Razan hit the hull. For a moment he didn't know if he was alive or dead, and then he realized it wasn't possible for a dead person to be in this much pain. The rain was in his face as he gingerly tested both arms and legs. Nothing was broken – somehow. The right half of the ship was still looming above him, and as his vision cleared, it seemed like it was leaning over toward him...

"Shanna!" he shouted. "Shanna!"

Her head popped up nearby and she staggered to her feet, limping and putting no weight on her left leg. "We have to go," he told her, pointing upward. "Look!"

She didn't protest as he put his arm under her shoulder, leaning on him as they hustled to the back of the ship, whose right half was creaking ominously. Then suddenly it was falling, collapsing on top of the left half – directly where Razan and Shanna were.

Razan helped Shanna the last few steps, and then wood was crashing all around him, splinters flying and screams echoing from those who'd still been on board. Razan's eyes were squeezed shut; if he was going to die, he at least didn't want to see it coming...

And then the crash was gone, though the deafening

rain continued, and then thunder bellowed so closely that Razan felt it in his chest. He and Shanna had survived, somehow – at least for the moment.

Now that they weren't in the ship, that wind was blowing salt water into Razan's eyes again, and he could just make out those bonfires on the beach. Arm still under Shanna's shoulder, Razan led her forward into the water, where the waves were even higher now, but at least they were washing Razan toward the shore instead of smashing him in the face like they had on the way out to the ship.

At last he and Shanna stumbled out of the waves, making it as far as the nearest bonfire before heaving themselves onto the sand. Rain was still pelting them, but Razan was so exhausted he couldn't even handle the thought of finding his pack, never mind putting up his tent. He just lay there on his side, one hand over his face to keep the rain out of his nose and mouth. Howls and shrieks from the wounded were the only thing that carried to Razan on the wind, and he wished they wouldn't.

The last few Introvertian soldiers were straggling back to shore too now, carrying injured Exclaimovians however they could. Above them, the gray sky had gotten almost completely dark. Though the equinox had passed and the nights were getting warmer, Razan edged close to the fire. Eventually the wind died down and the rain ebbed, and the stars even came out as the storm clouds began to dissolve.

Now that he could finally hear again, Razan asked Shanna, "How is your leg?"

She shook her head. "Something's wrong with my knee. I can't walk, and I can't bend it all the way."

Colonel Ezora was walking from bonfire to bonfire, and Razan stopped talking as she approached. "We've sent runners back to Tranquility to bring medics. We're going to evacuate anyone who can't walk or who needs immediate help. The others will stay here. Does anyone in this group need an evacuation?"

Shanna's hand went up.

"I'll go with her," Razan offered.

Colonel Ezora turned to him. "Request denied, Cadet, even though it was a thoughtful one. Those of us who are still here will have other duties."

"Yes, ma'am."

A few hours later, horse-drawn wagons were clattering through the woods, and Shanna was carefully loaded into one of them, waving goodbye to Razan.

Then a loud commotion came from one of the bonfires, where most of the rescued Exclaimovians had congregated. It was singing, and even at this distance Razan could make out the songs, and then the loud stories that followed – or that tried to follow, because every time someone made any kind of headway in the story, someone else would cut in with one that was supposed to be better. The noise was constant, and Razan was sure there were Introvertians trying to sleep. He didn't see Colonel Ezora or Captain Eriazan, so even though he knew he might be overstepping his boundaries, he rose and walked over to the Exclaimovian campfire himself.

"Excuse me," he said when he approached.

"Ah, one of them has come to join us!" said a woman about the age of Razan's grandmother. "Come, young one. Tell us your stories."

"Actually I was wondering if it might be possible for you to be a little quieter. We don't like loud noises, and it's very late."

The woman gave a dismissive wave. "Quiet!" she repeated, as if the thought amused her.

Several of the Exclaimovians exploded into laughter.

"You Introvertians have always been so misguided," the woman said with the shake of her head. "A few hours ago we were as good as dead and now we're alive, and you think the best reaction is silence!"

"Songs have a place," Razan allowed. "But many of us have risked our lives to save you. We're on the brink of exhaustion. Please, out of respect for us, can you stop being loud and annoying for one night?"

The woman appeared to be thinking, but one of the Exclaimovians behind her launched into another song.

She met Razan's eyes and held his gaze for several moments, but if she was trying to tell him anything, he wasn't getting what it was.

Razan shook his head in frustration. He should have expected no less. As he turned to leave, he raised his voice just loud enough that he was sure several of them could hear him. "Should have left you all on the ship."

"*Love or Potatoes*," Queen Annaya said, applauding. "Wonderful writing, Cammaina. I especially loved all the potato wordplay. I never expected to laugh so hard at a romantic drama."

Out of the corner of her eye, Cammie could see Eza wearing a self-congratulating smile. She was tempted to elbow him, but she had to concede he had been right. If the queen liked all the puns, that meant they'd been a good addition. "Thank you, Your Majesty."

"I think this is exactly what the kingdom needs right now," King Jazan agreed. "It's an uplifting message and it's lighthearted. You have my full approval. What is your first destination?"

"We're opening with two shows on Friday and two shows on Saturday here in Tranquility," Cammie told him. "Our stage manager has secured the amphitheater in Aurion Park, a mile north of the Music Square. We're leaving on Saturday after our second performance and taking Sunday morning to set up for a Sunday evening performance at the amphitheater in Grace Square in Dawnrise City." Cammie only had the vaguest possible idea where all these places were; Eza had written out the itinerary and, in response to her blank expression, had drawn a map. Dawnrise City appeared to be a western suburb of Tranquility, and the rest of their destinations formed a roughly westward line that ran parallel to the Rapidly Flowing River. Eza had told her once that about eighty percent of Introvertia's population lived along that line, with only scattered settlements in the rest of the kingdom. The fact that most of Introvertia was empty wilderness seemed oddly appropriate to Cammie.

Eza stepped forward to hand the king and queen copies of the itinerary, which Queen Annaya scrutinized with particular interest. "Have you already confirmed these dates with the venues?" the queen asked.

"Our stage manager has confirmed the four dates in Tranquility and the one in Dawnrise City, yes," Cammie answered. "She's drafted letters to the other venues but hasn't sent them yet."

"I would recommend taking Wednesday off," Queen Annaya said. "By then you'll have done seven shows in four different cities, and traveled thirty miles in the process. You'll probably be running low on rest, because no inn is quite same as your bed at home." She glanced at Eza. "You'll probably be fine; I bet you could go to sleep on the floor in here if you wanted to. But all three of you will benefit from having a down day. We call them zero days. Zero shows, zero rehearsal, zero writing your next play. Just a day for yourselves, enjoying whatever city you happen to be in. Trust me, if you try to do nine straight days of one to two shows a day, your performances will suffer by the end. You're expending too much physical and emotional energy in each show to sustain that pace."

Cammie already had her notebook in her hand, scribbling in the back of it. Everything Queen Annaya told her about acting or running a theater company would go into the book. "Thank you, Your Highness," she said, not looking up from her writing.

"You'll do fine," Queen Annaya said reassuringly. "You're going to bring joy to people, and when anything unexpected happens, because I promise it will, you'll handle it with grace and humor."

"I sure hope so."

Outside the palace, though, Cammie said what she was really thinking. "Is it normal that I'm more nervous about this tour than I was going to battle at Denneval Plain?"

"Yes," Eza answered immediately.

That wasn't what Cammie was expecting to hear, and she stopped walking and turned to Eza in surprise, sure that he was playing a joke on her. His face, though, was completely serious.

"I don't understand," Cammie said.

"At Denneval, things were simple," Eza said. "We had orders to stay alive and not upset the Telravians. If anything went wrong, it was General Nazoa's problem. No one was looking to us to craft a battle plan or keep soldiers out of trouble or figure out how to best use the spellcasters. The responsibility was somewhere else. With this...the responsibility is all on us." He thought about that. "All on you, really, since you're the only one who has a theater background. I've only acted in one play ever and Denavi has never been a stage manager before."

"Mmmmm," Cammie hummed. "I don't feel better."

Eza put an arm around her shoulder. "It's probably going to be difficult, but you've never backed down from a challenge. You were born for this, Cammie. Born to be on the stage, born to be applauded. When this goes well and you see the way people are enjoying your gifts, you'll understand that all the stress was worth it."

Cammie leaned into him. "You're so sappy sometimes."

"That explains why you're stuck to me."

A pained groan escaped Cammie's lips. "If you don't stop with those puns..."

"Then what?" goaded Eza.

"Then...I'm just going to keep on loving you."

Eza chuckled. "That's about right."

Cammie took Eza's hand, sliding her fingers between his and resting her head on his shoulder until they arrived back at Eza's house. "Do you remember," she said as they went in the front door, "when you and Gar showed up at my house in Exclaimovia, and you disguised me by turning my hair pink?"

That brought a fond smile of recollection to Eza's face. "I do. That was fun."

"Do you think you can do it again?"

Eza frowned thoughtfully. "I haven't tried since then, but I can make the attempt. We might want to wait till we're at home in case something goes wrong."

"Do it here," Cammie encouraged. "I believe in you."

"If you believe in me, then I believe in myself," Eza told her. He brought back to mind what Gar had told him on that occasion: empty your head of all your thoughts, and let Cammie's hair completely fill your mind. The color, the texture, the way the light shines off it...

Cammie was wearing her hair down except for one small braid on the left side, and Eza put his hand on the top of her head, then ran his fingers down through her hair, which turned pink as he went.

Denavi happened to round the nearby corner at that moment, having been off at the hospital using her healing magic on Shanna's knee and on the other

57

survivors of the shipwreck. Dimly Eza was aware of Denavi's mouth falling open in awe, but most of his focus was on Cammie, looking into her eyes, the blue one bright and the brown one dark, as she grinned at him, eagerly awaiting the results of his handiwork...

"What do you see?" Eza prodded Denavi.

"Your hair is pink, Cammie," Denavi said, sounding stunned. "Bright shiny pink."

"Is it really?" Cammie asked Eza excitedly.

He was busy admiring his handiwork. "It is."

"I knew you could do it," Cammie said. "My hair used to be down to my waist, you know. I cut it to my chin two years ago and let it go ever since."

"Do you want it longer again?" Eza asked impulsively.

An even bigger smile crossed her face. "What are you thinking?"

"Watch." Eza held her hair again, focusing all his energy on *growth*, and Cammie's hair began to lengthen in his fingers. She gave a delighted gasp, watching the part in Eza's hand get longer and longer until it had reached down to her waist again.

"Amazing," she said breathlessly. "Now I can cut it again tonight."

Eza laughed. "What?"

"It's simple, really. Now that I know you can grow my hair anytime you want, I can cut it back to my chin tonight. If I decide I want it long again tomorrow...you can do it in seconds. You'll have to color it brown again before we go out on our tour. I can't have pink hair and play an Introvertian."

Eza looked to Denavi, as if he needed confirmation that he was really hearing this. Denavi held up her hands in a "Don't drag me into this" gesture. "You're amazing," Eza told Cammie. "You have such a unique fashion sense and I'm sure being able to wear a different haircut every day will make you the happiest girl in the world."

"I'm already the happiest girl in the world," she told Eza. "But I think I just got happier."

FIVE

Taking these Exclaimovians into Tranquility was out of the question, Razan knew immediately. After that first night, every Introvertian in the camp knew it too. The Exclaimovians had spent the next two days hooting and cackling and singing at all hours of the day and night. If any of them had slept, Razan couldn't figure out when it might have been. Colonel Ezora hadn't asked the soldiers' opinion, but there probably would have been unanimous agreement in favor of keeping their visitors far, far away from Introvertia. As Razan had told the Exclaimovians, it wasn't that there was anything wrong with stories and songs. Yet he wasn't the only one who had asked them to be quiet, and every time the response had been along the lines of "you should all be louder and more like us," as if liking quiet and solitude was the sign of a defective mind.

By Wednesday morning the Exclaimovians were being loaded up into wagons and led northeast to a place where the soldiers could cross the Rapidly Flowing River and end up in the Very Large Forest. The river was naturally wider there, and it was even more furious than usual because of all the rainwater that had swelled the banks. That made the crossing difficult; several times

Razan was sure one of the boats was going to capsize and hurl everyone into the churning froth, but somehow all the soldiers and Exclaimovians made it safely across the river and then to the forest road.

From there one company of Introvertian soldiers – none of them dragon-companions, just in case the Exclaimovians got any ideas again – escorted the wagons eastward to Exclaimovia. The other four companies were dismissed back to Mazaren Fortress for the after-action report, while Razan and the rest of the Academy students were demobilized completely, free to go home or back to Carnazon or whatever they pleased.

Razan's first priority was to find out where Shanna had been taken; she was at the military hospital inside Mazaren, and after a quick stop by Carnazon to change clothes (he'd been right; the outfits in his backpack had been soaked and he'd been at least partially damp for two days straight), he made haste to Mazaren.

Shanna was in her ward, and she stood awkwardly when Razan entered the room. "Nice of you to come," she said.

"How's your knee?"

"They said I'd torn something inside it." Shanna's eyes drifted to her leg. "Normally that injury doesn't heal on its own. I might have walked again, but I'd never be able to run or lift or climb. I'd have been out of the army immediately. I mean, tomorrow immediately."

Razan frowned, perplexed. "But you're not?"

"No. Denavi Kiresti came, the Clairan who's living with Eza and Cammie. She does healing magic, and she was able to repair what had been torn. But I have a lot of work to do before it's as strong as it was before."

"You can stay in the army, then? And at the Academy?"

"It looks like it for now."

"That's good." Razan cleared his throat. "Do you think Exclaimovia will back down now that we've risked our lives to save some of their people?"

"Maybe," answered Shanna. "But I know someone who risked her life, who risked everything, to help people she didn't even know, and some of those people aren't grateful. So maybe the Exclaimovians will appreciate what we've done. Or maybe they'll be you."

They stared at each other.

"Speaking of grateful," Shanna said in a softer voice, "thank you. If you hadn't helped me, I wouldn't have made it out in time. I owe you my life."

"You owe me nothing. I'm a soldier and I was doing my duty. I know you'd have done the same for me."

"Maybe one day I'll have the chance." Shanna looked up. "Not that I hope you end up in mortal danger, of course..."

Razan laughed. "I wish you a quick recovery."

"Thanks, Razan."

Razan's family lived in Dawnrise, ten miles away from Carnazon, so he usually stayed at the Academy on weekends when most other students went home. It was only Wednesday afternoon, and there was still a week and a half before the term break ended, so Razan decided to head home the next morning. Carnazon was nearly deserted as he went through the south gate, but there was one man in the courtyard, making his way toward the gate.

"Cadet Enara!"

Razan snapped to attention, turning to his right. It was Colonel Naraza, the liaison between the army and the Academy. He was the one who organized the intensives, who assigned students to army units on their graduation, and who helped students with the transition from academic life to soldier life. "Yes, sir!" Razan said, turning and putting his right fist on his opposite shoulder.

"At ease, Cadet. I have some news for you. You'd have found it out as soon as the term break was over, but since we're face to face, I might as well tell you now."

"Sir?"

"No doubt you're aware that this is the time when third-year students are divided into squads and sent on reconnaissance missions so they can gain experience working as a unit. Part of my job is selecting the students who will be commanding officers in these squads."

Razan's heart started to pound and he could hardly keep a smile from coming to his face. "Yes, sir!"

"I've been examining your exam marks, and your performance in your Tactics class has been exceptional. I'd like for you to be executive officer, second in command, of Talon Squad."

"Yes, sir!" Razan said again.

"Your commanding officer will be Ezalen Skywing. I understand the two of you are friends, so I expect you'll work well together."

All the air left Razan's lungs. Eza would be ordering him around – and Razan had a sneaking suspicion that wherever Eza went, Cammie went too. He'd be stuck with both of them.

"Is something wrong, Cadet?" prodded Colonel Naraza.

"No, sir!"

"Good. Congratulations, Cadet. This is an excellent opportunity for your future army career."

"Yes, sir! If it's possible, sir, may I request a cadet for my squad?"

"Those decisions are made by the directorate. I'm afraid all has been decided." Colonel Naraza produced a piece of paper. "Here are the twelve soldiers who will be a part of Talon Squad. If there are any you don't know, I'd recommend introducing yourself. The commanding officer can afford to be a bit distant, but the executive officer is expected to be friendly with the entire squad and to represent their concerns to the commanding officer. Understood?"

Razan hadn't heard most of that because he was busy scanning the roster. Sure enough, there she was. Cammaina Ravenwood. *Of course* Eza could get his girlfriend on the squad, but Razan wasn't allowed to request Anneka. That was just so...

"Understood, Cadet?"

"Sir, yes sir!"

"Good. Make the most of this opportunity, Cadet. It may be your best chance to prove yourself."

Colonel Naraza continued out the south gate, leaving Razan completely alone. Overhead the afternoon was turning to evening; it was the "golden hour" when the blue sky and the sunlight from the west came together. Normally Razan would have cleared his mind and stood in awe, appreciating the glow of the sun off the stones of Carnazon Fortress and basking in the warmth of the spring that would soon be turning to summer. Now he was too distracted.

But Colonel Naraza was right. This was an opportunity, and it was one Razan had to take if he wanted to serve with distinction. His personal feelings would have to climb in the back of the wagon, with a tarp over them.

Razan made his way up to the Harmony barracks,

dumping his backpack in the empty third-year dorm and dropping heavily onto the edge of his bed. He should have been ecstatic right now. Over a single term-break intensive he'd managed to save the lives of four people, three Exclaimovians plus Shanna, and then be promoted to second-in-command of an Academy squad. It was tough for anyone, cadet or otherwise, to have a better week than that.

So why did he still feel empty?

The Friday morning performance of *Love or Potatoes* was basically a dress rehearsal for the Friday afternoon show, but Denavi had done her job well, getting notices posted in the squares and a few restaurants, and over a hundred people had showed up. That was smaller than the crowd they'd had for *The Ranger's Dilemma*, Denavi thought, but Cammie and Eza had been forced to prepare much more quickly for this play, and Denavi herself had a few small roles to act in this one too; she'd never so much as *looked* at a theater stage in her life, as far as she could recall, and the pressure was sitting on her chest like a rock.

But there was Cammie, on the front edge of the amphitheater, either thoroughly excited about the upcoming performance or else...well, or else putting on a *fantastic* act. After addressing the crowd, she ducked behind the curtain, and Eza came out, dressed in the simple clothes of an Introvertian farmer. This was it, Denavi thought, moving around the side of the stage and behind the curtain to wait for her own cue. There was no going back.

An hour later, legs shaking so badly she could hardly stand, Denavi staggered through the curtain to take her bow. Cammie and Eza stood on either side of her, raising her hands so that all three of them could bow together. Only then did Denavi notice: people were clapping, and some were even standing up. Cammie's smile was so huge it looked like it was going to wrap all the way around her face, and Eza looked just about as relieved as Denavi felt.

After the show, Cammie and Eza stayed at the front of the stage to greet the patrons. Most Introvertians who'd attended were already gone, content to enjoy a free play for an hour and then go on their way, but fifteen or twenty had stuck around to congratulate Eza and Cammie. Denavi couldn't help noticing that Eza was letting Cammie do most of the talking, and he'd also wrapped his Dragon Academy cloak around him; part of his task was to represent the army, which had lost ten percent of its strength at Denneval Plain and could use some new recruits.

"Can you really talk to dragons?" a young girl was asking him.

"I really can," Eza said. "I'll call mine right now. It'll

take her a few minutes to get here. Have you ever seen a dragon before?"

"No," said the girl, her eyes wide.

"Well, Aleiza is quite a bit larger than most dragons. We didn't know until recently that they get larger with magical energy. The stronger a spellcaster's magic gets, the bigger the dragon will become. So I'm learning Artomancy, and I'm trying to get better all the time so Aleiza can keep growing."

"Are you going to be a Ranger someday?" the girl asked.

Eza smiled over at Cammie, and Denavi knew they were sharing an inside joke. Cammie's previous play *The Ranger's Dilemma* was about a character who chose a life with his partner over life as a Ranger. "I haven't decided," Eza answered at last. "Life is full of possibilities."

The girl's father had been watching from a few yards away, and finally approached Eza. "You were present at the Battle of Denneval Plain, were you not?"

"I was," acknowledged Eza. "So was Cammie here. And we won thanks to intelligence provided by Denavi over there."

"What was the battle like?" asked the man.

Denavi saw Eza take a long breath in and out, then look over at her. "I would do anything I could never to see another one," Eza said at last.

"But Introvertia won," said the man, not seeming to comprehend.

"Losing a battle is the worst thing that could happen, but winning a battle is the second worst."

That brought an awkward silence to the park – Denavi had grown to appreciate silence and knew it was often comfortable, but this one was definitely awkward – before the man spoke up again. "I think you wasted an opportunity. You should have destroyed the Clairans and Esterians once and for all. Chased them down and showed no mercy. Maybe then nobody would ever come after Introvertia again. They'd just leave us alone to be ourselves."

"I don't want to talk about this anymore," Eza said.

As much as Denavi was getting used to Introvertia, it still caught her off guard sometimes when people simply said what they meant and it was accepted. "Okay," said the man. "I respect you and these other two for fighting to protect our way of life."

"Thank you," said Eza.

A few people remained who wanted to congratulate Cammie and Eza, but soon the crowd was gone. Eza sat on the front of the stage with his head in his hands. This should have been a happy occasion; they'd successfully performed their first play. Cammie went and sat next to Eza, gently nuzzling his neck with her nose. "What's wrong?" she asked.

"I still have nightmares," he admitted. "About Denneval."

That wasn't at all what Denavi was expecting to hear, and she found herself caught between wanting to know more and not wanting to pry. She settled for the middle ground, starting to fold the stage curtain and put the props into their box, taking care that her movements always kept her near Eza and Cammie.

"What kind of nightmares?" Cammie asked gently.

"Just dreams that you're in danger, or that there's nothing I can do to keep you safe. For as long as I can remember I've sometimes awakened in the morning with...this feeling of panic in my chest, like I can't breathe. I feel like someone's chasing me or like I've just gotten horrible news. That's not new."

"What's new is that I'm in these ones," Cammie observed.

"Please don't be upset." Eza's voice broke as he said it.

"I'm not," Cammie assured him. "That just means you care about me and you don't want anything bad to happen to me."

"I want you to be safe and happy forever."

"It's okay," Cammie said, wrapping her arms around Eza. "I'm here for you no matter what happens and no matter what dreams you're having."

Eza didn't respond, but leaned into Cammie, and the

two lapsed into silence. Denavi stopped pretending to clear the stage. She hadn't been expecting to find the same tightness in her own throat.

Eventually all three of them finished boxing up their things, and before long Denavi was pulling the wagon of curtains and props back to Eza's house as Eza and Cammie walked in front of her. The wagon got stashed in the backyard, while Cammie went upstairs to change and Eza parked himself on the sofa in the living room.

Denavi sat on the other sofa to his left, looking at the floor for a long time and then looking up to see that Eza was watching her. "You're not feeling alright," he said. It wasn't a question.

"Why do you say that?"

"Your boots are on," he said, pointing. "You're always barefoot inside, and half the time you're barefoot outside too."

Denavi gave a half-nod. "Very observant, Eza."

"That's what Introvertians do. We observe. We might not always tell you *what* we observe, of course. We may hide that information in our back pockets and pull it out later. This time, though, I thought the right thing to do was ask about it."

Denavi blew a long breath out and then met Eza's eyes. "How many people died at Denneval?"

"Four thousand Introvertians. We don't know the others for sure, but we think twenty thousand

Telravians, thirty thousand Clairans, and fifteen thousand Esterians."

"Thirty thousand Clairans," repeated Denavi. "Dead because of information I gave you."

Silence hung in Eza's living room.

"That's a lot of kids who don't have a dad tonight because of me," Denavi concluded.

She really, really wished Ezarra was there to hug her at that moment. Ezarra was the father she'd never had, and his smile made her entire world light up. When he was around, Denavi could pretend her childhood hadn't been stolen from her, could pretend that her father dying in a pointless war had just been a bad nightmare and that Ezarra was the father she was supposed to have enjoyed all along...

"Not because of you," Eza said quietly.

Denavi frowned at him. "But I told you all about Clairan tactics. You told me yourself when you returned that your people would have shifted to the right to meet the Esterian charge, except that you knew it was a fake and that Claira was coming for your left."

"Did you make the decision to attack Introvertia?" Eza asked.

"No..."

"Did you make the decision for Claira to ally with Exclaimovia?"

"No..."

"Did you send a hundred thousand Clairan troops to Denneval Plain?"

"No, I didn't," Denavi said.

"Then how exactly do you figure this is your fault?" Eza asked.

Denavi couldn't answer.

"It might *feel* like it's your fault," continued Eza, "but that doesn't mean it *is* your fault. You can look at the outcome and say it happened that way because you warned my people what your people were going to do. But what if you hadn't done that? How many tens of thousands of people would have died if you'd kept your mouth shut?"

"I don't know," admitted Denavi.

"Nobody does. So you can't blame yourself for the way things happened." Eza looked at the ceiling, then back at Denavi. "This is just my opinion, but I think there's a difference between fighting a defensive war and fighting an offensive war anyway. Claira was attacking Introvertia for no reason, just because they could, because they made a bunch of assumptions about us and about our motives and didn't bother trying to find out the truth. But we were fighting for our homes, for our people. If there's a more righteous side in that battle, if there's a side that's more deserving of help, it's the people who are defending themselves and didn't do anything wrong."

73

The pressure in Denavi's chest, which had sat there ever since the play, was beginning to fade. "I suppose that makes sense. Thanks, Eza." She pulled off her boots and socks, hurling them all into the corner of the living room. "I've noticed something about you, too. You're the kind of person who's happiest when all the people around you are happy."

"My mother used to say the same thing."

"That's a gift," Denavi said. "A gift and a curse at the same time, really, because you can't always make everybody happy. Sometimes the people around you will be unhappy and there's nothing you can do, and those times will be extremely hard on you. But on days like today, it's a gift."

Eza nodded. "I'll take the gift even if it's a curse sometimes."

Cammie finally came down the stairs, and Denavi would never have known something was unusual except that Eza stood, a stunned look on his face. "Cammie," he said in awe. "You look *amazing*."

That got Denavi's attention, and she turned around to see that Cammie had cut her long pink hair up to her chin. The bright hair and the short cut were very striking together, Denavi had to admit, and she smiled at the look of childlike excitement on Eza's face as he walked over to her as if in a daze, putting his hand on the back of her neck. That was the other thing, Denavi suddenly realized

– Cammie wasn't wearing her glasses.

"I'll be outside with Aleiza," Denavi announced, strolling out the back door as quickly as she could so the two of them could be alone.

SIX

Razan's sword cracked against his opponent's, and he staggered backward. He'd thought this was going to be a lot easier. Sweat was already collecting around his eyes, cooling him as a spring breeze from the Impassable Mountains teased his face.

Shanna was visibly limping, and the grimace on her face had been there for the past half hour. But her footwork was still perfectly accurate even if her forward thrusts weren't as fast as they could be since her left leg wouldn't let her push off.

"Do you need a break?" Razan asked, keeping the tip of his wooden scana in the guard position.

"Do *you*?" Shanna responded, circling him. "The doctors said I have to get my leg back up to strength."

"Right, but...you can't tear it again, can you?"

"If I do, Denavi will just fix it like she did the first time." Shanna lowered her sword. "See, this is the thing that doesn't make sense about you, Razan. You're kind and thoughtful. There are a million things you could be doing but you're here with me helping me train, and you're looking out for my leg. You have a good heart."

Razan knew where this was going.

"Which is why the way you treat Cammie is so out of

character. It doesn't fit you, Razan. Some Introvertians are so inward-focused that they don't think about how others feel. They're rude out of apathy or out of arrogance or whatever. But you're not like that. You like being kind, but you're being mean to Cammie for no reason."

"You were there," Razan said defensively. "You heard the way those Exclaimovians were so rude to us after we saved their lives. Do you want more people like that here?"

"Nobody's saying we have to invite them all to Introvertia, or open the borders, or anything like that. We're talking about the *one* who's already here, and who – let's just be honest – is nothing like that. Is she?"

Razan rested his scana on the ground. He had a feeling the swordfight was going to be over for a while – and that a different kind of duel was just beginning.

"She's not shrieking in the middle of the courtyard, or running down Broad Avenue hugging strangers. She's doing her best to be one of us, and you and Anneka aren't even giving her the benefit of the doubt." Shanna put the point of her wooden scana in between two cobblestones, leaning on it like a crutch for her left leg. "See, here's the thing about being that kind of person. Who's going to want to spend time around you? Nice people, or other mean people?" She waited for a response, but Razan was silent. "Nice people don't want to be in situations where people are being mean to each other, so they're going to avoid you. The only ones who will want to be around you are other mean people. So you're going to be stuck, surrounded by fools and donkeys."

Razan didn't want to admit that she might have a point.

"People always attract more of whatever they are," Shanna continued. "Soldiers spend time with soldiers. Athletes seek out other athletes. Musicians find musicians. Quiet people want to be near other quiet people, which is why Introvertia exists. If you want to be a mean person, that's fine, but you need to know you're going to attract other mean people, and you're going to be miserable because that's not who you are. You're kind and thoughtful and it's going to drive you crazy if you have a bunch of friends who only want to hate Cammie together. Their negativity is going to drag you down and smother you."

"Maybe," allowed Razan.

Shanna seemed to sense it was best not to push him any further. He wanted time to think about all of this and make a decision when he was ready, and Shanna had been his friend for years. That must have been how she knew to back off.

"I'm going to be seeing a lot more of her anyway," Razan said. "I talked to Colonel Naraza a few days ago, and he told me Eza was going to be commanding officer of his own squad. I'm Eza's second, and Cammie's in the squad too."

"Am I?" Shanna asked hopefully.

"No. I'm sorry."

Shanna looked down. "I'm sure my squad is great. I'd better get back to training if I'm going to be ready to join them by the time they deploy." She put her weight on her left leg again and raised her wooden scana. "No going easy this time, okay?"

Their swords clacked together again, Razan surging forward in the footwork of the Tiraza offensive. But that attack was easily countered with the mirror parry and the Gerazi counterattack, which Shanna executed perfectly, sending Razan backward more than he expected. Shanna lacked the speed to take advantage of him on her weakened leg, but she went for it anyway, and Razan only just got his wooden scana up in time. They were both back on neutral footing now, and Razan probed, feinting to Shanna's left and then circling around to the same side, forcing her to put her weight on that left knee. A twinge of pain clouded her face, but she kept following Razan's movements.

Something clobbered Razan in the back and he staggered forward into Shanna, who touched her sword to his chest in victory. "Nice job," he heard Shanna saying as he picked himself up off the cobblestones and looked around.

She wasn't saying it to him. A purple dragon was hopping up onto her shoulders. "That's my boy, Evaza," she cooed. "Who's a good boy? You're a good boy." The dragon chirped and rubbed its snout against her head.

"That might be considered cheating," Razan observed.

"It also might be considered winning. Where's your dragon? You should be spending time with her. They grow when they're around magic, you know."

"She's in the stables. I don't think she likes me very much. She doesn't listen."

"I think the two of you would build an understanding if you spent more time together. The fact that she doesn't know you very well means you need to get closer, not pull away."

Razan shifted uncomfortably. He didn't like the way Shanna was staring at him. "You're talking about Cammie again, aren't you?"

"Yep. That's probably going to keep happening until you start doing the right thing."

Eza saw the girl staring at him from across the park – well, probably not at *him*, but at Aleiza. It wouldn't have been polite for the girl her to approach a stranger without knowing whether he wanted to be spoken to, so Eza waved her over with a smile. She looked to be about twelve, the same age Eza had been when he'd started at the Dragon Academy, and her eyes were wide with wonder as she approached.

"Are you a dragon-companion?" she asked.

"I am. This is my dragon, Aleiza." He opened a mind link to Aleiza, asking if she would mind being petted. The dragon had a funny personality, Eza was beginning to realize. She didn't like loud noises and was still, months later, reflexively skeptical of Cammie, but she also loved attention. Eza had lost track of the number of times he'd come into a room to find Aleiza wrapped around Denavi like a blanket, or Denavi using her as a footstool. Even on this tour so far, Aleiza had let people pet her before every show.

There was pure awe in the girl's eyes as she reached a hand up toward Aleiza's snout, resting her fingers on the tough, leathery skin. "Wooooowwwwww..." Her eyes drifted lower. "What's this mark on her stomach?"

"She was wounded in the Battle of Denneval Plain. I healed her the best way I could, but she was attacked with primal magic and those injuries always leave a scar."

"You're a healer?" the girl asked, her eyes somehow even wider.

"No," Eza said with a small laugh. "I'm an Artomancer, and I have some small ability to heal with that. Denavi over there knows actual healing magic."

"Could I be a dragon-companion?"

"Normally companions are taken from certain families who have been doing it for centuries, but I'll tell you what. I have these forms people have been using to sign up for the army. You can fill one of those out, mention that you want to be a companion, and I'll pass it along."

"I should probably ask my mother first." The girl turned toward the playground, where several children were playing on something that looked like a scaffold, with metal bars running vertically and horizontally. Eza had loved playing on one just like it at the park near his house, and a distant smile crossed his face as he remembered jumping from the higher bars and his mother telling him to stop before he hurt himself.

Suddenly a clang reached Eza's ears, and the woman near the scaffold was sprinting toward it, looking very alarmed. The girl was running too, and Eza followed her. One of the boys had fallen from the top of the scaffold and evidently hit his forehead on another bar as he was falling. The skin on the child's forehead was split and blood was leaking down the side of his face as he sat with a dazed expression on his face, as if he were too stunned to even cry.

Denavi was looking that direction, as if unsure whether she should get involved, and Eza waved her over. Denavi arrived a few moments later, with Cammie on her heels. "What happened?" Denavi asked.

"He just fell," the child's mother said, panic on her face.

Denavi had lowered herself onto her knees next to the boy, sitting on her feet, and she reached out to take his hands. "What's your name?"

"Erian."

"And where are we right now, Erian?"

"On the playground," he said, looking at her as if she were crazy. "In Dawnrise City."

"That's good," Denavi told the boy's mother. "He's aware of his surroundings and his speech is clear. It means he doesn't have a serious head injury. That cut on his forehead is really something, though." Denavi held her hand about two inches above the cut, with her palm open. Aleiza had followed them, curious, and hopped her way over next to Denavi. There must have been some healing magic going on, Eza thought.

Sure enough, when Denavi pulled her hand away, Erian's forehead was no longer bleeding or bruised. He put his hand up to it, then looked at Denavi with awe. "How'd you do that?"

"I'm a healer," she told him. "You can go back to playing now."

"Thank you," he said over his shoulder, already reaching up to climb the scaffold again.

Eza leaned down and put his hand on Denavi's

shoulder. "Great job."

But she was watching Erian, who had now made his way back up to the top of the scaffold. "That felt really good," she said distantly.

"What did? Helping the boy?"

"Exactly." Denavi stood up, wiping off her knees. "I like children. I feel...I don't know. I feel like I'm doing something important when I help them."

"You never really got to have a childhood," Cammie pointed out. "You want to help other kids have what you missed out on."

"Yeah," Denavi agreed, nodding. "Yeah, it's exactly like that."

"I think a lot of people do that," Cammie said. "The thing they get excited about is the thing they needed the most when they were younger."

"Are you that way?" Eza asked. "The thing that gets you really excited is theater, right?"

That made Cammie stop and think. "You're right," she said slowly after several moments. "I told you, Eza, way back when we first met, that I had always felt out of place in Exclaimovia. You made fun of me for thinking I might be a little bit Introvertian."

Shame washed over Eza and he put his head down. He'd been so rude to Cammie, so unkind. He still did things like that – not being mean on purpose, not to her and not anymore, but just not thinking of her needs as well as he should have. It always made him feel...like he'd never be good enough to deserve her. Disappointment crashed over his heart like the Rapidly Flowing River making whitewater on the rocks, and that feeling was followed shortly by hopelessness. She was so amazing, and he was such a *failure*, and he'd never stop being a failure...

You always mess up, he chided himself. *No matter how hard you try to make things better, you only make them worse.*

Some part of him knew those thoughts weren't right. Cammie told him she loved him, told him he made her happy, and Cammie wasn't a liar. Eza trusted her enough to know that. But what if today was the day? What if today she finally decided it wasn't worth putting up with him anymore, and she just walked away?

Cammie was still talking, and Eza forced his attention back to her, where it should have been all along – *just another thing you can't do right, busy feeling sorry for yourself when you should be focused on someone else.* "So I think the theater was the one place I really felt free. I could be loud, I could be quiet, I could be outgoing, I could be reserved, and no one ever questioned me. It was...nice. If I can help other people feel that same way, it'll make me really happy."

"That does sound nice," Denavi agreed. "What about you, Eza?"

He really didn't want to pull himself out of his spiral

long enough to answer, so he forced a smile. "I still don't know what gets me most excited."

"Being a Ranger, right?" Denavi prodded.

"I used to think so, until I met Cammie. You've read *The Ranger's Dilemma*. Maybe we'll act it out for you sometime." He raised an eyebrow at Cammie. "At least the last scene."

"My favorite," she said with a mischievous smile, leaning her head against him.

"I told Cammie I'd give up everything for her, and I meant it. Nothing to me matters as much as the people around me being happy." *If you can keep from messing it all up, you failure. You really think you can make them happy? They're going to see right through you and be so disappointed...*

"You're the best," Cammie told him.

Eza couldn't see her face well, since she was next to him with her head on his shoulder, but he could hear the delight in her voice and forced himself to believe her. "Thank you." He put his fingers on the back of her neck – her hair was back to being short today – and gave her a gentle massage.

"We should get set up, though," Denavi informed them. "We only have two hours until curtain."

"You go ahead," said Cammie. "Eza's going to be doing this massage for a little while."

That made Eza laugh. "Am I?"

"I sure hope so."

SEVEN

This was it, Cammie thought – the last performance of *Love or Potatoes* on her first ever theater tour. They were in the city of Rushwind on this Saturday evening, all the way in the southwest corner of Introvertia where the Rapidly Flowing River leaped and crashed its way out of the Cloudscraper Mountains and started its long run to the Great Sea. The Saturday afternoon show had gone off without any hiccups – in fact, almost all of them had. That horrible storm from the week before had apparently been a one-off, and weather had been great ever since their first day out. Cammie had taken to performing without her glasses on, and that had caused a problem in one show when she'd accidentally kicked a prop box and Eza had caught her before she fell on her face, but they'd both played it off like it was on purpose and the crowd had loved it.

"Rushwind is really pretty," Denavi said.

They were seated in the city's Mountain Park now. Tranquility and most of the other cities they'd played in were pretty flat, but the rolling foothills of the Cloudscrapers gave Rushwind a wavy look. The houses were built with blocks made from local clay mixed with stone, so the whole city was reddish, except for a few of the taller buildings which were constructed entirely from stone.

"It really is beautiful," Cammie agreed.

"Not as beautiful as you," Eza told her.

Cammie swallowed. Back in Exclaimovia, compliments were used to manipulate people, and there were rigid social rules about who was allowed to compliment whom. For her entire life, her immediate reaction had been suspicion whenever someone tried to build her up the way Eza just had, and that suspicion had tried to bubble up in her as soon as he'd spoken. She'd fought hard to get to where she could accept compliments from Eza – and she thought she'd gotten there. By the time of the Battle of Denneval Plain, even though she might turn a little bit red, she could thank Eza and enjoy the kind words. Why had she gone backwards? She'd fought this fight, and she'd won it; why was she back where she started?

Maybe the stress of the theater tour had brought back some old habits – she didn't think she felt stressed, but Queen Annaya had said a tour like this wouldn't be easy. Maybe it was something else. Cammie didn't know...and that bothered her, too.

Eza seemed to sense Cammie's inner tension, and he put an arm around her shoulder. "I'm sorry. I should have been more considerate. I thought you'd gotten to where you were okay with me talking like that."

"Wait," Cammie said immediately. "I don't want you to stop complimenting me. I want to learn how to handle them the right way. Just like I learned to reject them, I want to learn to accept them when they come from you. You're a kind person and I want to be able to receive that."

Eza slid his fingers in between hers and squeezed her hand. "Then I'll say it again. You're really beautiful. Your smile is one of the most captivating things I've ever seen and I can't believe you love me."

Cammie was ready for it this time, and felt the avalanche of skepticism that crashed down on her heart. But another part of her wanted desperately to believe what Eza had said, wanted to know without any doubt that someone really did cherish her that way, really did smile with delight at the thought of her. She pushed back against the skepticism, making room in her heart for the compliment...and it stuck there. Cammie looked into Eza's eyes and knew he meant it, and that was enough for her. The feeling was strange, unreal, but Cammie liked it and wanted more of it. "Thank you, Eza."

"You're welcome, my treasure."

Cammie felt herself turning bright red, and looked down with a smile. "One compliment at a time, please."

The seats were beginning to fill in preparation for the evening show. "Shall we take our places?" Cammie asked.

"Let's go," Eza agreed.

There was a cool breeze blowing down out of the mountains, not strong but just enough to make them all grateful for the warm sun that was easing its way toward the horizon. Tall jagged peaks rose into the sky to the northwest, casting long shadows on the plains north of the city. This was...relaxing, Cammie thought, breathing in deeply. She suddenly had an extremely vivid mental image of herself and Eza, living in a farmhouse by that lake she could see in the distance, and she could see herself sitting under a giant maple tree and writing a play as their kids played around her...

Cammie blinked in surprise. That had been unexpected. Besides, these cities were quiet enough; could she really handle the solitude of living in the country?

Focus, Cammie.

"You look contemplative," Eza said as they sat behind the curtain, waiting for show time. Aleiza sat next to him, rubbing her snout against his neck and making him giggle. It might just have been Cammie's imagination, but the dragon looked even larger now.

"Just thinking about something I said to you back in Dawnrise City," she said. "About the theater making me feel free. Here in Introvertia, the stage is as close as I get to being an Exclaimovian. I can be loud, stomp around, fling my arms in the air, shout, and cry, and people love every moment of it."

"You bet they do," said Eza.

"In Exclaimovia, the theater was the closest we got to being Introvertians – everyone is only allowed to say certain words at certain times, can't blurt out whatever they're thinking on stage or even backstage, can't interrupt anyone else unless the script calls for it."

""Hmmmm," Eza said.

"Now *you're* the one looking contemplative," Cammie teased. "But I'm serious. Maybe that's the whole point of theater; it takes people out of their own worlds and into a different world. And maybe that's what King Jazan meant all those weeks ago when he said my art could be the bridge between our people."

"Maybe your next play should be about an Introvertian and an Exclaimovian falling in love," suggested Eza.

"Yeah, great. They'll riot against me in *both* kingdoms."

"Curtain in five," Denavi said from a few yards away.

"Ready?" Cammie asked Eza, taking her glasses off and stashing them on one of the empty prop boxes. Eza was just staring at her, and she tilted her head to the side. "What?"

"With your hair like that, and your glasses off so I can see your eyes clearly..." A huge goofy smile hung itself on Eza's face. "You're just so stunning."

Ugh why is he always –

He doesn't mean it he's just –

Doesn't he know how uncomfortable this –

Once you really truly trust him he's going to stab you in the back –

Cammie shoved all those thoughts out of her mind.

"Thank you, Eza."

Cammie didn't know why Denavi had picked this particular curtain time; the stage faced south, which meant the sun was setting to their right and would be in the eyes of whichever actor had to be facing west during a scene. Well, it was Denavi's first time being stage manager; these were the sorts of things Cammie could explain to her before the next tour, whenever it was.

The play went *perfectly* for the first two acts, and Cammie was feeling good as the final scene of the third act was about to begin. This was the pivotal moment of the whole play, and one of Denavi's biggest scenes. Cammie was behind the curtain for this part, but her cue was coming up, so she always had to listen carefully during this part.

"Don't you see how much Niranna loves you?" Denavi was asking passionately. She'd gotten louder and more forceful as the week had gone on, and by this point her acting was very passable. "Erila, how can you be so blind?"

"I'm not blind," Eza said, sounding wounded. "I have

more eyes than this potato. I can see just fine."

That line always got scattered chuckles from the audience.

"Niranna *loves you*," Denavi told him, intensity in her voice. Cammie had coached her through the delivery of those lines, and she knew Denavi was thinking back to her conversations with Eza when he was unsure whether to court Cammie. "Have any of those potatoes ever loved you, Erila?"

"They always seem to find me pretty a-peel-ing," protested Eza.

Groans and giggles usually followed that line.

"Stop making jokes!" Denavi demanded. "This is serious! We're talking about true love here and all you care about is making potato puns."

Eza heaved a huge sigh and stomped his way to the other side of the stage. "It's not that simple, Leza," he said, just loudly enough for the people in the furthest seats to hear. "I'm good at selling potatoes. I never feel not-good-enough when I'm selling potatoes. Potatoes are simple. But love, Leza...love is messy. I adore the way I feel around Niranna but I keep worrying that I'm not good enough for her. I'm always scared she'll walk away and decide I'm not worth it anymore." Eza's voice always caught in his throat during this part. "So I choose the potatoes because they're easy and predictable."

"Maybe you should take a risk," Denavi urged him.

"Do you love Niranna?"

That was Cammie's cue, and she silently pushed the curtain back, appearing on the side of the stage where Eza couldn't see her.

"Yes!" he shouted. "I love Niranna! I love her more than I've ever loved anyone or anything."

"And I love you too," Cammie said, sweeping to the center of the stage. Eza whirled in pretend surprise and Denavi disappeared behind the curtain, leaving the two of them alone onstage.

Suddenly the sunlight shone on Eza and his face glowed in the afternoon light. *This* was why Denavi had chosen that curtain time, Cammie realized. The golden hour had arrived at the perfect moment. Eza's eyes were so green, so impossibly bright, that they nearly took Cammie's breath away, and the sunlight on his skin...

"Niranna..." Eza stage-whispered.

"I heard it all," Cammie told him. "Everything you said to Leza." Her breath was getting faster now, looking at the way Eza was smiling at her in the setting sun...

"Oh, Niranna. I love you from my head to my...potatoes!"

The audience laughed and groaned at the pun and then exploded into applause as Cammie leaped into Eza's arms. They probably didn't *have* to kiss; the scene would have worked just fine if he'd hugged her and whirled her around a few times, but Cammie had written it with a kiss *because she could*, so Eza put his hands on the back of her neck and their lips met. Goosebumps covered every inch of Cammie's arms and legs, and she wore an enormous smile as he eased away from her, his eyes looking into hers. The golden sunlight bathed them both and Cammie felt so warm and so *perfectly alive* in that moment. She never wanted it to end.

"Niranna," he said again when the applause had died down, "I choose a life with you. I don't know what the future holds, but I know if you're there with me, we can face anything together."

Cammie was supposed to have another line after that, but the crowd was on their feet, applauding and cheering. Cammie waited as long as she felt comfortable, and then whispered to Eza, "I'm going to grab Denavi." The three of them went ahead and took their bows, the final performance of the play one line shorter than any of the others.

But just as they were rising up from their bows, Denavi noticed something. "DADDY!" she screamed, sprinting off the stage and toward the back rows of seats. Cammie looked up just in time to see her burying her face in Ezarra's chest, then looking up at him with a smile that radiated absolute delight. Over the applause and the shouts of the crowd, Cammie couldn't possibly hear what they said to each other, but their body language said everything.

Eza and Cammie finished their bows, and Cammie stayed on the front of the stage to talk to the crowd as Eza ducked backstage to put on his Dragon Academy cloak and bring Aleiza in front of the curtain. It *wasn't* just Cammie's imagination. Aleiza was taller than Eza now, several inches taller in fact. Cammie had seen the damage Aleiza had done at Denneval Plain; the dragon must have killed several dozen people and more than a hundred magical creatures herself. There was no telling what Aleiza would be able to do as she grew even larger.

Maybe it was just Cammie's relief at having the tour over with, but it seemed like the residents of Rushwind were the kindest and most welcoming out of all the places she'd been. Eza told them all up front that Cammie was from Exclaimovia, and rather than being repulsed or horrified, every last one of them welcomed her to Introvertia and talked about how much they loved her play. Cammie felt herself getting misty-eyed by the end; it was one of the first times, away from Razan and Anneka and the others like them, that she'd felt unconditionally welcomed in Introvertia. The feeling made her so comfortable and relaxed that Cammie would have been content to linger here and soak in it forever.

Denavi and Ezarra were walking toward the stage, with Denavi's arms wrapped all the way around Ezarra and the two of them nearly joined at the hip. Eza hugged both of them as they reached the stage, and Cammie joined in to complete the group hug. "That was *really* good," Ezarra said. "That was such a great play, Cammie, and so well acted. Eza, you did a marvelous job. Denavi...I'm so, so proud of you."

Denavi looked up at Ezarra, her eyes shining. "You're proud of me?" she repeated.

Ezarra kissed the top of her head. "That's right."

And then Denavi was crying, sobs shaking her body like she had the world's worst case of hiccups. Cammie pulled back a step in surprise and Eza came with her, freeing up Ezarra to hold Denavi close. "Are you okay?" Ezarra asked softly. Denavi couldn't answer right away, so Ezarra gently rubbed the back of her neck (so *that* was where Eza had gotten it from, Cammie thought triumphantly) and swayed back and forth slowly.

But seeing the two of them made Cammie's heart sink, and she turned away to gaze at the intense purple and orange of the sunset. Eza's hand touched the small of her back and Cammie jumped. "Sorry," Eza said. "Is everything alright?"

Cammie nodded. She didn't really want to talk about it because she knew she was going to start crying, and she *hated* crying around people. That reminded her of the time the Exclaimovian diplomats had come to declare war and Eza had closed his eyes so he didn't see her crying. *That* memory made her start laughing. Eza was the best kind of goof. Now he was really confused, though, so Cammie shook her head. "I'm sorry. I just miss my family so much. It makes my chest hurt sometimes. I want to see my mom's smile. And I want to see Aed. I wonder what he's wearing today." She paused, looking at Eza in the fading dusk. "But what I really want is a big strong hug from my daddy. It's not fair, in a way. Denavi came here and found the family she never had. I came here and got torn away from mine."

Eza was quiet – *very* quiet, in fact. Cammie had noticed he had several different types of silence; there was comfortable silence, and thinking silence. This was "not sure whether to say what I'm thinking" silence. It dawned on her that being able to recognize different kinds of silence meant she was *way* more Introvertian than she'd realized, and she was surprised to find that the thought made her proud.

"Out with it," she ordered.

Surprise flickered across Eza's face as he realized she'd just read him like a book. "It just makes me sad that you're not as happy as you could be. I wish there was more I could be doing."

This reminded Cammie of the way he'd overreacted after accidentally teasing her too hard about liking silence. "Are you getting all insecure on me again?"

Eza nodded, looking like he was on the verge of tears.

"Eza, I *am* happy. I've told you. I'm happier with you than I've ever been in my life. But nothing..." She pointed at Denavi, who still hadn't managed to control her sobs enough to get a word out. "Nothing can replace a father's hug. That doesn't mean you're doing something wrong, or not good enough, or anything like that." She paused. "Is that what you feel? You wrote all those lines in the play because you really think them?"

Again he nodded. "Not all the time. But sometimes those thoughts just...*come*, and they sit on me and they won't go away no matter how hard I try."

"But you haven't always been like this."

"No. It just started recently. I've never cared about anyone or anything the way I care about you, and I guess...I don't know how to handle all this love."

"Aww," Cammie said, leaning her head on his shoulder. "That's sweet. But please don't handle it by doubting yourself or beating yourself up, okay? I promise to tell you if there's something I want you to do differently. Do you trust me to do that?"

"I do."

"It's just," Denavi was saying from behind them, and Cammie whirled to see. "I never got to hear my daddy say he was proud of me. If he did, I don't remember it. This is the first time I've ever heard that..." She was crying again, the sound muffled by her face in Ezarra's thick cotton vest.

Cammie's hand reached for Eza's. "I love you," she told him. "Believe it and don't doubt it, okay?"

"I'll try."

She looked at him, searching his eyes. "That's...really pessimistic coming from you."

"I'm sorry. Those thoughts are really powerful when they come. I...don't always feel strong enough to fight them off. But I'll try."

"I'm here for you."

Cammie had doubtful thoughts too, like the ones that soared into her mind when Eza complimented her, but that skepticism was a learned behavior, drilled into her by years of conditioning. Eza wasn't talking about something like that. He was talking about something that *happened* to him. Cammie didn't know exactly what was going on, but she was going to keep an eye on it.

"I want you to be happy," she added. "If you're not, tell me so I can help you, okay? Don't keep it all to yourself."

"But it's so stupid," he said, sounding angry at himself. "You tell me you love me. You tell me you're happy. And I keep thinking the opposite, and I don't know why and I can't make it stop. It's embarrassing. I don't want you to..." He swallowed. "To be burdened by that."

"You can't ever be a burden to me," Cammie told him. "It's never a burden to care for the people you love.

It's never a burden to help them when they're weak or to make them smile when they need it. That's what love is *made* of, Eza. It's the opposite of a burden. It's a blessing." She patted him on the shoulders. "Excuse me please. I have to write all that down *right now.*"

Eza laughed. "Go!"

EIGHT

Eza was awake at dawn Monday morning, alone with his thoughts as usual, wishing his body knew how to wake up later. The forty-mile trip back from Rushwind had occupied all of Sunday, from early in the morning until so late at night that Cammie and Denavi had fallen asleep in the wagon while Eza was driving the horse. Being able to spend the night in their own beds had helped, but Eza would still have been *very* happy with two more hours of sleep.

The doubts and feelings of failure were gone at the moment, and in their place were...shame, and embarrassment. How had he ever been so weak that he allowed those thoughts to sink into his head? Why hadn't he been strong enough or confident enough to kick them out right away? This was *stupid*. Eza was a trained soldier, a dragon-companion. He'd fought Azanna the rogue dragon trainer one-to-one, and been victorious. He'd snuck into Exclaimovia, resisted their attempt to torture him with small talk, and helped Cammie free Introvertia's stolen dragons. He'd visited Telravia, been attacked by Clairans on the way back, then fought at the Battle of Denneval Plain. He'd protected Cammie from Arianna's death mist. And after all of that, it was *thoughts* that were wrecking him, his own mind doing what swords and beasts couldn't.

This was miserable.

Eza changed his clothes and wandered outside. Aleiza was already awake; she'd sensed his uneasiness and met him at the back door, probing through the mind link to see if she could help. She couldn't – at least not with these thoughts – but Eza had thought of something on tour that he hadn't wanted to try for the first time in front of people. If Aleiza could get it figured out, though, she'd be incredibly dangerous the next time they found themselves in a fight.

"Okay, girl," he said out loud. "Trust me on this one."

Aleiza soared into the air, where the pink and orange rays of dawn were just cresting over the Impassable Mountains to the east. She followed Eza out of the garden and over the street outside. "You're going to need lots of space for this one," he told her. "Go full speed and don't stop no matter what, okay?"

Eza had only been speaking to dragons for a little over a year, and couldn't express thoughts so precise through the mind link yet. It wasn't much good saying them out loud either, because Aleiza almost certainly couldn't understand his language, but perhaps she could hear the confidence and comfort in his tone of voice.

Aleiza went a few blocks down the street and began flying toward Eza, building up incredible speed as she soared about ten feet above the cobblestones. When she was almost to Eza, he reached up. A flowing multicolored circle opened in front of Aleiza, with a second one sixty feet down the road. With no time to react, Aleiza flew straight into the first circle and instantly popped out of the second. Confusion howled in her head and she appealed to Eza for an explanation, spinning around in the air to face him.

There was really no way to explain the concept of Artomancy and the rainbow door to her, other than that she'd seen it a few times before, at Denneval and also while bringing the captured dragons back from Exclaimovia. At Denneval, she'd been attacked by primal magic while flying low; with no time to think, Eza had opened a rainbow door below and above her, and the primal lance had passed right through both doors, missing her. She hadn't understood then either.

So Eza cast the spell in midair again, about forty feet in front of her, and held it rippling there for as long as he could. Aleiza nosed her way toward it, investigating, then looking back down at Eza, easing her way into it and emerging from the other end right over Eza's head.

The dragon settled back to the ground, face to face with Eza, seemingly content now that she'd had the chance to examine the thing on her own terms. Eza could tell from the mind link that she was still mystified, but just like he'd asked her to, she trusted him and knew he wasn't going to deliberately harm her.

"Stick out your wings," he told her, saying the same thing through the mind link. She did, and Eza stepped up to her with his own arms outstretched. "About eight feet," he said. "Whew. That means you've still got another four feet to go before you're as big as Mazaren Tiranna's dragon, Arjera."

Aleiza would be *fearsome* when she got that huge. She'd probably be about nine feet tall by that point, and if she and Eza got their communication perfect and he could rainbow door her on top of enemy troops from a long distance away and then rainbow door her back out again before they even knew what hit them...their enemies, if they still had any by that point, would be in for a very bad time.

That made him want to redouble his efforts in Artomancy. He needed to get stronger, needed to project that rainbow door further. Way back when Eza had gotten kicked out of Pride and thought his mission to free the stolen dragons was over, Gar had rainbow doored to him from ten or twelve miles away. Granted, Gar had also said there were only two or three Artomancers in the world who were that strong, but if Eza could get even a quarter of that distance...well, it would have made yesterday's journey back from Rushwind a lot more bearable if Eza could have hopped them home several miles at a time instead of waiting for a horse to pull their wagon.

He and Aleiza kept drilling, switching from speed to precision. Eza started telling Aleiza just before he was going to open the rainbow door, having her pull up as soon as she was through it. After a few passes of that, Eza decided to raise the stakes.

"You'll be diving this time, girl, alright?"

Aleiza flew way up into the sky, which by now was almost entirely blue. The sun caught her silver scales, making her shine in a way that left Eza breathless. She paused momentarily, then hurtled down toward him.

He gave her the signal through the mind link, then popped the rainbow door open in front of her, with the other end about ten feet over his own head. If Aleiza's timing was off, she'd crash into him and maybe into the ground itself – but if everything went right –

WHOOSH went Aleiza, just a few feet above his head, the breeze blowing his hair as her wings flashed past him. Eza started laughing in delight, and he could tell Aleiza was pleased with herself, too. "Great job, girl," he told her. "Let's go wake up Cammie so we're not late for our nine o'clock class. She's probably going to want her hair turned pink again now that we're not on tour."

Eza was close: Cammie wanted purple this time. She certainly knew how to keep him guessing. After a leisurely breakfast and a little bit of quiet time on the couch, they entered through the south gate of Carnazon

Fortress. They had just enough time to drop by the barracks and leave their duffel bags of clothes before taking their backpacks and textbooks to class.

There was something on Eza's bed when he arrived in his dorm, though, and he dropped his duffel to pick it up. It was an envelope, thick paper with gold embossing. Careful script addressed it to "Ezalen Skywing and Cammaina Ravenwood, Dragon Academy, Carnazon Fortress, Tranquility, Introvertia."

The long-winded address made it sound like it'd come from outside the kingdom, and Eza was immediately curious. He resisted the temptation to tear the envelope open and forced himself to take it back out into the lounge so Cammie could be there when he read it. After all, her name was on the front, too.

"A letter?" she asked when she saw it. Eza showed her the address, and Cammie impulsively grabbed the envelope out of his hands, ripping it open and pulling out a folded paper. That made Eza smile; no matter what Cammie said, she would always be at least *part* Exclaimovian. "It's from Colonel Ennazar," she said in shock, almost dropping the paper.

Eza went behind her, peering over her shoulder with his hands around her. The paper looked like a wedding invitation, or a graduation announcement, very formal and decorated with an official-looking stamp. "Be it known that ARIC ENNAZAR, Elemental Archmage, has ascended to Telravia's COUNCIL OF THE SEVEN, with all the rights and responsibilities thereof."

Below it was added, in what Eza assumed was Ennazar's own handwriting, "Told you so," and underneath that the signature "Aric Ennazar," with all the proper flourishes that Eza associated with royalty or authority.

"He really did it," Cammie murmured in disbelief. "He really did it."

"He's probably just as surprised as you are," joked Eza. There was no time to ponder the implications of that news at the moment, though; he and Cammie had to rush to Professor Ozara's History class. They'd have to tell the king and queen later, just in case the knowledge wasn't already common.

However, the day wasn't finished dropping surprises on them yet. After History, Survivalship, and lunch, Eza and Cammie found themselves in Tactics, where Professor Rizara was seated in the corner because Colonel Naraza was at the front of the room. "At ease, Cadets," the colonel said. "As many of you know – and, indeed, as many of you have been looking forward to – we have reached the point in your third year where you will be divided into squads."

Introvertians, as a general rule, didn't *murmur*, but Eza could somehow sense the heightened energy. Several of the students traded looks with each other, unable to control their smiles.

"The rosters are posted on the north wall of the classroom," Colonel Naraza said, pointing to his left. "Please locate your squad, and if the captain is not personally known to you, introduce yourself to him or her as soon as possible. You'll receive orders for your first set of maneuvers within the next week, after the Company Games are over."

It was the second time in three hours that Cammie's excitement beat Eza's, and she arrived at the wall a half-step ahead of him, scanning the papers. "Found you!" she declared. "You're the commanding officer of Talon Squad."

"And we're together," Eza observed, pointing at her name.

"YES!" she shrieked, throwing her arms around him. Most of the other students had grown used to Cammie's periodic outbursts, and even if she was the only one who shouted for joy when she found out who she was with, there were certainly others who'd wanted to. Razan, though, rolled his eyes and looked away. "I'm already going to be the only one in the entire school who doesn't have a dragon of her own," Cammie explained. "I don't want to be around strangers, too."

"I'm glad to have you," Eza assured her. But there was another conversation he needed to have. He stepped away from Cammie, coming face to face with Razan.

"Are you up for being my second?" he asked Razan.

"I'll do my duty," Razan answered.

"I expect no less. You're to treat every member of this squad with the respect their position deserves."

"I said I'd do my duty," Razan repeated defensively.

"I'm sure you'll do a great job and I'm glad to have you along."

That seemed to catch Razan off guard. At last he responded with a simple, "Yes, sir."

Denavi had been evasive when Eza and Cammie had asked her what she was going to do while they were off at school. It was true that she'd read nearly every book Eza owned, and it was true that she was going to take some of her share of the leftover tour money and buy some new books. But that wasn't really what she needed. She was a soldier, and even though she didn't want to fight anymore, she was still used to having a purpose, having a direction, training for something. The first few weeks of sitting around Eza's house with nothing to do had been *wonderful*, but then it had gotten aimless, and Denavi didn't like feeling aimless.

The staff at the military hospital where Shanna was treated had given Denavi directions to a hospital that specialized in treating children. The closer she got, the more Denavi felt excitement bubbling up in her – along with fear. She knew a specific healing magic, for treating

111

battlefield injuries. Nothing had prepared her to treat a cold, or a virus, or tumors, or to help a child rehabilitate after an amputation. Would she really be any good to these people at all?

Denavi had almost talked herself out of the whole thing by the time she entered the front door and explained why she was there, then sat in a chair with her legs jiggling ferociously while the receptionist went to find Director Oleizen, who was expecting Denavi. After a brief introduction, Denavi was ushered to a room where a young boy was recovering from some serious burns.

Director Olaizen stood near the door, hands clasped behind her back, her face neutral as Denavi made her way up to the boy. Burns. Okay. "What's your name?" Denavi asked.

"Renaeza," the boy said, though it looked like the burns on his face hurt him when he talked.

"Where does it hurt the most?"

"Everywhere."

Suddenly Denavi felt the pressure, felt the director staring at the back of her head. Would her magic be good enough? "I want you to close your eyes, Renaeza," she said in what she hoped was a soothing voice. "Picture something that makes you very happy."

"Okay..."

The boy's eyes scrunched up and Denavi reached deep inside herself for healing energy, feeling it as it built in her chest and then passed out through her hands into the boy's face. Immediately she could see the wrinkled and scarred flesh start to smooth out, and in moments his face looked like a normal child's. Next Denavi went to his arms, where the wrinkles also disappeared. The exertion had taken a lot out of her, though, and the magic faltered before she could go on to his chest or legs. Why hadn't she thought to bring some food with her?

"Can I open my eyes now?" Renaeza asked.

"Please do."

The boy took a look at his arms, a frown of disbelief coming to his mouth a split-second before a wide smile of delight. "And my face?" he asked hopefully.

Director Olaizen handed Renaeza a mirror and he examined himself, wide-eyed and wide-mouthed. "How did you do this?" he asked.

"Magic," Denavi told him with a wink. "I trained in healing magic."

"Can I hug you?"

Of course; this was Introvertia, and uninvited physical contact was off limits. Denavi's only answer was to put her hands out, and Renaeza got to his knees on the bed, wrapping his arms around her neck. "Thank you," he said.

"You're not all the way healed yet," she told him. "Your chest and back..."

"Perhaps you can return next week for a final round

of treatments on him," suggested Director Olaizen. "For now, there are other patients..."

But Renaeza wasn't letting go, and Denavi wasn't about to pull away from him. "How long ago were you burned?" she asked him quietly.

"Two months. They tried everything. I was starting to think I'd be like that forever."

"I'm glad you're better," Denavi said. "And I'm glad I could help."

It had been a long time since she'd felt proud of herself the way she did when Renaeza finally let go of her and beamed at her. With a final wink she left his room and followed Director Olaizen to the next room.

Several hours later, and with several full meals worth of food in her stomach to replace the energy she'd burned, Denavi was walking out of the hospital feeling more satisfied than she could ever remember. She couldn't wait to tell Ezarra everything about her day and about how she'd helped those children.

There was one stop she had to make first, though. A quick right turn took her to the Music Square, then a left onto Broad Avenue took her through the Reading Square and past the palace. Cammie had said something about going back there later tonight to give the king and queen an after-action report on their tour. But that wasn't what Denavi was after. She kept going down Broad Avenue, almost to the gates of Tranquility, until she reached

Cappel's Bookstore.

The shop had only two other people in it on this Monday afternoon. Eza hadn't been joking when he'd said it was a house that had been turned into a bookstore. The front room even still *looked* like a living room, with shelves along every wall and more shelves where the couches would have been in a normal home. To her left was a staircase, with shelves lining the wall all the way to the door at the top.

An old man with white hair poked his head out of what had probably been the kitchen. "Be with you in just a moment..." Then he spotted Denavi. "On second thought, Traiza, I'll be back momentarily. I have a new customer."

He really knows I've never been in here before? thought Denavi.

"I'm Cappel, and you're not Introvertian," said the old man by way of greeting. "But you're a soldier, or at least you used to be, and 'used to be' is a very interesting phrase to use on someone who's...what, eighteen? I bet you have quite the story."

"Do you do this to all your customers?" Denavi asked with a smile.

"Only the ones who have a tale worth telling. So, out with it. Dark hair means you're not Esterian, and you haven't offered to give me a hug yet so you're probably not Exclaimovian. So...Clairan?"

"Vagrani, actually," said Denavi, spontaneously deciding to see if she could fool him. "My family and I are traders from the capital city of Evara. We tagged along with an Introvertian convoy to see if we could get a look at Tranquility from the inside, since I know your kingdom doesn't allow visitors."

Mr. Cappel guffawed. "A most excellent story, my young Clairan friend. You have a gift for creating, I can tell that. Now, the truth, if you please."

His pure, bright laugh brought a smile to her face. "How did you know?"

"I have my ways."

"Very well, then. I'm Denavi Kiresti, and I'm friends with Ezalen Skywing."

Mr. Cappel slapped his knee. "Ah, yes. One of my favorite people. Anyone he likes, I like too. How did you end up here? Is he just collecting people from other nations now that he has an Exclaimovian for a friend?"

"Oh, they're not friends anymore. They're courting now."

"Courting!" repeated Mr. Cappel in astonishment. "For how long?"

"Ah...about three weeks."

"That's wonderful. I'm thrilled for them. I'll have to get them a special present for the next time they poke their heads in here. However, we were talking about you."

Denavi saw why Eza and Cammie liked Mr. Cappel. This wasn't just a store owner talking to someone about to spend money. His interest was genuine, and the way his eyes examined hers told her that he was truly eager to hear what she was going to say.

"I'm seventeen years old, and I was a healer in the Clairan army. My company was annihilated in a fight against Introvertia, while your troops were on their way back from sealing the alliance with Telravia. I was the only survivor because I hid to save my life. Clairans believe in death before dishonor, so I could never go home again. Being the lone survivor would have brought shame on my entire family. But Eza and Cammie persuaded the king to let me live with them, and now I'm here."

"Tell it again," said Mr. Cappel. "But don't tell me the facts. Tell me the *feelings*."

Denavi blinked. "I'm sorry?"

"You told me information, events, in a logical sequence of order. I want you to tell it again, but focusing on *emotions*. Tell me how you *felt* to be a Clairan soldier. Tell me how you *felt* when you saw all your friends slaughtered around you, how you *felt* when you realized you could never go home again."

This was...strange, but then again, both Eza and Cammie had warned her of the old man's strangeness, too. She thought for a moment. Cammie always told stories in a certain way, as if she were acting them out on a stage, with body movements and exaggerated voices, her eyes wide during parts that were exciting or scary. Denavi pondered that, then told her own story in the same way – hands wide, moving closer to Mr. Cappel during happy parts and withdrawing during the sad parts.

She didn't realize until the end of the story that she had an audience. The two other customers had left the kitchen by the other door and had doubled back around into the living room where Denavi was standing, off to the left so that she couldn't see them while she was focused on Mr. Cappel. Only at the end, when Mr. Cappel was nodding and smiling approval, did she catch sight of them, and a wave of embarrassment washed over her.

"That was very good," Mr. Cappel said. "I've seen plays in several different kingdoms, and your delivery was excellent. All that time you're spending around Miss Ravenwood – soon to be Mrs. Skywing, I suppose – must be benefiting you. Let me encourage you in that gift, young Miss Kiresti. Is there anyplace where you could practice telling stories?"

"At home with Eza and Cammie, I guess," Denavi said, and then suddenly a thought leaped into her mind. She could tell stories to the kids in the hospital while she was healing them! Even if she couldn't heal some child's injury or sickness, she could at least tell stories and entertain them for a while. This was *spectacular*. Denavi made up her mind to ask Cammie that very night about how to tell stories even better.

Eza and Cammie weren't yet back from class when Denavi returned, but Ezarra was, sitting on the couch when Denavi opened the front door.

"Daddy!" Denavi shouted, running to him and leaping over the arm of the couch. She landed next to him, grinning expectantly.

"How was your day at the hospital?" Ezarra asked, smiling down at her as she tore off her boots and socks and dropped them by the side of the couch.

"It was *wonderful!*"

A huge smile of delight and pride sprang to Ezarra's face. *He makes that face when he thinks of me*, Denavi thought, and that realization made her so happy her throat got tight and she nearly cried.

"Tell me everything," Ezarra said excitedly.

NINE

Cammie hadn't grasped just how *huge* a deal the Company Games were until she'd seen Eza and the other third-year Harmony students stay awake until ten at night on Tuesday debating who would compete in which events. Eza had explained that the Games consisted of around twenty different events, each of which was broken up by year, meaning the third-year Harmony students would be competing against the third-years from each of the other companies. Beyond that, Cammie didn't really know what was going on, and had stayed at the edge of the room, away from the excitement, while the other students set the roster.

There had been a surprising amount of disagreement for a group called Harmony, but bragging rights were on the line, as well as a trophy which would be in the winning company's barracks until the next year's Games. Cammie was tempted to retreat to the dorm, but she didn't think she'd be able to fall asleep in a quiet room knowing there was fun being had next door. It was times like this when she realized she wasn't fully Introvertian, and although the thought didn't normally bother her – Eza loved her just the way she was, after all – on this particular night it made her feel even more excluded, when she already felt left out because she didn't know much about the Games.

Eza had been at the center of the chaos, though, trying to referee the whole thing, and eventually when the roster had been set and everyone had voted on it, he brought the finished paper over to Cammie. "I got you into two events," he said proudly. "Technically four, if you count all the variations..."

Cammie searched for her name. "Dance?" she asked. "Wh – I – thank you, Eza, but why is there even a dance event at a military academy?"

"I think you'd be shocked how many students take up dance as a way to improve their swordfighting footwork. I bet eighty percent of the people in this room can hold their own on the dance floor." He tilted his head at her. "Why are you surprised, anyway? You danced with me at the Equinox Festival."

"Yeah, you're right. I'm just in a strange mood tonight."

"We can talk later if you want. I also got you into Recitation."

"You mean doing a monologue in front of people?"

"Sort of. There are three variations and you're doing all of them. There's Existing, where you perform a bit from a speech or play or poem that's already been written. There's Original, where you write your own and then perform that. And then..." He couldn't hide his smile. "There's Group, which is two or more people reciting together. I was thinking you and I could –"

"The final scene from *The Ranger's Dilemma*," Cammie said, cutting him off. "It'd be perfect."

"Exactly," Eza told her.

"Thank you for thinking of me, Eza." She took her glasses off and put them on top of her purple hair; she knew he always loved being able to look directly into her eyes without anything in the way. "You really are the best, even when you don't think you are. What events are you doing?"

"I'm part of the foot race relay, and I'm also doing dragon aerobatics. I think Aleiza and I can really put together something special. I'm also on the ringball team and I'm an injury alternate for swordfighting."

Cammie was looking around the room. "There are more than eighty Harmony third-years, but I'm in four events and you're in three more – well, actually four, if you count the one you're doing with me. There aren't enough events for everybody to do one."

"You'd be surprised how many Harmony students don't want to participate. Most of us aren't very competitive. Harmony people tend not to like situations where one person wins and everyone else loses. We'd rather all work together."

"But you're the most competitive person I've ever met."

"That's why I'm doing so many events," he grinned. "Most of Harmony doesn't really care whether we win or lose as long as everyone gets along at the end, just like most of Sun doesn't really care whether they win or lose as long as everyone has a good time. Excellence wants to win, but even they don't really care whether they win as long as they know they did their best. It's only Victory who take the results seriously. Losing drives them nuts." Eza held up his hand to Cammie. "And we're going to drive them nuts."

She took his hand, folding her fingers between his. "Thank you, Eza, for always making sure I feel welcome here."

"I try."

"You succeed," she insisted, gently spinning him around and digging her thumbs into his shoulders. "By the sun, Eza, why are you so tense?"

His only answer was to groan in satisfaction as Cammie's hands broke apart his muscle knots. "I don't know, but this is really amazing."

"I'll go a little longer, and then you need to get to bed if you're going to be well rested in the morning."

Eza craned his neck to look backward at her. "Yes, mother."

"MOTHER?!" Cammie screeched, digging her fingers into his ribs and dropping on top of him when he sprawled to the floor to get away. "MOTHER?!"

"People are sleeping!" Eza protested between laughs and squirms.

"Then laugh quieter!"

Eza tossed her off easily, as he always did. "I won't call you mother again. Probably. But that was funny."

"Go to bed, you goof. I'll finish your massage tomorrow. I love you."

"I love you too."

It probably would have made more sense to do the Games during one of the two-week term breaks, Eza thought, but so many students did intensives and went home to visit family that it would have been difficult to organize. Taking a Wednesday, Thursday, and Friday off class seemed to work well enough, although Eza and Cammie had been away from the school so much in the past month that Eza honestly would have enjoyed spending those days in class, just taking notes and studying like a normal person.

Because the Games were played not just between companies but between years, each event actually happened five times. The first event was the rope climb, where students had to go from the courtyard to the second floor walkway. The first-year students competed right after breakfast (an agile Sun girl named Liriana Oreza took first prize), the second-year students after that, and up through the years until all five had competed. After the rope climb, though, things got really wild, with ringball being played in the courtyard at the same time that several of the survival events, such as shelter construction and zero-to-campfire, were being conducted outside the city, all while the cooking competition with mystery ingredients was going on in the mess hall. Every year there was at least one student who was supposed to compete in some event but forgot the schedule or got so caught up in cheering for classmates that they didn't make it on time.

That was why Eza was waiting on standby at the swordfighting event just outside the city gates while the first-years were playing ringball. Harmony's swordfighter, Torea Nizeara, fought hard, and he ended up defeating Sun's fighter easily in the first round before winning a thriller against Victory Company's Lahan Meara in the final. It was hard to know where any company stood before all the events were over, but with victories in third-year swordfighting and the second-year rope climb, Harmony was looking good so far.

But then it was time for third-year ringball in the courtyard, and Eza hustled over, as did Torea, who somehow didn't seem fatigued after a swordfight that had lasted longer than any Eza had ever been in. Victory had won the first- and second-year ringball, and they were out for a win in their third-year semifinal match against Harmony. For the Games, a regulation field had been measured out, with actual metal rings and retaining nets rather than hand-drawn rings chalked onto the walls during pick-up games.

Eza usually played on the right wing, where he could cross the ball to the central attackers or else cut inside and shoot with his left foot. That put him against Victory's left defender, Gezan Nirea, who was taller and heavier than Eza. Both of them knew what that meant: Gezan would be using his physicality, trying to bodily keep Eza out of the attacking lanes without drawing a foul, while Eza would be using speed and agility to get past him and get a clean run on goal.

It was funny, Eza thought, how both of them could know exactly what was about to happen, and the only question was which of them could do it better when things counted.

The referee's signal blew and instantly Eza had his back in Gezan's chest, arms out, calling for the ball. Harmony's center was Anneka Azoana, playing in place of the injured Shanna; despite Anneka's inexplicable hatred of Cammie, Eza had to admit that she was a quick thinker and a capable attacker. As soon as she planted her feet to pass, Eza was already rounding Gezan, leaving the defender in the dust as Anneka's pass went straight to the point where she knew Eza would be. He took the ball on the outside of his left foot, dribbling it forward with his head up.

Victory's other defender, Rizanna Cana, shifted over to meet Eza, who spotted Anneka making an attacking run. At top speed, Eza dribbled right at Rizanna, and as soon as the defender had committed to getting in his way, Eza flicked his foot outward and sent a pass right to the feet of Anneka. Before Eza could even blink, Anneka's shot was blasting right through the metal ring and into the net. Eza sprinted toward her, trading high-fives as they made their way back to midfield for Victory's kickoff.

Victory attacked aggressively as soon as the referee signaled for the restart, sending the ball forward to their center and then sideways to their wings. As a winger himself, Eza wasn't supposed to pull back and play defense; he was supposed to stay high and ready for the counterattack, but Victory was moving the ball with confidence and the Harmony defenders never had a chance to break up a pass. Eza waited for the perfect moment to pounce, and then sprinted toward Victory's left winger.

But his approach was too loud and the Victory player scooped the ball up with her hands, heaving it back toward her midfield, where their central midfielder distributed the ball back to Gezan to attack down the left sideline. Eza rushed back toward Gezan, hoping his foray into defense hadn't pulled him too far out of position. Gezan picked up the ball and held it for a few moments. For some reason, Eza just *felt* like Gezan was going to make a throw back toward the opposite defender, and he tensed. Sure enough, Gezan cocked back to throw and Eza took off at full speed, intercepting the pass before it was halfway to Rizanna and faking a cross before blowing past Rizanna and scooping the ball right into the ring.

Victory never recovered from that opening salvo, and Harmony opened a five-goal lead before Victory pulled a few goals back. The final score at the end of half an hour was Harmony nine, Victory five. That result meant that Harmony was through to the final, which would be held that night after dinner, against whichever team won the Sun-Excellence semifinal that was about to start.

But Eza couldn't stick around. Still sweaty, he took off for the east side function room, the same place where he and Cammie had performed *The Ranger's Dilemma*, so he could watch Cammie compete in Dance. It turned out that Cammie was waiting for him at the door. "Did you win?" she asked excitedly.

"We crushed them. I had two goals and two assists."

"I still don't really understand the game but that sounds impressive and I'm proud of you." Cammie's eyes wandered toward the front of the stage. "I'm pretty nervous at the moment, though. I found out about this thing last night and I didn't have time to choreograph a dance, so I'm doing one I made up while I was still living in Exclaimovia. I hope it's not too..."

"Loud?"

Cammie giggled. "Exactly."

"Do your best. We chose you because we believe in you."

"Can you make my hair just a little longer, like to my shoulders? I want it to flip out when I twirl and I don't think this is quite long enough."

Eza placed his fingers on her hair, reaching out with his Artomancy magic and trying to eyeball the length. Cammie's hair grew, and Eza stopped it at what he thought was the perfect time. "I have to recolor the top," he told her. "The new stuff came with your natural color, so it's brown on top and purple below."

"Hurry, because –"

"Cammie Ravenwood, Harmony Company!" someone called from the front.

Cammie pulled away from him, her hair still brown. "Wish me luck!"

"You won't need it because you're great!" he called as she rushed to the stage.

As soon as she began, the room got even more silent than a room of Introvertians would normally be. The only sounds were Cammie's shoes on the stone floor and the whooshing of her clothes as her arms swayed. There was passion in the movements, and even though no music or words accompanied her, Eza felt like she was telling him a story with her body. She edged her way to the front of the stage, arms wide and head forward with open body language – then suddenly she slid backward, head low and to the side as if she'd been burned by flying too close to the sun, low and compact like she was hiding. She stayed low, moving around the back of the stage, seeming like she was trying to find her place there away from all the eyes, then came to a halt, her body radiating language of exhausted defeat. Just when the crowd seemed to wonder if she was done, her head came up again, slowly, but confidently, and then she burst out, elbows bent and palms out as if pushing away all the voices that had told her to stay low and scared, then reaching high with a smile on her face, twirling – her hair spinning out from her just like she'd said she wanted it to – and at last coming to a halt on the front of the stage, arm out and palm up as if inviting the audience to take her hand and come with her on the journey.

It was like nothing Eza had ever seen before, and he found himself applauding even before he knew what he was doing. He was still standing at the back of the room, but he found a seat and then got to his feet again just so he could say he'd stood up for her. Cammie was looking for him, and Eza moved away from his seat and into the side aisle, walking toward the stage.

Cammie ran off the stage and into his arms just like Denavi had done to Ezarra after the final performance of

Love or Potatoes. "Did you like it?" she asked breathlessly. "I've never seen you dance like *that*. I had no idea you could be so emotional with just your body!"

"Maybe I can show you how," Cammie said, hope in her voice.

"I'd love to learn."

TEN

The ringball final was going to be against Sun Company, much to everyone's surprise. Excellence had been heavily favored, but Sun had used a quick counterattack and long, direct passes to neutralize their opponents' skill, and Excellence had never found an answer. There had been some grumbling afterward – not just from Excellence students, either – about how the "kick it long and hope for the best" strategy made for ugly play, but until the referee started giving points for beauty, winning the game was all that mattered.

The Harmony players had met before the game and agreed that the only way to beat Sun was to play tight, compact defense and not leave any space behind midfield for them to kick into. Sun would be expecting Harmony to play four defenders and leave three on offense, but Harmony would actually be playing five on defense, with Anneka dropping back – Eza had never in his life seen a center forward playing defense, but today was going to be the day – leaving Eza and Razan, the wing players, in a two-man attack. It was a big gamble, but this was the final of the Company Games. It was time to win big or lose big.

Sun took possession first, and Harmony dropped

back into their unique formation – two defenders in the center, two on the sides slightly in front, and Anneka in front of them with Razan and Eza still wide. Sun's midfield held the ball for a few moments, as if trying to figure out what they were looking at, before launching a hopeful ball toward the sideline just behind Eza.

Harmony's right-side defender was already retrieving the ball, so Eza sprinted forward, checking over his shoulder for the pass he hoped was coming toward him. It came, but not exactly into his path; he had to slow his run and move to his left to retrieve the pass, controlling it with his left foot. Anneka was advancing toward him, in a hesitant attack that left her plenty of room to withdraw in case Eza lost possession. He held up his left arm, then passed the ball back to Anneka.

His left arm was the signal for a forward run. As soon as the ball came off his foot, Eza whirled to his left, blasting past the defender who'd been expecting him to go the other way. Eza was in the center attacking lane now, and he glanced backward for Anneka's pass. Sure enough, she'd played the one-two with him, passing forward into the attacking lane as soon as the ball had come to her, and Eza ran onto the ball with no difficulty, scooping it into the unguarded ring and wheeling away for a celebration.

There were spectators standing all around the perimeter of the court and on the second floor walkway above the courtyard, and loud cheers with a few groans echoed off the walls of Carnazon. The sound was pure energy to Eza; he loved every moment of it, slapping his hands against Anneka's and Razan's as they came over to congratulate him on his move. *This* he could get used to.

But Sun's next possession was more focused, and they patiently probed for weaknesses in the Harmony defensive line before finally lofting a hopeful pass in toward the center of the goal area. A miscommunication between the two Harmony central defenders let one of Sun's attackers race onto the ball and level the score immediately. Eza put his hands on his hips. "Come on!" he shouted. "We can't be beating ourselves now! Tighten up!"

Anneka's restart went to Razan, who tried passing forward to Eza only to see the pass intercepted and a long ball sent back toward the Harmony goal. This time the defenders were ready for it, though, and after a brief scuffle the ball was cleared out to Anneka, who tried to get it to Eza on the right.

But there were two defenders rushing toward Eza, so he picked the ball up, which he almost never did, holding it to his chest. Hand passes could only go sideways or backward; he'd taken a lot of options away from himself by holding the ball, but he felt like time was more important than speed here. Anneka drifted toward him, but so did one of the defenders who'd been at his back. Eza took his left hand off the ball, meeting the eyes of his right-side defender and pointing to the right. The defender nodded, and Eza rolled the ball hard toward him. Just as Eza had hoped, the defender immediately crossed the ball to Razan on the opposite side of the field, switching the attack to the place where the opponent had fewer defenders. Razan raced toward the ring and smashed the ball through before Sun's defense could react to him. Eza punched the air in celebration. He wouldn't get credit for an official assist on the play, but he'd made the goal happen, and everyone who understood the game knew what they'd seen. That was enough for him.

Sun's attacks got more desperate, which meant less careful, and every time they tried a high ball into the Harmony defense, two or three bodies were there to break it up and counterattack. By the twenty-minute mark Eza was drenched in sweat from sprinting forward at full speed every time one of his defenders collected the ball, but the scoreboard didn't lie. Eza finished with four goals and three assists, not counting the one on Razan's goal, as Harmony scored ten goals and held Sun to just the one.

After losing in the final both of his first two years, Eza hardly knew what to do with himself. As soon as the referee gave his signal for the end of the game, Eza put his hands on his head and dropped to his knees on the cobblestones. They'd really done it. Razan and Anneka were shouting in victory, running toward Eza, who forced himself to his feet and wrapped his arms around both of them. "We did it!" shouted Razan. "We won the final!"

"It's amazing what we can do when we're united," Eza agreed.

Instantly Anneka pulled away. "What's that supposed to mean?" she snapped.

Eza frowned in confusion. "What?"

"Why do you have to go and bring Cammie into this?"

"No one's talking about Cammie," Eza said, beyond bewildered. All around them, their teammates were cheering and their fans on the second floor walkway were going crazy. Why was Anneka choosing this moment to pick a fight?

Anneka heaved a sigh of disgust and walked away shaking her head. "Do you have any idea what she's going on about?" Eza asked Razan.

"I..." It could have just been Eza's imagination, but it looked like Razan was being torn in half, as if he wanted to say one thing but knew he should have been saying something else. "I don't. I'm sorry."

Eza shook his head. "Later. For now, let's celebrate."

Cammie came sprinting up to Eza, and he grabbed

her under her arms and twirled her around. "You were amazing!" she shouted over the cheers.

"Thank you," he said.

"But you can put me down now. You're really sweaty."

The ringball final was the last event of the day, and the courtyard began clearing out after the celebrations died down. Cammie and Eza usually stayed in the barracks during the week, but Eza smelled very strongly of sweaty boy, so Cammie had convinced him to go back to his home for a proper bath.

It was normal for everyone in the house to take a few gallons of warm water up to their bedrooms and wash off there each morning, but Eza needed submerging, and that meant bathing outside in the garden, because there was no way to carry that fifty-gallon cauldron up the stairs and it wasn't safe for Aleiza to heat up the water indoors. Eza went upstairs to change into some cotton shorts, then slipped on a pair of socks for the walk downstairs.

Cammie was waiting for him by the cauldron, pouring something that smelled like flowers into the water. "I'm afraid soap by itself might not do the job," she said apologetically. "This may help."

"Oh, please!" Eza laughed, peeling his socks off and lowering himself into the cauldron. "When we first met, I'd been in the forest without showering for a *week*."

"And I didn't get close enough to find out how you smelled, did I?" she asked, sitting on a stool next to the cauldron. "But now that we're walking arm in arm everywhere we go, it's a different story."

"Fair point," agreed Eza.

"Who do you think is winning the Games right now?"

"I don't have any idea. Based on the events I saw, I think we're just about tied with Victory, but I didn't see everything."

Cammie handed Eza a bar of soap, and he began scrubbing his arms and then his armpits. "When do you think I'll know how I placed in Dance?"

"Tomorrow morning. The professors get together after the event to discuss what they saw and decide who should win, and the results will be posted in the mess hall when we go to breakfast."

"How do you think I did?"

"I'm not a dance expert by any means, but I swordfight, and like I told you, they're very similar. Your footwork looked perfect, and your motions were very expressive but very controlled. I don't see how you could possibly have done better."

Cammie smiled. "Thank you, Eza. I just hope the judges liked the style. It was really different from the other performers. But you liked it, and your opinion matters more."

"Cammaina Ravenwood, did you just accept a compliment and then *offer one back?*"

"N – uh, maybe?"

Eza just winked at her.

"So we're teasing each other now," Cammie said. "Alright." She bent down, picked up Eza's socks, strode to the door, and flung them inside, an enormous smug grin on her face as she sat back on the stool. "Enjoy walking inside barefoot."

"You *monster*," Eza joked.

"I'll bring them back for you if you let me give you a foot rub like the ones you give me."

Eza froze, blinking several times.

"I know how you feel about being vulnerable," Cammie continued. "But it's me, Eza. I want you to trust me."

"I do..."

"Not all the way. Not yet. You wear two pairs of boots, Eza, one on your feet and one on your feelings, so you can run away and hide whenever something threatens you."

"I –"

Cammie set her glasses on top of her head, her blue and brown eyes fixed on Eza. "You say you trust me, and I've never given you a reason to distrust me, but you won't let me do something as simple as *touch your feet.* And let's not even talk about the way you've been hiding all those doubts and fears and negative thoughts from me, or at least trying. I want you to talk to me about those things. If we're going to get married someday, we have to think with one mind and feel with one heart. Anything that delights you delights me. Anything that grieves you grieves me. Okay?"

Eza was tempted to get out of the bathtub and go fleeing inside, but that would only have proved Cammie's point, wouldn't it?

"I bet I know why you're like this," Cammie continued. "Back in Rushwind we were talking about the things we needed when we were younger, and you didn't say anything – which isn't unusual, of course, but it got me thinking. What happened to you when you were younger? Denavi lost her dad, and I felt out of place in Exclaimovia. What was your big wound?"

"My mother dying," he said instantly.

"And how did you react to her being gone?" Cammie prodded. "By sharing all your deepest feelings with your dad?" Eza made himself meet her eyes, and Cammie examined him. "No," she concluded. "Because your dad was hurting too, and you didn't want to burden him. So you buried your feelings, pretended you didn't feel the pain. You thought it was the best thing for your dad, and you've always been the type who loves to make other people happy, so you did what you thought he needed even though it was tearing you apart."

Eza's eyes were getting watery, but he forced himself to keep looking at Cammie.

"Right?" she asked.

Eza nodded. Tears found their way out of his eyes and down his cheeks.

"So you put boots on your feelings and ran away from the pain. And now, after...how old were you when she died?"

"Eight."

"So after seven years of doing that, it's all you know how to do. You put on a strong face even when you're dying inside because it's never been safe for you to let your feelings out. Sometimes that really does help you, too. You've done some pretty incredible things by pretending you weren't scared. But I don't want you to pretend with me. I want to know the *real* Eza."

"What if you don't like what you see?" The words were out of his mouth before he'd even thought about them, and he wished he could take them back – but part of him didn't, because that fear gnawed at him, and if Cammie could help chase it away...

"Do I have to repeat your own words back to you, what you said when I was worried about us growing apart? You said you made a promise to me and that you don't break your promises. I made the same promise to you, Eza. I'm here *for you*. And if it turns out you're hurting inside, then I'm here for that. In fact, it's what I want." She laughed at herself. "I don't want you to be hurting. But if you are, then I want to be a part of the healing. Even if it scares you. Even if it scares *me*. I want you to let me in. I'd rather be deep inside your heart where it's messy than have you hold me at arm's length so everything looks perfect."

Eza didn't even know what to say. He knew what the right answer was – to let her in, let her see the brokenness, let her see the scared little boy who still wanted a hug from mommy. But it felt so...so hard to do, after years of running and hiding...

"Please?" Cammie said softly.

All Eza could do was nod. "Okay," he managed at last. "I promise. I won't always do a good job at it, but I promise to try."

"Your best will always be good enough," Cammie assured him. "Now, wash your hair and get out of that cauldron so I can rub your feet."

ELEVEN

Cammie had gone to bed the night before even more in love with Eza than she'd ever been before. He'd talked to her, really *talked*, about his mother's death and how badly it hurt and how he'd tried to keep everything inside afterward. He had cried, and Cammie had cried too imagining Eza as a terrified little boy. Hearing his doubts and fears didn't make him seem weaker to her – it made him seem *stronger*, because she knew everything he was fighting inside. She made sure he knew it, too, and when they'd both gone to bed (far later than they should have, given how little sleep they'd gotten the night before and how busy they'd both be on Thursday), the hug they shared at the end was Cammie's favorite hug ever.

However, she was still absolutely dragging as she and Eza made their way back to Carnazon on Thursday morning, with Aleiza lazily banking from side to side above their heads. Eza and Aleiza hadn't been able to find any extra practice time for their acrobatic routine, and Eza was hoping the rainbow door's novelty was enough to scrape out victory for them. Cammie would have her hands full the entire morning, with the Existing and Original recitation events followed by her Group performance with Eza.

They arrived just as breakfast was ending, but food was the last thing on Cammie's mind. She hustled to the spot on the wall where the Dance results were posted, hunting for her name.

"Second place," she said, feeling pleasantly surprised. "I – that's really wonderful."

"If you look at the scores, you very nearly won, too," Eza said from over her shoulder. "You lost to Victory's dancer by half a point."

"And I beat two others," Cammie reasoned. "I'd say that's good for my first event ever in the Company Games. And, you know, for finding out the night before that I'd be performing, and not having any time to prepare something or practice."

Eza laughed. "You always exceed expectations."

Cammie reached behind her, trying to poke him in the stomach. "You're too kind."

"There's no such thing as too kind."

"That's...probably true. What time do you have to be in the courtyard for Dragon Aerobatics?"

"Ten. I should be able to see you do at least one of your recitations before then."

The two of them headed to the same east side function room where Cammie had danced the night before, taking two seats near the back of the room. The first performers were *good*, Cammie had to admit, and she leaned over to Eza. "Who were the first two?"

144

"The first one, from Sun Company, was Tiazen Aviana. You might have recognized her from the ringball game last night; she played in the center of defense and I torched her pretty hard on a couple of goals."

"She had good stage presence just now. I want to talk to her about joining the theater company."

"Ooooh, that's a good idea. The one from Excellence was Jaraza Auberan. He wants to be an officer when he graduates, so he's been used to projecting his voice with authority and confidence."

"He'd be a good actor, too. Eventually I want to do plays with more than just two or three people in them, so I'm making a list in my head now." Cammie took Eza's hand. "Or rather, in your head, since I don't know who all these people are just yet."

"Your list is safe up here," Eza promised her.

Cammie's selection was a little different than either of the first two. Tiazen had performed a poem and Jaraza a monologue from an Introvertian play that Cammie had read recently, but Cammie had opted for a passage from...well, a book that meant a lot to Eza.

Her name was announced, and she made her way to the stage and bowed to the judges before launching into her recitation. "'You're a fool, Mazaren Tiranna,' the sorcerer said, sounding exhausted. 'You could have been great in my kingdom, a dragon-companion whose name and deeds would live forever, but you've chosen death on a nameless field...'"

She saw Eza gasp in delight, and it took all of her focus to keep from smiling. The passage was from *Heroes of Introvertia*, the book Eza had been reading on the day he first met Exclaimovians. Forcing her gaze to the other spectators, Cammie continued reciting, eventually coming to the end of her selection, the part where the dragon Arjera was grievously injured.

"'Arjera!' Mazaren screamed, running around to her front and putting his hands on her cheeks," Cammie said, passion in her voice as if it were her own child who'd been wounded, dropping to one knee and pantomiming the action. "He looked up frantically to see if any Introvertian soldiers had seen the fight and were coming that direction. 'Help! Someone help!'"

She screamed it with such intensity that three people actually did come sprinting in through the side entrance, scanas drawn like they were expecting to see someone being attacked. Again Cammie nearly laughed, and had to look down while she regained her composure. "He locked minds with Arjera and felt pain, but faintly, at a great distance, as if the dragon were slipping away. 'No,' he whispered quietly, telling her without words how much he loved her and how much he needed her to live. 'Arjera, stay with me...'"

There was absolute silence in the room as Cammie stood, bowed to the judges, and made her way off the stage. Only then did the thunderous applause kick in, and she smiled as she skipped her way back to Eza, who was standing to meet her. "That was absolutely incredible," he told her, taking both of her hands in his. "I'm glad you liked it. I picked that story because it means a lot to you."

"You're so thoughtful. I love it."

They sat down together and Cammie leaned her head on his shoulder to watch the remaining performance.

Before long, though, Eza wriggled out from underneath her. "I have to go. Dragon Aerobatics is coming up."

"Come back as soon as you can, okay?"

"Anything for you."

Aleiza joined Eza in the courtyard, swooping over the walls with her enormous wingspan and settling down next to him, nuzzling him with her snout as usual. Eza wrapped his arms around her neck, gently pouring magical energy into her the same way he did every time they were together. He was sure that's why she'd grown so huge – but as he'd told her before, there was still work to do if she was going to become as large as Arjera in the old stories.

Eza was the first performer in Dragon Aerobatics, which meant he had no idea what his competition would be doing. He'd be the one setting the bar, for better or for worse. "Ready, girl?" he asked Aleiza. Through the mind link, he received back confidence and calm. She was as ready as she was going to be.

The judges signaled to Eza and the crowd grew silent. It didn't matter whether the cheers were deafening; Eza had commanded Aleiza on a battlefield, with soldiers fighting below her and combat falcons screaming above, and the noise had never distracted him. She flew up into the warm spring sky, sunlight glinting off her silver scales, then suddenly swooped down toward Eza.

Instantly he was locked in on her, telling her what was about to happen, and then a rainbow door opened below her with a *fwoosh* and she barreled through it, emerging so close to Eza that he could almost reach up and touch her. Just like it had when they'd practiced on the street, a rush of wind tugged at his clothes and hair as Aleiza pulled up just over the top of him. *That* was when the crowd roared.

But Eza wasn't done. Aleiza was pulling up, gaining altitude, and suddenly *fwoosh* she was on top of the spectators, bellowing out a deafening roar as she passed within ten feet of their heads. She wheeled over on one wing, banking into a tight left turn and then dropping out of the air as if strafing some enemy infantry. A furious blast of fire raked the cobblestones, and then Aleiza was swooping into the air again, radiating pure joy to Eza through the mind link. She was *loving* this, he realized, and he was loving it too.

For another ten minutes he and Aleiza played in an aerial dance, with her bursting in and out of rainbow doors, surprising the audience and delighting herself and Eza. The judges *had* to be in awe. Eza was biased, of course, but he didn't know how it was possible for anyone to score higher than him and Aleiza.

As with Cammie's Dance scores the night before, though, no one would know who had won Dragon Aerobatics until dinnertime that night, after the judges had discussed the scores and come to a consensus. Before that, though, Eza had something else to do. He sprinted off toward the Harmony barracks, emerging a few minutes later in his costume for the Group Recitation performance with Cammie.

By this time the east side function room was packed, with all the seats taken and people standing wherever they could find empty space. Eza knew the word had spread that Cammie had been sponsored by the king and queen, and that this final scene of *The Ranger's Dilemma* was the one that had first gotten Queen Annaya's attention. Expectations were through the roof, and it was up to Eza and Cammie to deliver.

Again, Eza was biased, but he couldn't imagine anyone performing better than he and Cammie had. They'd done an excellent job on the night of the original performance, and the week-long tour had only given Eza more experience and more confidence. Rather than just acting, he felt like he *commanded* the stage, striding back and forth with a confidence he finally felt rather than just pretended.

"I'd give up all my dreams for love," he told Cammie, projecting the feelings with his face as well as with his hands. "But I wouldn't be giving up anything at all, not really..." He let his voice drop, trying to make it break the same way it had the night of the performance, and thought he might have succeeded. "If I gained the kind of love people wrote poems about."

Normally Cammie was standing face to face with him during the scene, but in this performance she had wandered off across the stage, looking down with her shoulders slumped as if expecting the worst news of her life. As soon as he said the word "but," she looked over her shoulder with hope in her eyes, turning her whole body to face him on "if," and allowing relief and excitement to break over her face as soon as he finished talking. The script called for him to move to her, but she sprinted the three steps to Eza, hurling herself into his arms as he spun her around and put his hand on the back of her neck to kiss her. Suddenly he was thinking of their talk the night before, and he was crying, unable to stop. The audience roared, apparently thinking Eza was a master of the stage, and he wasn't about to correct them if it meant winning the event for Harmony.

"Nice job on the tears there," Cammie told him as they left the stage.

"They were real."

"Mmmm. I did tell you that kissing was more convincing if you really meant it. Crying is the same way. Are you okay?"

"I'm great."

Cammie took him at his word, and the two of them sat back down to watch the other performances.

If she was being really honest, Cammie would have to admit that she neither knew, nor particularly cared, which events were happening when, other than the events she was competing in. Eza had managed to be present for most of them, and Cammie had gone with him because she wanted to be wherever he was all the time, but it really didn't matter to her whether she watched the shelter construction event in the Very Large Forest, or the campfire construction event in the foothills of the Impassable Mountains, or the obstacle course in the courtyard, or the cooking event with mystery ingredients in the mess hall. Harmony was Eza's group; he cared how they did because he'd been with them for years, but Cammie had barely been with them for a month – and only because Eza was there. All that mattered to her was that he was happy, and if these Company Games made him happy, then she was fully into it.

By Thursday evening the results of that day's events had been posted in the mess hall, and after quite a long wait to get at the papers, Cammie was finally able to find out how she'd done. "I WON!" she screeched at the top of her voice, making several students cover their ears and scramble over tables to get away from her. "RECITATION, EXISTING: FIRST PLACE, CAMMAINA RAVENWOOD, HARMONY COMPANY!"

"Keep it down," Anneka Azoana chided, disgust in her voice.

"Don't you see how many people are waiting to see the results?" Eza asked. "Cammie's doing them a favor by reading it out loud."

"Just because she's your girlfriend doesn't mean you need to defend every little thing she does."

"Just because you're jealous and bitter doesn't mean you need to attack every little thing she does."

Cammie really wanted to laugh but felt it wouldn't have been helpful, so she pretended to cough. She kept scanning the papers. She'd finished second in Original Recitation. Maybe that wasn't worth bragging about. But...

"RECITATION, GROUP: FIRST PLACE, FIFTY POINTS, CAMMAINA RAVENWOOD AND EZALEN SKYWING, HARMONY COMPANY!"

Scattered cheers greeted this comment, and Cammie

beamed. "We did it!" she shouted to Eza, throwing her arms around his neck. "I'm proud of us!"

"I'm proud of us, too," he agreed.

Anneka let out a loud groan, turning to face the posted results. Cammie was about to leap forward and say something rude, but Eza held her back. "Let me," he said quietly.

"Okay."

"So," Eza said in his stage voice, projecting loud enough for everyone to hear. "That's two first-place prizes for Cammie. Anneka, how many first-place results did you get?"

Anneka threw her hands up in disgust and strode away, with Razan behind her, looking like he was trying unsuccessfully to convince her of something.

Cammie giggled. "That was so deliciously petty of you. I love it."

"Hey, she started it. Don't start something if you don't want to finish it, right?"

"Exactly. How did you and Aleiza do this morning?"

Cammie and Eza searched the papers for the Dragon Aerobatics scoresheet. "Here you are," Cammie said, finding Eza's name at the bottom. "Last place. Disqualified for excessive use of magic." She turned to him in disbelief. "What does that mean?"

Eza was staring at the paper. "I think it means exactly what it says. The judges must not have liked how often I used the rainbow door with her. Maybe there's a written rule against using magic. I don't know. I should have looked before I built my whole routine around it."

"You're not going to beat yourself up over this, okay? Promise me. You won ringball, and you won our Group Recitation event. You did a good job."

Eza nodded. "I'm fine. Really. I'm not feeling those thoughts today."

"Good. You'll tell me if that changes, right?"

"I promise."

The afternoon was free time, which Eza spent conducting magical duels against a few of his classmates while Cammie lounged on the side of the courtyard with Aleiza. The dragon had never liked Cammie, but seemed to have finally realized that Cammie wasn't going anywhere and that the two of them might as well get along. Aleiza was...well, not exactly shoulder to shoulder with Cammie, but at least not deliberately ignoring her anymore, and Cammie was trying her best not to make any of the sudden movements or noises that always upset Aleiza.

Dinnertime was what they were all waiting for, when the final scores for all four companies would be announced. Eza had explained that the winning team for each event got fifty points, the second-place team got thirty points, the third-place team got ten, and the last-place team nothing. Armed with that knowledge,

154

Cammie sat in the mess hall, which was filled with an anticipatory silence.

General Leazan, the head of the academy, rose to a podium at the head of the room, smiling as she spread out a score sheet in front of her. "First, students, please accept my congratulations on a hard-fought Company Games. I've presided over several of these events, and I'm satisfied to say that this was the closest and most competitive out of any of them."

Polite applause greeted this comment, but Cammie could tell the students were really just eager to know who'd won.

"And now, it is my pleasure to announce to you the results. For the first time in recent memory, the Games have ended in a tie according to points scored."

"A tie?" Cammie repeated in surprise, turning to Eza as a murmur spread over the mess hall. "What does that mean?"

Eza pointed at General Leazan, who was about to continue. "The two companies who have tied for first are Harmony and Victory!"

An explosion of cheers greeted this comment, at least from half the students in the mess hall. As quickly as the cheer had broken out, though, it was stifled by the general motioning for calm. "The rules of the Games state that the first tiebreaker is the number of events won outright by each company. In all the events, from first-year through fifth-year, Harmony Company won thirty events."

Several of the Harmony students seemed as if they wanted to cheer, but weren't sure whether this number was enough for victory or whether the general was about to lead with a "but."

"Victory Company," said General Leazan, "won thirty-one, and are this year's Company Games champions!"

Cammie's eyes drifted to Eza, who had clenched his teeth and grimaced, shaking his head. "So close," he said. "If I hadn't been disqualified...even third place would have meant we won instead of going to a tiebreaker."

"Hey. You said you weren't going to beat yourself up over it."

He smiled. "I'm not. We still have two more years. We'll do even better next time."

"That's the spirit," Cammie said, satisfied. "And besides, you won two other events, when half your company wouldn't even compete. That has to count for something."

"It counts for you being the most amazing girl in the world," Eza said.

All the old voices were rushing into Cammie's mind, like unwanted guests to an Exclaimovian dinner party. *He's lying. He doesn't really mean it. He's just messing with your head. Why is he saying these things? What does he want out of you?*

"Thank you, Eza," she said with a smile. "I like when you say kind things to me."

TWELVE

Starting the next Monday, all the students in Talon Squad stayed after classes, drilling together just outside the city gates until the sun started going down. Twelve students and eleven dragons made for a pretty fearsome attack force, Eza had to admit, even if most of the dragons were half Aleiza's size. Now that all the students at Carnazon had been learning magic for a month or so, the dragons were growing, and had also gotten stronger at breathing fire.

Cammie was the only one without a dragon, but she was also far and away the strongest spellcaster in the group. Eza was getting to where he could do some pretty impressive things with his Artomancy, but Cammie could obliterate dragons and those weird spellcasting bears and Claira's combat falcons, and that counted for a lot. It would take *years* of learning before any of the Introvertian students or soldiers managed to reach the level of natural ability that Cammie had enjoyed even before she'd ever cracked open her elemental magic textbook.

By Friday afternoon, Eza was satisfied with how well prepared the group was. By his count, the third-years had been divided up into somewhere between twenty-five and thirty different squads. Every Friday afternoon for the rest of the spring and summer, the squads would engage in mock maneuvers against each other, doing pretend battles and being graded on their tactical knowledge and their execution under pressure. This was where Colonel Naraza, General Leazan, and the other high-ranking officers would decide for themselves who would be put on the army's fast-track leadership path. Talon's first maneuver was against Spear Squad. Fantastic, thought Eza. It would be Razan versus Anneka.

The two squads met, with a group of judges almost as large as one of the squads, on a field a few miles east of the Tranquility gates. "The scenario is this," one of the judges informed all the students. "Spear Squad are the attackers. Your objective is to divide the defending army in half by taking that hill in the woods. Talon Squad are the defenders. You are the only thing that stands in the way of Spear Squad. If you fail, your army will be completely obliterated." The judge paused for dramatic effect. "And Talon Squad will have no dragons."

Eza's mouth fell open.

"How are we supposed to defend without our dragons?" Razan demanded as Talon Squad trudged toward the objective. "We can't possibly win."

"Okay," Eza said. "Let's think about that for a minute. Squad, on me!"

The other students formed a circle around him.

"Razan says we can't possibly win. I know we don't want to believe that, but he may be right. So, if we can't win, what's the next best thing?"

"A delaying action," Tiazen Aviana said. "Buy time for the rest of our army to fill the gap."

"Exactly. So if we fight smart, and we make Spear pay for every inch they take, we could win on the judges' score sheets even if we don't win in the field. How do we do that?"

Eza knew the answer, had already decided where he was going to set up his soldiers and who he was going to assign to which job. However, he wanted his people to feel like the solution belonged to them. Anyone could follow orders, but sometimes people followed orders halfheartedly, especially if they thought the outcome was hopeless. If they created the strategy themselves, though, if they felt like they owned it, then they'd fight to the death for it.

Well, not to the death *here* of course, but the idea carried over to anywhere – the battlefield, the ringball arena, probably even Cammie's theater company.

"We'll want to set up in the woods," Razan said. "The more branches and junk we have over our heads, the harder it'll be for their dragons."

"Right," agreed Eza. "I'm expecting the dragons to come after us first, so we'll want to focus all our magic on them right away. If we can take out a good number of them, that evens the odds quite a bit."

"What if Cammie and I split off and set up a flank defense?" Tiazen asked.

"Split our forces while outnumbered?" Razan wondered skeptically.

"We'll camouflage ourselves on the left flank and hit them from the side when they go straight for the hill, which they probably will."

Eza chewed his lip. "I like it. Let's make it happen, people."

A chorus of "Yes, sir!" echoed from the company and they moved into their defensive positions. The judges were scattered around the field, in brilliant robes of yellow – probably the brightest clothes anywhere in Introvertia, Eza thought with a smile – so they weren't mistaken for fighters. Several minutes remained in the preparation period before the fight started, so Eza let his gaze wander over the battlefield. Colonel Naraza was there, off on Eza's left. That was very interesting.

A loud horn call signaled the start of the match. Eza motioned his people to crouch in the holes they'd hastily dug, watching for movement from the enemy lines. The attacking force was considered to win if they achieved their objective in one hour or less, while the defenders won if they killed all the attackers or held out for an hour. Because of that, Eza knew Spear Squad was going to have to get moving.

But for fifteen minutes, nothing happened, and Talon's fighters were starting to get restless. "What are they waiting for?" Razan asked no one in particular.

"They're waiting for us to lose our focus," Eza said, loudly enough for his whole squad to hear. "Stay sharp."

Five minutes later, the sound of rustling wings reached Eza's ears, and then the sky was thick with dragons, all twelve of Spear's aerial warriors surging toward Talon's line. Elemental magic flew out to meet them, and several of the dragons were hit by deliberately underpowered fireballs or bolts of electricity. "Orange dragon down!" one of the judges declared from the middle of the field. "Red dragon down!"

The dragons' companions sent them flying to the spot on the sideline where Colonel Naraza was standing, where all the casualties were supposed to gather. The remaining dragons kept coming, though, and in moments they had made their way through the barrage of magic and were blasting weak fireballs at Talon's cover holes. "That one's hit!" a judge shouted, and one of Eza's fighters got up and trotted to the sideline.

Talon downed one more dragon as it tried to escape the woods, but then Spear's entire squad was rushing their lines, the dragons swooping back around for another strafing run. It looked like Spear had spotted Tiazen and Cammie off to the left and were sending their full strength directly at them –

Eza's heart slammed in his chest. Cammie was in danger! Not real danger – but if this were an actual battle, she would be – and he was close enough to watch her die but not close enough to help –

His spellcasters knocked off three of Spear's attackers, but lost two of their own in the process, and then the other squad was practically on top of Cammie and Tiazen...

"CAMMIE!" Eza shouted, taking off at a dead sprint toward his flank. He arrived at full speed, punching one of Spear's attackers in the side of the face and leaping onto the back of another one, arms around the boy's neck, trying to strangle him. An explosion of protests erupted from Spear's fighters and from the judges nearby, but Eza didn't care, couldn't care – Cammie was in danger – he was screaming furiously, without words now –

At last someone pried him away from the fighting, saying something to him that he couldn't hear because of the blood rushing in his ears. He staggered a few steps and then he was crying, sinking to his knees with his head in his hands, gasping for breath and smearing dirt all over his face as he tried to wipe the tears away. His hands were shaking and he couldn't think, couldn't do anything. The only thought in his head was Cammie being attacked while he was powerless to prevent her –

you couldn't save her, you failure; she's dead because of you, because of your plan, because you weren't fast enough or strong enough –

Dimly Eza was aware of himself being escorted to the infirmary, barely able to support his own weight. Accusations crashed around in his head – *this is all your fault; you always mess up; why did you ever think you were good enough to command a squad?* His hands still wouldn't stop shaking, and he forced himself to take long, slow breaths. Screeching came from outside the door and Cammie burst in with a nurse behind her. "I'm sorry," the nurse apologized, embarrassed, "she refused to wait outside."

"She stays in here," Eza said, the first words he'd managed since – well, since whatever it was that had just happened to him.

Cammie sank into a chair in the middle of the room, opposite Eza, who was seated up on the examination table. "Hey," she greeted him. "So, what was that?"

"I don't...I don't know." He stared at Cammie in silence for a few moments, hoping that her Exclaimovian side would take over and she would start rambling, but she was sitting back in the seat, plainly ready to wait until he spoke again. "I just...they were attacking you and there was nothing I could do to help, and if it were a real battle you would have been dead..."

Before Cammie could respond, a doctor in a medical

cloak entered. It was Dr. Deraza, who Eza saw a few times a year for his regular physicals. "Hello, Cadet Skywing," she said, taking a seat across from Eza. "Colonel Naraza has already briefed me about the circumstances of your arrival. First, I'd like to hear it from you. What would you say happened on that field?"

"I don't know," Eza repeated. "I...something happened in my mind and suddenly I was afraid and angry and worried and a bunch of other things all at the same time. I stopped thinking and...I don't even know what I would call it, to be honest."

"You were brought here, to the infirmary. Do you think that what happened is a medical issue?"

Eza's eyes drifted to Cammie. He felt for some reason that the question was a trap. "I...don't know?"

He'd said the words so many times by now that they were starting to lose their meaning.

Dr. Deraza leaned forward. "You said you were afraid and angry and some other things at the same time. Has this happened to you before, Ezalen? Have you ever felt these doubts or fears or accusations come into your head suddenly, and had a hard time dismissing them?"

Eza didn't mean to gasp out loud, but he did, looking at Cammie again.

"That sounds like a yes," said Dr. Deraza with a slight smile. "But I want to hear it from your mouth."

Eza was *so tempted* to lie, to run away and hide from

these thoughts and feelings that scared him. They were so strong they'd made him lose control on the battlefield. What if he *couldn't* control them? What if they were just going to seize his mind whenever they wanted for the rest of his life and things were never going to get better?

"Ezalen?" Dr. Deraza asked, jolting him back to reality.

"Yes," Eza said. Out of the corner of his eye he saw Cammie nodding in approval. "Never before in my life. But over the past month or two, they started, and I – I think they're getting worse."

"Have they ever interfered with your life before?"

Eza considered that. "They make me unhappy a lot. But what just happened during the maneuver, no, that was new." There was silence for a few seconds. "Doctor, what's wrong with me?"

"It's called anxiety, Ezalen. Many things can cause it, but you don't care about that right now. What you care about is whether it can be beaten, and the answer is yes, it can. You can learn how to control it and have whatever life you want for yourself. You may always struggle with it; I can't promise that it will go away, but I promise that we can help you not feel as hopeless as you feel right now."

"That sounds wonderful," Eza blurted. He'd never imagined himself as a blurter before, and didn't know whether to blame Cammie or this anxiety. Suddenly something occurred to him. "Doctor, does this mean I'm going to be removed from command of my squad?"

Dr. Deraza shifted in her seat. "When we're treating anxiety, we've found it best to keep exposing patients to the source of the anxiety. If you confront the fear, it tends to diminish. If you flee the fear and do not put it back in its place, it tends to grow, and that is exactly what we don't want for you, Ezalen. Colonel Naraza is going to ask me whether you're fit to continue your duty, and my recommendation, at least for now, is that you remain in your post. In the meantime, I'm assigning you to daily sessions with me, since I'm our specialist on staff when it comes to...matters of the mind like this. You'll report here after your final class each day."

"But Doctor, my squad trains every..."

A raised hand from Dr. Deraza made him trail off. "Do you want to be well, Cadet?"

"More than anything," he said immediately, not expecting to be quite so honest. He could see the faint smile on Cammie's face.

"Then put yourself first. Your health has to be your priority. Understood?"

"Yes, sir!"

"I'll see you here on Monday. Enjoy your weekend, Ezalen."

Dr. Deraza left, and Eza was alone with Cammie. "How'd we do?" he asked.

"Got wiped out. Seeing you..." Cammie stopped, obviously trying to figure out how to describe what had happened in a way that wouldn't make him feel worse. "We lost focus," she said at last. "The flank collapsed, and Razan couldn't pull everyone together. The attackers kept us pinned while the dragons wiped us out."

"I don't know why they're even having you fight," Eza said abruptly. "You're not going to be in the army when you graduate. You're going to run a theater company. You don't even need to be out there. And I'm – I don't want to be a Ranger anymore. I guess I should tell them that sooner or later so they're not expecting me to –"

"There you go," Cammie said quietly, cutting him off. He was used to being interrupted by her, but it was usually loud when she did. The softness in her voice was what grabbed him. "You're putting boots on your feelings and getting ready to run. The thought of losing me in battle scares you, so you're going to run away from all that instead of facing it."

Eza tried to answer, but his bottom lip shook and tears burst from his eyes. He didn't know what he was thinking anymore, or what he was feeling, and he was so embarrassed that he just wanted to go to sleep and wake up a few months down the road when all this was a distant memory. He jumped when Cammie's arms wrapped around him.

"This has to be so scary for you," she said, rubbing the back of his neck just like he always did for her. "You've spent your whole life trying to feel like you're in control, and now everything is out of control and there's nothing you can do."

The lump in Eza's throat was so huge that he had trouble breathing, so he just nodded his head against her shoulder.

"I need you to know I'm here for you," Cammie continued. "The good, the bad, and everything in between. I made a promise to you, remember? When you're feeling weak, I'm here to help you be strong, just like you do for me. Okay?"

"Okay," Eza said in a voice like a wheeze.

"We're together, and when we get married we're going to be together forever. That means we do this together too. I'm not going to get scared and walk away. I'm here."

"You might need to repeat that a lot," Eza told her. "Like...ten or twenty times a day."

"If that's what you need, then that's exactly what I'll do," she said, pulling back from Eza and pushing her glasses up on top of her head. "And if you need me to help you, to listen to you or encourage you or whatever you need, I expect you to say so, even if it's ten or twenty times a day, okay?"

"I promise."

THIRTEEN

"If that Exclaimovian hadn't gotten second place in Dance or Original Recitation, we'd be lifting a trophy right now." Anneka Azoana stood in the Harmony lounge, her hands on her hips, staring out the east side windows at the rapidly darkening sky.

"Oh, come on," Razan said in exasperation. "If you're going to blame someone, blame Eza. He got disqualified from Dragon Aerobatics."

"Yeah, but nobody knew he wasn't allowed to use magic. That was an old rule, still on the books from before the ban was lifted. How was he supposed to know that?"

"That's not the point. I'm just saying that if you're looking for blame, you should probably start with the only event where we finished last."

"It sounds to me like you're defending Cammie. Surely I'm mistaken."

Something shifted in Razan just then. Maybe it was the tone of superiority in Anneka's voice, or just the negativity in her words, but he suddenly saw what Shanna had been trying to say to him. Cammie had a lot of flaws, and Razan still privately believed that Harmony would be better off if she weren't there. But Cammie had won two events in the Company Games, and finished second in two others, earning a hundred and sixty points for the team. Razan had checked the score sheets afterward and found that no one had scored more – for any team.

Yet here was Anneka, practically frothing at the mouth with rage, so biased that she was willing to blame *the entire Academy's highest scorer* for their loss.

In that moment he knew it was wrong.

"Look," he said, "I don't like her either, but don't you think that's being a little unrealistic? She scored a hundred and sixty points for us. You don't have to like her personality, but trying to pin the loss on her...that just doesn't make any sense. I feel like you're only saying that because you don't like her."

"It sounds to me like you're taking her side!" accused Anneka.

"There are no *sides*," Razan snapped. "We're all Introvertian here. We're all on the same side."

"*She* isn't Introvertian."

"She's doing her best, isn't she? It's not like she's running down Broad Avenue hugging strangers. She's trying to be one of us. And yeah, she's still loud a lot, and it's still really annoying a lot, but considering you and I only have dragons because of her, because she committed treason and got kicked out of her own country, don't you think we should at least *try* being a little patient with her?" Razan could hardly believe the words that were coming out of his own mouth. Almost all of it was exactly what Shanna had said to him before. Apparently he hadn't been lying when he'd told her he would think about the things she'd said. His mind had been thinking about them all by itself, and was notifying him what conclusion it had reached.

"This is incredible," Anneka said in disbelief. "It sounds almost like you want to welcome her in."

"I – I don't, really, or at least I don't think I do. I cringe the whole time I'm around her, wondering when she's going to do that screeching thing she sometimes does. She drives me up the wall, and I wouldn't be sad if I never saw her again." Razan took a deep breath. "But Shanna pointed out that even when we've been rude to Cammie, she's only ever been kind to us. And I guess – if I have to choose between Eza and Cammie thinking I'm too mean to Cammie, or you thinking I'm being too nice to her...well, I'd rather be known as someone who's too nice. I'm sorry, Anneka. If you're looking for someone to be angry and bitter with, I can't do it anymore. I want to be around nice people, not angry and bitter people."

"So you're choosing the Exclaimovian over me."

"No. I'm choosing kindness over meanness. If that means you get left behind...then that's your choice and not mine."

Anneka just stared at him, and Razan was worried

about losing his composure if he stuck around, so he pretended to storm off, out of the Harmony lounge and out through the south gate of Carnazon. He knew where Eza lived; Eza and Razan and Shanna had spent dozens of laughter-filled nights at that house reading books and playing games together over the past two years. This wasn't going to be fun, but with every step Razan felt more and more like it was the right thing to do.

Fear still gripped him as he stood on the front step with his hand over the door. What if everyone laughed at him? What if they rejected him? Would he be forced to go back to Anneka, heart in his hands, begging her to forgive him and take him back?

Knock knock knock.

A dark-haired girl he didn't recognize answered the door. "Hi," Razan greeted her. "I'm a classmate of Eza and Cammie's. Are they here?"

The girl opened the door wider to reveal Eza on the couch, apparently getting a foot massage from Cammie. Shanna was walking back into the living room from the kitchen as well, moving easily and without a limp. *Great. Literally everyone is here.*

Razan took a step into the living room, his chest tight. This wasn't going to be easy, so he might as well get it over with. "Cammie...I just wanted to say I'm sorry. I haven't been kind or reasonable to you, and I regret it. Please forgive me."

Silence wasn't unusual in an Introvertian house, but this was *silence*. Shanna and the dark-haired girl had both turned to Cammie to see how she would react, while Eza just appeared to be trying to hide his feet. At last Cammie stood. "This isn't a joke?"

"No. Anneka's mad at me right now because I told her to take it easy on you. But if she's mad at me for being too kind, I think I can learn to live with that. I'd rather be known for too much kindness than too much meanness."

"Can I hug you?"

"I'd rather you didn't..."

"Then I won't. Thank you for the apology."

Razan fidgeted. "I mean...you can if you want to."

Cammie cracked a smile and hugged Razan, and Shanna piled on a moment later. Eza stayed on the couch, cross-legged with his feet underneath him, but he was grinning, too. This felt *right*, Razan thought. It felt way better than sitting in a dark Harmony lounge discussing Cammie behind her back with someone who didn't smile enough.

"Want to stick around a while, Razan?" asked Eza.

"No, thank you. I have studying to do." *And I feel I've made things awkward enough already*, he didn't add.

"See you on Monday, then."

"Bye, everybody," Razan said, disappearing out the front door and walking back to Carnazon with an enormous smile on his face.

"Who was that guy?" Denavi asked as soon as the door had closed again.

"Razan," answered Eza and Cammie and Shanna all three at the same time.

"He used to be friends with all of us," Shanna continued. "But at some point he decided he didn't like Cammie..."

"Which is quite frankly inconceivable," Cammie interrupted, flipping her purple hair out to the side. Denavi giggled at that.

"Anyway," Shanna said through a smile, "he basically decided to be the pettiest person in the five kingdoms for the next couple of months."

"There was one time he waited outside our history classroom for an hour after the lecture ended just to harass her as she was leaving," Eza added.

"He sounds...kind of horrible," Denavi said.

"I guess I managed to talk some sense into him during our last intensive," Shanna said. "I pointed out that Cammie had risked everything to help us, and gotten nothing in return except for bitterness from Razan and a few other people like him."

Denavi sensed Cammie closing off, in a way, at that remark, as if Cammie didn't like being reminded that she could never go home again.

"I'm glad he came around," Eza said. "It was really fun watching Cammie destroy him every time they got into an argument, but I'd rather everyone be getting along."

"Oh," said Denavi. "That's why they put you in Harmony Company."

Eza nodded agreement. "Yep. Can't get away from it."

The conversation lapsed into a comfortable silence for a few moments, and then Denavi cleared her throat. "So, tell me more about this...anxiety."

"Can you heal it?" Cammie asked, hope in her voice. "Is it...I mean, can you..."

"I don't know how to heal wounds to the mind," Denavi said apologetically. "This isn't something that can be dismissed with magic. The only way is for Eza to learn how to overcome it."

"And I will," insisted Eza. "But for now I think it's bedtime. Thank you for the massage, Cammie."

"Anything for you, my love."

Eza bent down and kissed the top of her head. "You're the best."

"You are."

"I usually leave when people start kissing," Shanna said, "so I'll see you all on Monday."

Eza went upstairs, leaving Denavi and Cammie alone in the living room. Cammie collapsed on the couch and took a deep breath. "I think of this is my fault, Denavi."

"All of what?" Denavi asked, feeling like she'd missed something important.

"Eza's anxiety. All of it. He never felt this way before I was around. He's suffering because of me." Cammie put her hands over her face.

"It's not like that at all," Denavi assured her. "We know this disease in Claira, too. A lot of our soldiers come back from war with it, or with something like it."

"So you're saying being in love with me is like fighting in a war," Cammie said sourly. "Great. Thanks."

"Isn't it?" Denavi asked. "When you're in love, don't you have to fight jealousy and insecurity? Don't you have to fight feelings of not being good enough? And don't you sometimes even fight each other and have to make peace afterward? I think being in love is a lot more like combat than people realize. But – not combat against each other. You're fighting on the same side. It's your love against all the things that can destroy love." Denavi looked into Cammie's split-colored eyes. "Doesn't it make sense that someone who's never been in love before might not be used to the strength of those feelings and find them hard to deal with at first?"

"Yeah. It does."

"So that doesn't mean it's your fault at all. It's really a compliment, when you think about it. It means your love is so strong that it's overwhelming to Eza. He doesn't just like you a little bit. He's crazy in love with you. He's never cared about anyone or anything as much as he cares about you, at least not since his mom died."

Cammie's head snapped up. "He talked to you about his mom?"

"No. I was trying to read the other night and you two were...perhaps not aware of how loudly you were speaking. I heard everything."

"Sorry. I guess we thought you were asleep."

"It's okay. We're family. We should know what's going on so we can be there for each other."

With a huge sigh Cammie shook her head. "I still feel like it's my fault. What you said makes perfect sense...but I still feel it."

"Just like Eza feels like a failure? Just like Eza feels you deserve better than him?"

Cammie seemed to understand the point Denavi was making. "I guess you're right. Both of us are feeling things that aren't true, and both of us have to learn how to fight. I need to go talk to Eza."

"No, you don't." Eza's voice came from the staircase as he came halfway down. "I was eavesdropping at the top of the stairs."

"You HEARD?!" Cammie shrieked.

"Why not? You sat at the bottom of the stairs when I told Denavi I was going to ask you to court. And then you pretended like it was a surprise when it actually happened, you magnificent actress you."

"YOU KNEW ABOUT THAT?!?"

"Of course! I heard you skitter back up the stairs as soon as I told her my plan. Don't look so surprised, you goof. You know I have incredible hearing and I'm always paying attention."

"AND YOU JUST LET ME ACT ALL AWKWARD PRETENDING I DIDN'T KNOW ANYTHING?!?"

"Yeah," Eza chuckled. "It was...pretty funny, actually."

Cammie tilted her head at him, a huge smile making her eyes wrinkle. "How could you ever think you're not the best?" she asked. "How could you ever think I could do better than you?"

"I don't. Not really. I don't think that stuff because I believe it's true. I think it because I'm afraid it might be true."

"Well...it's not. And I'll repeat it until you get sick of hearing it."

"Go right ahead," Eza told her.

FOURTEEN

Cammie had wanted very badly to accompany Eza to his therapy sessions, and Eza had said he wanted it too, but Dr. Deraza was adamant. "I'm his court-mate though," Cammie had argued unsuccessfully. "If we're going to be married one day, I need to know how this is going to affect him and what I can do to help him."

She'd thought it was a great point, but Dr. Deraza had refused. "Ezalen will tell you everything in time. But for now, our priority must be him."

And Eza always came out of those sessions looking absolutely exhausted, and sometimes looking like he'd been crying. He never wanted to talk afterward, and Cammie's curiosity meant that she was dying inside, wanting to beg him to share even though she knew that it wouldn't be helpful to force him. So she made herself wait until he was ready to talk.

Cammie did have to admit that it seemed to be helping. Once Eza had taken an hour or two to collect himself at home – they were spending the entire week at Eza's house rather than bunking in the barracks – he was more...present in the moment, Cammie thought, quicker to smile and not seeming as if he were carrying an enormous weight.

Yet the real test was coming on Friday, when Talon would be conducting their second maneuver – not a simulated combat scenario against fellow Carnazon students, but a night-time reconnaissance of some of the outlying farms. "We've received reports lately of odd activity to the north of here," Colonel Naraza had said. "Scattered movements, like enemy scouts, moving southward from Claira. There's a chance you may intercept this scouting party, if it's really out there. If you do, you're authorized to take whatever action you see fit. Capture anyone you can, if possible. If not, do what needs to be done. Of course, there's a greater chance that you have a pleasant evening stroll under the full moon and the stars and return here with a boring action report, having seen nothing more exciting than an owl attacking a rat."

This time there were no contrived restrictions on Talon Squad, and they were marching out with their full strength of twelve students and eleven dragons. Cammie hadn't heard any of them murmuring about Eza behind his back, and she knew she probably never would. Introvertians were generally too polite to gossip like that, although she knew a few who would have done it. If the other students under Eza's command had any doubts about his ability, or were wondering whether he would come apart at the seams again under pressure, they hadn't said it.

The fact that Colonel Naraza had sent Eza into what might potentially be an actual fight, though, said that the colonel himself was firmly on Eza's side.

Of course, the colonel could have been lying about there being danger. Most Introvertians didn't do *that*, either, but if there was a such thing as "lying for a good reason," applying some mental pressure to Eza while sending him into a completely safe situation certainly fit that description. Cammie had no idea at all what to expect. But Eza seemed to have taken the colonel at his word, and didn't seem to be particularly bothered at the idea of real combat against actual enemies. Maybe the therapy was working, or maybe he was just back to running away from his feelings, pretending he was okay while he was really scared shirtless.

Evening had already fallen before Talon Squad gathered at Carnazon's south gate in preparation to march out. "Razan's the wayfinder," Eza told everyone. "We follow his directions without question. Keep your dragons up as scouts and report everything to me. I mean *everything*. If you see the mountain corn is two weeks behind schedule, if you see someone's farmhouse is missing a shingle, I want to know about it. Understood?"

A chorus of "Yes, sir!" greeted this order.

"Alright," Eza said. "Then we march."

Cammie knew she was probably in the worst physical

shape out of all of them. She'd never done anything remotely athletic or outdoorsy in Exclaimovia, and her natural thinness had come from not eating very much while she was spending long hours studying or memorizing scripts. Eza's thinness, on the other hand, came from eating everything in sight while also climbing every mountain in sight and hiking every trail in sight and chasing every animal in sight. Cammie knew she'd gotten faster and stronger since arriving in Introvertia – but she also really hoped she could stay up with the group and not be left behind.

Razan, as Eza had said, was on the point, out in front of the group. Eza and Cammie were about ten yards behind him, with the rest of the squad spread out to each side and behind, in a shape that looked vaguely like the head of an arrow. "It's a gorgeous night," Eza told her in a whisper.

"It really is," she agreed. "Out away from the city, you can really see all the stars, can't you? And the moon...it's so gorgeous."

"Not as gorgeous as you."

Cammie giggled. "Quiet, you sap. You're going to make me squeal when we're supposed to be sneaky."

Every once in a while something would fly between Cammie and the moon, casting a dragon-shaped shadow on the ground. Eza waved the squad in and they all huddled up around him. "Watch your dragons," Eza warned. "Keep them above us or to the south. If the folks we're tracking are coming from the north, someone might see one against the moon or against some brighter stars and realize we're out here."

Murmurs of approval greeted this comment, and the group dispersed again. They passed one farm, where rows of mountain corn were neatly planted (and, it appeared, the farmhouse was not missing any shingles). One of Talon's fighters and her dragon stayed there, keeping an aerial watch, while the other eleven continued on.

"Do you really want to be spreading your people out so widely if there might be enemy soldiers in the area?" Cammie asked softly.

"It's a risk," agreed Eza. "But with our dragons in the sky, we should be able to spot any hostiles from miles away, even at night. Even if they get to within a mile before we see them, that still gives us a minimum of ten or fifteen minutes to re-form."

The late spring days might have been warm and comfortable, but the evenings were still cool, and Cammie pulled her Academy cloak tightly around herself against the wind that blew down out of the Impassable Mountains. A narrow river ran just to the north of the second farmhouse along their route, with a small stand of trees on both sides. Eza led the remaining eleven squad members toward the trees, ordering them to take cover and have their dragons observe from above.

"Contact, four miles northwest," said Miraza Alenna, a girl from Victory Company. "It looks like six to eight people, coming this way. They're definitely not Introvertian."

Cammie had no idea how a dragon could tell someone wasn't Introvertian from four miles away, but she'd learned not to second-guess a dragon's sense of vision.

"Details?" demanded Eza. "Any creatures with these people, uniforms, anything the dragons can see from this distance?"

"Negative, sir," Miraza answered, and the word was repeated from all the others within earshot of Eza.

His voice was carefully even, but Cammie could see the tension in his shoulders, the way he immediately closed off his body language. She touched him on the arm. "Are you okay?"

Eza didn't answer.

"Spread out along the stream," he ordered. "As soon as they try to cross, hit them from the front with magic and from the rear with dragons. Confuse and disorient them. We have surprise, as far as we can tell."

"Do you want us to try and capture any, sir?"

Eza hesitated. The silence lengthened. Were the other squadmates wondering if Eza had lost his composure? Were they doubting his leadership? Cammie caught herself breathing hard, and made herself pretend to be calm, even though she was panicking inside...

"No," Eza said at last. "No, I won't place any of us at risk. We'll gather what information we can from their bodies and their belongings afterward. Hit them hard and *win*."

"Yes, sir!"

Eza went distant then, and Cammie suspected he was watching through Aleiza's mind link as the enemies grew closer and closer. "Shift west," Eza told his squad. "Don't be seen. They're going to try and cross near where we left Rizian. Cadet Ravenwood, you're with me."

He'd addressed her by her official title for the others' benefit, but Cammie knew what Eza really meant. He was scared, and he wanted her near him. She wanted to reassure him, but her own heart was thundering. This was going to be real combat. She had cast her spells against enemies before, but she was courting Eza now. So much could go wrong; she could be killed, or he could be killed, or...

The splashing of water jolted her back into the moment, and Eza was shouting, "Open fire!"

Suddenly Aleiza roared, the sound echoing off the trees and across the open farmlands as a ferocious belch of flame from her mouth ignited two of the attackers immediately. Aleiza surged upward, disappearing back into the night sky as the other dragons followed behind her, their weaker breaths of fire turning the creek to steam and bringing panicked howls from the enemy.

"Magic!" ordered Eza, and Cammie cut loose with a salvo of lightning. Her magic was still linked to her emotions, and she hadn't realized how terrified she was until she heard herself screaming and saw the way her lightning brightened the entire night. In its glow she could see looks of horror on the faces of the enemy scouts, and screams reached her ears as Aleiza circled back around for another pass and Cammie's eyes burned from the orange glow of flame. When her eyes adjusted to the darkness again, there was silence, apart from the hiss of steam rising from the water and the burbling of water around the dead bodies that rested in it.

"Send the dragons back up," Eza said immediately. "Make sure there aren't any other scouts in the area. Let's drag these enemies out of the creek and see what they can tell us."

Cammie kept her distance for this part, but even from several yards away she could hear Eza gasp. "Cammie," he said, as if struggling to get the words out. "Look..."

She rushed to Eza's side and looked down, blinking hard and looking down again in disbelief. "It can't be."

The face staring up at her, eyes open in death, was that of Azanna, the rogue dragon trainer who'd attacked her and Eza on their way to Exclaimovia all those weeks ago. That was the day Cammie had first learned how strong her magical powers were, when fear had exploded in her and she'd roasted his dragon in a fit of rage. Eza had wounded Azanna in the ensuing swordfight, and neither of them had seen the man again since then. Where had he gone? And why had he suddenly turned up on the border of Introvertia?

"I don't like this," Cammie heard herself murmuring.

Eza was going through his pockets, pulling out a few coins, a survival tool, and then a crumpled piece of paper. "What's that?" Cammie asked unnecessarily, as Eza's fingers were already unfolding it.

"It's a code," Eza told her. "I think. I can't make sense of it."

"Let me copy it, then."

Eza nodded his approval, and Cammie reached into her pack to pull out paper and something to write with. In minutes, while the rest of Talon Squad was searching the bodies of the dead, Cammie had written down whatever message was on the page.

"What did we find?" Eza asked.

"No uniforms, no insignia," Razan reported. "We don't have any idea who these people were or what they were doing, other than that they were in our territory and they obviously didn't want to be seen."

"Any guess where they were from?"

"They all look Clairan," said Razan. "Except for the one you were searching. We can't figure out where he was from."

"Don't worry about him," Eza answered. "Let's get these bodies buried. It may take a few hours, but I don't want to just leave them here for the birds. The farmers might ask questions."

Cammie was getting exhausted by this point, either from all the hiking or from her magical exertion, which might have been why she didn't think before she spoke. "Why don't I just burn the bodies?"

There was silence, and Cammie wondered if she'd said something wrong.

"That is...a way better idea," Eza said. "Do you think you can? Most of them are still wet."

"Is that a challenge?" she answered with a grin. "Cause if you want to put some money on it, I'd be happy to place a bet."

"I bet you a foot massage," Eza told her.

No one else in the squad would have any idea how meaningful that truly was to the two of them, and Cammie laughed out loud at the secret joke they'd just shared. "I take you up on that bet," she said. "Let's go."

The bodies were gathered together in one spot, and Cammie took a deep breath. "Here we go."

Just as she was about to cut loose with the strongest elemental magic in her arsenal, Aleiza landed just a few yards from the bodies and roared flame onto them. Instantly the wet clothes caught fire and the dead were cremated, ashes drifting up into the night breeze. "THAT'S CHEATING!" Cammie whisper-screeched indignantly, trying to explode with rage but not give away their position to anyone else who might be nearby. Those two things were tough to do at once.

"What's cheating?" Eza asked innocently.

"YOU OWE ME A FOOT MASSAGE, YOU GOOF. I GET TO GIVE YOU ONE AND YOU HAVE TO GIVE ME ONE, BOTH. I WIN. YOU CHEATED!"

Eza was laughing by now. "Okay. I accept your terms, Cadet Ravenwood."

The plains were calm once again, and Eza kept his squad by the river with their dragons in the air just in case these scouts had merely been the vanguard of a larger group. "I wish we could have found out what Azanna was doing," Eza mused out loud. "I know we only met him twice, but he seemed like a thinker, a planner. He must have been up to something."

"What about that code he was carrying?"

"We'll pass it on to Colonel Naraza and let him do what he wants with it."

"Why did you make a copy?"

Eza shrugged. "It might be fun to try and decode it ourselves. Maybe it's a treasure map or something. He tried to kidnap us for ransom, after all, so we know he liked the thought of easy money."

"A treasure map?" Cammie asked excitedly. "Do you

really think so?"

"It could be anything. Maybe Azanna and these other guys got hired to scout Introvertia's defenses for the war, and that code was his observations so far. Maybe he was making a list of what crops we're growing so he could buy something cheaply and sell it for a profit. There's really no telling."

"We *have* to crack that code, then!"

Eza kept the squad in position until midnight, when he sent the dragons forward a few miles to scout. There didn't seem to be any other movement. It truly appeared as if Azanna's small group had been alone – which really only heightened the mystery, didn't it?

"What do you think he could have been up to?" Cammie asked Eza an hour later as they were nearing Tranquility. She knew she'd just had the same conversation with him, and she knew he hadn't learned anything on their silent march that might have given him new insight, but sometimes her mind got stuck on an idea and she just *had* to talk about it. "It can't have been something important, because he only had a few people with him. Or...does that mean it was something *really* important, and they thought a smaller group would have a better chance of slipping through and not being seen?" Cammie thought about that. "And who even is *they* in that sentence? Who sent him? Did he go on his own?"

"The fact that they were on foot is a clue," Eza

reasoned. "If they were going to bring something back, it had to be something small, because they didn't have any horses or wagons."

"Ooooh. Good point."

"But it's also possible they were only sent to bring back information. Did you see how they were dressed?"

"No uniforms..."

"That too, but also no armor. They weren't expecting to get into a fight. They went, or were sent, on a mission where they would go to a place, do...something...without the threat of resistance, and return." Eza chewed on the inside of his cheek. "Or maybe not return. Maybe they came from Claira and were going to take their findings to Exclaimovia. We just don't have enough information right now."

"I can't wait to start working on that code."

They were entering the Tranquility gates now, and Eza rushed to catch up with Razan. "You did a good job tonight, Razan. Excellent performance. I'm glad to have you in the squad."

"Thank you, sir."

Eza made dismissive wave. "I'm only *sir* out in the field. Here in the city...we're just friends."

They hugged, which surprised Cammie since she knew Introvertians weren't big on physical contact – but immediately realized that was a clue about how close the two of them had been before Razan had distanced himself. Eza was clearly happy to have his friend back.

"Can you get this to Colonel Naraza tonight?" Eza asked, handing over the code paper they'd taken from Azanna. "Cammie and I are heading home, and since you're staying at Carnazon, it'd be on your way. Let him know I'll have my action report in by tomorrow."

"Will do."

Cammie had *said* she couldn't wait to start on the code, but the closer they got to Eza's house, the more she felt her eyes drooping. Just as they neared the Music Square, though – which was silent in this pre-dawn hour – the silence was broken by the thundering of horses' hooves coming from the north, where Mazaren Fortress was.

Eza and Cammie stepped off to the side of the square while a full company of Introvertian soldiers tore past them, going *somewhere* in an incredible hurry.

"Wh..." Cammie began, trailing off immediately.

"They're heading toward the eastern gate, by the Very Large Forest," Eza said, craning his neck to see which exit they'd taken from the square

"An invasion?" Cammie asked, her hands and feet going instantly cold. She'd lived in almost constant dread of this moment for weeks now – ever since Exclaimovia had threatened war because Introvertia refused to return Cammie to them to stand trial. There hadn't been any more fighting in over a month, since the Battle of

Denneval Plain, and Cammie had *almost* allowed herself to believe that the big battle was, somehow, the end of the war. She knew her people; they liked to bluster and pose, and they liked to make threats, and those threats didn't always turn into action. As likely as not, Exclaimovia would never end up actually fighting at all.

But then again, maybe they would, and maybe today was the day...

"I don't think so," Eza said, his words breaking through her terror. "We wouldn't fight an invasion with only one company."

"That's...true."

She felt Eza's hand take hers. "Just like you're here for me, I'm here for you, okay? We do everything together."

Cammie nodded. "Can we sleep on the couches in the living room, though? I don't...want to be alone right now."

FIFTEEN

Eza couldn't remember the last time he'd slept in until eight in the morning, but that Saturday was the day. Cammie was still snoring, lying on her side on the couch with Eza on the floor right below her, and Denavi was on the opposite couch, sipping from a cup of juice. "Late night?" Denavi whispered.

"Early morning," Eza corrected. "We got back here at around two."

"Whoa. So Cammie probably won't be up for a while, then."

"Speaking of," Eza said, reaching into his pack for the code paper Cammie had copied. "Have you ever seen anything like this before?"

Denavi stared at the paper for a few moments, then at Eza. "Where did you get this?"

"I...don't think I can tell you the details. I haven't been debriefed by my colonel yet."

"Oh, so this is from your mission last night. You fought Clairans?"

"I..."

Denavi grinned. "You said you couldn't tell me. You didn't say I couldn't figure it out."

"True. They weren't Clairan soldiers, though. They

195

weren't wearing uniforms. And the guy who had this on him wasn't Clairan."

"How do you know?"

"He was Introvertian. Cammie and I had met him before."

"Now *that* sounds like a story." Denavi lapsed back into silence while she examined the paper. "This is a Clairan military code. There are a whole bunch of different ciphers that can be used to encrypt the message, and in theory I'd have to try them all in order to find the right one."

"You've *memorized* all those code ciphers?" Eza asked in astonishment.

"Not all of them, obviously, but a few of the more common ones. Healers tended to double as message-writers and message-readers, so I got pretty quick at decoding."

"Isn't that dangerous, to just have people running around on the battlefield with codes memorized like that? What if someone managed to capture one of you and force you to give up the ciphers?"

"Death before dishonor," Denavi reminded him. "Clairan soldiers would never permit themselves to be captured. In theory, at least."

Eza was already grimacing even before she'd answered. He should have known the answer, shouldn't have said something so insensitive. Denavi had gone against the ideals of her entire nation when she'd panicked in battle and allowed herself to be captured. She'd done the one thing no Clairan was ever supposed to do, and that's why she would never be welcomed home again. For the crime of surviving a battle, she would bring shame to her entire family and probably her friends too – if anyone ever learned that she was still alive. Reminding her of that, even accidentally, was so stupid of him. *That's you, Eza, always hurting the people around you with your stupidity. Nice going.*

"Stop that," Denavi ordered.

Eza blinked and met Denavi's eyes. "Stop what?"

"You're doing the anxiety thing again. I can tell from the look on your face."

"I have a look?"

"Don't change the subject," Denavi scolded him. "I don't know what you were telling yourself just now, how you thought you hurt my feelings or whatever, but stop. We're friends."

"I know we're friends," Eza said, embarrassed that she'd seen right through him and even more embarrassed at how silly his fears sounded when they were coming out of her mouth.

"If it was about the way I ended up here, yeah, I was ashamed of that for a while. But I forgave myself. I made the choice I wanted to make, I did the thing I thought was right, and now I'm here with the best family I've ever had. I'm not going to get all bitter every time someone reminds me I was supposed to have let myself die on that battlefield." Denavi stared into Eza's eyes. "And you're going to learn to forgive yourself too, okay? You don't have to be perfect. You don't have to say the perfect words every time. You don't have to keep everyone safe all the time, and in fact, you can't. You're just going to do your best, and that will be good enough, okay?"

Eza hadn't been expecting to get an earful from Denavi, of all people, so he just nodded.

"As I was saying," Denavi continued, looking back at the code paper as if that whole conversation hadn't just happened, "since you said these people didn't appear to be soldiers, and the one carrying the code wasn't even Clairan, I'm going to guess they used one of the simpler ciphers. The complicated ones have a lot of math involved, where the value for each letter changes depending on what letters come before it. The really gnarly ones change depending on what letters come before *and after*, which mean you have to know the first couple words of the message, usually the name of the specific officer it was addressed to, or else you literally can't decode it. But like I said, those are for high-ranking military directives. This is probably a child's game."

"I'll leave you to it, then." Eza stood and stretched, unsure how they hadn't awakened Cammie with all their whispering. She must *really* have been sleeping hard.

But she wouldn't be sleeping for long, because loud thudding sounded on the front door. Eza sprang over to it, aware that he'd gone to bed in his rumpled and dusty Academy uniform and awakened with bed-head, or rather floor-head. He hoped it wasn't anyone important, but he knew that most times when someone knocked on their door first thing in the morning, it was –

A royal messenger nodded at Eza, handing over a piece of paper. "Miss Ravenwood's presence is requested at the palace at her earliest convenience."

"Is it about the theater company?" Eza asked, examining the summons. "Do they want Denavi and me to come, too?"

"You know everything I know," the messenger said apologetically.

Ezarra had come down the stairs by this point; Denavi moved over to him and wrapped her arms around his waist, leaning against him. "Cammie is a little indisposed at the moment," Eza told the messenger. "But we will come, as you said, at our earliest convenience."

"Very good," the messenger said, nodding and stepping out of the doorway.

"I made you breakfast, daddy," Denavi was saying as she steered Ezarra toward the kitchen and out of the living room. "Eggs and grilled onala. Your favorite."

"Anything you make is my favorite," he told her, and

she beamed up at him.

Eza rounded the couch, kneeling next to Cammie. "Good morning," Eza said, gently shaking his court-mate.

"Nope," she said, her eyes squeezed tightly closed.

"The king and queen want to see us."

"They can't. I'm sleeping."

"You're not sleeping. You're talking to me."

Cammie stopped talking.

"I have...ways of persuading you," Eza told her.

"No tickles. That's a horrible way to wake up."

"Alright. No tickles." Eza searched his brain for something that his Artomancy could do. He could do heat...could he take away the heat in an object and make it cold instead?

Cammie had fallen asleep with her socks on the night before, so Eza concentrated on them, trying to pull all the heat out of them that he could. He touched them hesitantly, not wanting Cammie to think he was breaking the rules and attempting a tickle, but immediately Cammie was leaping out of bed and yelping. "EZALEN SKYWING, DID YOU PUT SNOW IN MY SOCKS?!"

"I – snow?" he asked, playing innocent.

Cammie stared at her socks, which she had torn off and hurled away, as if it were somehow their fault.

"I win, though," Eza pointed out. "You're vertical and with no tickles."

Cammie tried to glare at him but broke out into a smile instead. "Then we're even for what happened last night, you cheater. Quick, turn my hair...ah, maybe strawberry blonde this time. I know the king and queen wouldn't mind if it were purple, but I want to look the part."

Eza was ready to leave in about five minutes, after a quick dash upstairs to change into his customary gray pants and green shirt with his Ranger cloak around him. Cammie had opted for an ankle-length green dress with gold accents. "Where did you get that from?" Eza asked in wonder.

"It's...kind of a long story."

"We have time," Eza told her. "Denavi, are you coming?"

"Nope. Gonna have some daddy time. We're going to weed the garden together."

"Have fun!"

"She's really opting for *weeding the garden* over an audience with the king and queen?" Cammie wondered.

"You know the answer to that. It's not the garden she's choosing. It's my dad."

"Yeah. Dad time is really powerful." Cammie swallowed hard.

"Besides," Eza said, quickly changing the subject, "Denavi's had a hard life. She's been a soldier for years. I think she's done with all that, really. She's done doing important things and being around important people. She just wants to be a kid, to have the childhood she never got to have." *And to have a dad,* he added mentally, but that had obviously been a sore spot for Cammie, so he didn't say it out loud.

"What do you think the king and queen want, anyway?" Cammie wondered.

"It could be they want to talk to us about our next theater tour. Either that or Colonel Naraza told them about the code sheet and it's more important than we thought. Or neither of those. They have a funny way of surprising us, don't they?"

"They definitely do," agreed Cammie. "It's really warm this morning."

"It sure is. That's a problem. Warm mornings during the spring usually mean thunderstorms later when cool air comes down from the mountains. The worst storms blow in from the sea during the summer, but we get hit occasionally during the spring too. It can be scary, but it's not all bad. After all, those crops we saw last night need watering."

Cammie was quiet for a few moments. "It's not fair, you know."

"What's not?"

"That someone as optimistic as you should have anxiety. It should go to someone who worries all the time or who already thinks the world is awful. You,

202

though...you try to find the bright side in everything, except for yourself. You keep talking to yourself like you're the worst person who's ever lived, like all you know how to do is disappoint people. It's just not fair."

Eza didn't know what to say to that, so he said nothing.

"Think about it, Eza. You told me a few days ago that you feel like you're a failure. Would you ever look someone else in the eyes and tell them they're a failure?"

"Of course not," he said instantly. "That would be..."

"Would be what?" Cammie prodded. "Mean? Horrible?" Eza didn't answer. "And yet you say it to yourself all the time," she continued. "You say things to yourself that you would never dream of saying to other people, and you believe those things, and you take ownership of them. Why?"

"Because I'm afraid they might be true." Eza looked up at the sparkling blue sky. "Can we please not talk about this right before we go to meet the king and queen? I have a feeling they'll know if I've been crying."

"Okay." Cammie took Eza's arm. "Let's see if we can catch a dance in the Music Square."

"But the king and queen said to come at..."

"At our earliest convenience, yes. But you know Queen Annaya. If we tell her we were late because we were dancing together in the Music Square, do you really think she'll be upset?"

That made Eza smile. "Good point."

All four of the bandstands were occupied on this Saturday morning, and the one nearest Broad Avenue was host to a folk three-piece band playing quiet, thoughtful songs. Eza loved that type of music, and he knew Cammie probably preferred something louder and more assertive, but she pulled him in toward the quiet songs.

"Empty your mind," she ordered him. "I know you can do it, because you've told me over and over that's how you learned to hear what the dragons were saying to you. Well, now I want you to hear what *I'm* saying to you. Not just my words. All of...everything."

Cammie set her glasses on top of her head, wrinkles in the corners of her split-colored eyes as she smiled at him and offered her hand. Eza took it, beginning to lead her in the steps of a slow dance. "No," she told him. "Follow *me*."

That made Eza curious, but he did what she'd said, pushing every thought out of his head so that his only focus was on her. She led him confidently, but in steps he didn't recognize. From time to time his feet would falter, and whenever he stumbled, Cammie would get even closer to him, her heart beating against his until he'd gotten his balance back.

That *meant* something, he realized. She was talking to him through dance, telling him that whenever his anxiety made him weak, she'd draw closer to hold him up. "I feel you," he whispered to her. The smile of delight that crossed her face made his heart leap for joy.

Then she led him round and round in wide circles, pulling away from him a little and then coming back in, then pulling even further away and coming closer than before, then drawing so far away that only their fingertips were just barely touching before whirling back in toward him, her back against his chest. Reflexively he put his hand over her stomach and they moved together in perfect unison before the song ended.

Again Eza could *feel* what she meant – that whatever struggles they went through together would only bring them even closer than they had been before. That wasn't a new thought to Eza. He'd heard that soldiers often shared a bond of brotherhood and sisterhood closer than anything an ordinary person could even imagine, and Cammie was telling him that the same was true of them. They would fight Eza's anxiety, and they would win *together*, and they'd be closer than they ever would have if his life had been perfect and he'd never *needed* her so desperately.

Cammie seemed to sense that he was working through all the things she'd just told him, so she didn't force him into another dance, instead taking his arm as she had before and following as he started walking toward the Reading Square where the palace was. "That was *incredible*," Eza told her. "I had no idea dance could speak like that. You're...really amazing."

The joy in her eyes was pure and radiant. "Thank you, my love."

Eza was sure they drew some looks as they neared the palace, with his arm around Cammie's waist and her head on his shoulder as they walked. That was fine. People could stare. He was going to love Cammie the way she deserved to be loved, and people could write poems about it if they wanted.

As usual, the two of them were waved past the guards at the front gate of the palace and directly into the throne room. "Ah!" King Jazan said when they appeared. "Welcome, welcome, both of you. I'm sorry for summoning you here so early in the morning after you'd only just returned from maneuvers, but please accept my assurance that it could not be helped."

"We are, as always, in the king and queen's service," Eza assured him.

"You have a guest," King Jazan said, gesturing to the side of the room.

Out from one of the side corridors came a tall figure in a red-and-gold traveling cloak that was dusty and wrinkled. The figure was looking down, with the hood of the cloak covering its head, but in one smooth motion it pulled the hood back. Eza had seen the face before, and his eyes got huge. How – this was impossible –

"Hello, Cammaina," said General Barin Ravenwood.

SIXTEEN

"DADDY!" Cammie screamed, just like Denavi had after the final performance of their play, exploding into sobs and sinking to the ground as tears burst out of her eyes.

She felt her father picking her up. The smell of his clothes filled her lungs and she squeezed him so tightly that it had to be hurting him, but he just chuckled that low chuckle of his.

"Good to see you again, my firebug."

"You're late to the family breakfast again," she teased him through the tears, her voice breaking.

His only response was to rub his strong hands over her back.

Cammie was aware of Eza approaching the thrones and saying something to the king and queen, but they were speaking quietly and she couldn't hear. He looked...really worried, she thought, and suddenly she was upset with him, because she was concerned about him instead of focusing on her dad being here in front of her. "Wh – how –" she spluttered, a million thoughts trying to land on her tongue at the same time as she wiped her cheeks dry.

"No one in Exclaimovia knows I'm here," Barin said.

A Fury Like Thunder

"I told the High Command that I was going to make an inspection of our defenses, and that I was going to do it by stealth so our soldiers would not know they were being observed. Instead, I snuck out and came to Introvertia. I arrived before dawn this morning."

"The soldiers!" Cammie gasped. "We saw a company of soldiers galloping through the city while it was still dark out. They must have been on the way to greet you."

"I don't know if *greet* was the right word for it," Barin said philosophically. "They thought I was a spy at first, and the meeting was not going to end well. At last I managed to convince them of my identity, and they brought me here – although, truth be told, I suspect your king and queen had some doubts themselves until they saw your reaction just now."

"So – what are things like in Exclaimovia?" Cammie asked.

"It's still not safe for you to come home," Barin said sadly, and out of the corner of her eye Cammie saw Eza stiffen. "The government has doubled down on their accusations of treason. You know how we are, firebug. We don't like to back down and lose face."

"I didn't mean that," Cammie said, trying to hide the way her insides had just gone numb from devastation. "I meant – how are mom and Aed?"

"Your mother and Aed miss you very much, but we received the letter you sent a few weeks ago and we are relieved to know you're being well taken care of here." He examined her outfit and hair. "I must say you're looking especially radiant."

"Daddy," she said again, wrapping him up in another hug.

"As for the war," Barin continued, "the High Council remains divided, as do the people. You know that the government accused you of treason and demanded your return from Introvertia, but has refused to say exactly what the treason was – because to do so would require that they admit causing the hostilities in the first place by stealing Introvertia's dragons, and that information is still not public knowledge." Barin looked up at King Jazan and Queen Annaya. "I do not believe any of my people have ever apologized, Your Highnesses, so allow me to do so now."

"It is already forgiven," Queen Annaya said gracefully.

"Our people are perceptive, as you are well aware, Cammaina. They know they're being manipulated, and they don't like it, so they do not support the war. As long as the High Council does not have the support of the people, they will not commit to action. They do not *require* popular support, of course; King Dorran and the Council may do as they please. But to risk alienating such a large percentage of the populace, in a war with no benefit – we're not likely to gain territory or money or anything like that – well, that is rightly considered foolish. While that remains the case, and while I remain the loudest and most influential voice against war, there is not likely to be any fighting."

"I believe in you, daddy."

"If you will permit me to ask, what then does this mean with regard to Claira and Esteria?" asked King Jazan. "Are you able to persuade your allies to lay down their weapons as well?"

"Not while we remain indecisive," Barin said, his voice full of regret. "Simply put, we must make a choice for either war or peace before we can tell our allies to choose war or peace. At the moment they will act however they see fit."

"Can daddy come back to Eza's house with us?" Cammie asked the king. "Please?"

King Jazan and Queen Annaya turned to speak quietly with each other, and it was Queen Annaya who answered. "You will enjoy a military escort along the way. General Ravenwood, we must request that you do not speak or draw any attention to yourself en route."

"I accept. I have no desire to disrupt your way of life."

King Jazan smiled. "I appreciate your thoughtfulness, General, and I wish more of your people felt that way. I did not mean it like that, though. We were merely concerned with a practical matter. If word somehow gets out that there is an Exclaimovian in Tranquility, visiting Cammaina...it would not take much for your cover to be blown, and the consequences would likely be severe."

"You have the mind of a true tactician," Barin said, and Cammie blinked in amazement. Her father had just given a genuine compliment to someone other than his family! She had never heard him do something like that before. "There are many reasons I pray we do not meet in battle, and this is among them."

The walk home was the hardest part for Cammie, because she couldn't hold her father the whole time like she wanted to. She passed Eza, who had been walking at the front of the line, and set the fastest pace she could manage back to his house, with him and her father in tow and a guard of soldiers following far enough behind that they could *almost* pretend to be minding their own business.

At last they were through the front door, and Cammie turned to her father, leaping up onto him and hanging on with her arms and legs. "I love you, daddy," she said.

Denavi sat up abruptly from the couch, where she'd had her head in Ezarra's lap as he read a book to her and played with her hair. "Daddy?" she repeated in shock.

"Dad, Denavi, this is General Barin Ravenwood of Exclaimovia," Eza said formally. "General, this is my father, Ezarra Skywing of the Introvertian army, and my sister Denavi."

Denavi threw her hands over her mouth and started bouncing up and down at those words, looking up at Ezarra, who smiled back at her before rising to shake Barin's hand. "It's an honor to meet you, General," Ezarra said. "Cammie has spoken highly of you from the first moment she came under my roof."

"The pleasure is mine, sir. And you, Ezalen! What are you doing, calling me General instead of Barin, like we've never met before?"

Barin clapped him on the shoulders and Eza flinched – and it didn't look like he was merely drawing back from surprise contact, but that he was *afraid*. That didn't make any sense to Cammie; Eza knew Barin, and knew that he was an honorable man. What was to be afraid of?

"Eza and I are courting, father," Cammie told him.

"Is that so?" Barin looked down. "He treats you well, firebug?"

"He makes me the happiest girl in the entire world," she said, staring into Eza's eyes as if the force of her gaze could make it sink into his brain for good.

"Then I'll have to spend some time with my future son-in-law while I'm here. I must head back tomorrow, though."

"So soon?" Cammie asked, the devastation returning. "But daddy...I haven't seen you in so long..."

"I told you, firebug. I'm supposed to be on a mission.

If I'm gone for too long, people will get suspicious – and the anti-war faction in the High Council needs my leadership." He put his hand on Cammie's cheek. "But the risk was worth it, to see you again and to let you know how much I love you."

"I love you too, daddy," she told him, holding him again as the tears came against her will.

Barin held her until she stopped crying, and then reached into his pack. "Here. I brought something for you."

"My spices!" Cammie shouted, taking the huge glass jar. "You're the best, daddy!"

"Just a little taste of home."

Ezarra and Denavi had left after the introductions, and Ezarra reappeared after the back door. "General, can I interest you in some breakfast? We have grilled –"

"Everything, please," Barin interrupted him. "Thank you."

That one interruption was just foreshadowing for the rest of the meal. Cammie and her father spent the *entire* time shouting stories at each other, happily cutting each other off, hurling accusations of exaggeration and falsehood, shrieking laughter, pounding fists on tables, and all the other things that usually made Introvertians uncomfortable. Neither Eza nor Ezarra even attempted to get a word in, but they laughed along at the funny parts and shared skeptical glances at the parts that (even

Cammie had to admit) were probably not *entirely* true. Denavi, who had most likely never met an Exclaimovian before, looked a little overwhelmed, and excused herself as soon as her plate of food was empty.

At the moment, Cammie couldn't possibly care.

When breakfast was over, Ezarra followed Denavi out into the garden to do the weeding. Cammie was surprised, but grateful, when Eza went out with them, leaving her to have some precious alone time with her father.

"Tell me more about this Dragon Academy you mentioned in your letter," Barin said.

So Cammie told him everything, about the classes and the professors and the barracks and the Company Games and Talon Squad – and her theater tour with Eza and Denavi.

"It sounds as if you've enjoyed your time here very much," he observed.

"I have, daddy. Except for not having you and mommy here, it's been almost perfect."

"That makes me happy, firebug. I miss you more than you can understand, but knowing that you're truly satisfied here makes things easier to bear."

"Stay here, daddy," she begged. "Send for mommy and Aed and come live here. We can all be together again."

Barin smiled distantly. "I doubt very much that King

Jazan and Queen Annaya would allow an entire family of Exclaimovians to come here."

"They welcomed me."

"Yes, but you're the quiet one in the family, aren't you? You heard what breakfast was like, with only two of us."

Loud laughter came from outside, and Cammie's eyes drifted out the window. Eza had pinned Denavi's hands behind her back and Ezarra was tickling her ribs, although Denavi didn't seem to be trying very hard to get free. "But I want that," Cammie said, pointing. "It's not fair that they get to have a daddy and I don't."

"None of us knows what the future holds, firebug," Barin reminded her. "There may be peace between our kingdoms yet."

"Queen Annaya said that once. She said my art, my acting, may be what brings peace."

"I believe in you. If anyone can do it, it's you. Work for peace, firebug. I'll do the same. Okay?"

"Okay, daddy."

Eza had offered his bed to Barin that night, but the general had opted for taking Cammie's bed so that Cammie and Eza could sleep in the living room together as they'd done the night before. Eza hadn't just gone outside with Denavi so that Cammie and her father could have some alone time. He'd gone outside because of the crushing wave of thoughts and feelings that crashed over him. All the insecurities about Cammie choosing home over him had reignited at that moment, and Eza had spent the rest of the day absolutely miserable, so nervous he wanted to throw up. He knew Cammie had seen him flinch when Barin grabbed his shoulders, and he was pretty sure she knew the reason – not because he wasn't prepared for someone touching him, but because Barin was the living embodiment of Eza's fear that Cammie would abandon him.

It didn't help that Cammie's mind seemed to be split just like the colors of her eyes. One day she'd be telling Eza that nothing could replace a father's hug, but the next day she'd be saying Eza made her the happiest girl in the world. So which was it? Did she need her father, or could she be content with Eza?

She'd cried in front of the *entire throne room*. Cammie *hated* crying in front of people, including Eza, but the mere sight of her father had made her gush like the Rapidly Flowing River. *That's how much her dad means to her*, he thought. *That's what she'd be giving up if she stayed here.*

How can I possibly fill that hole?

Around and around in his head the thoughts danced. None of the therapy techniques he'd learned from Dr. Deraza made a dent in the wall of doubt. He was supposed to try saying his fears out loud in a funny voice, but he didn't feel like being funny right now. He was supposed to imagine his fears coming out of someone else's mouth, and imagine himself explaining to that person why they were wrong, but that imaginary person *wasn't* wrong. Cammie really was in pain every day she didn't get to be with her family, and it was Eza's – well, not his fault, in truth, but it *felt* like his fault. At the very least, he felt helpless to do anything for her, to ease her pain – she said he made her happy but there was nothing he could do about this...

Eza was instantly alert at the sound of bare feet on the stairs, light footsteps that couldn't be his father. "Denavi?" he whispered. "It's almost midnight. Why are you still awake?"

"Why are *you*?" she asked.

"I asked first," Eza answered, hoping she would say something interesting so that he could talk more about that and not have to answer her question.

"Barin snores."

Eza covered his mouth to keep from laughing. "Oh, yeah. I forgot about that. He and Cammie's brother, both."

"Yeah. But I can't hear him down here, so what's keeping you up?" A particularly loud snore sounded from upstairs, and Cammie let one out as if in sympathy. "On second thought, maybe we should talk in the garden."

Silently, Eza eased the back door open and he and Denavi crept into the freshly weeded garden, taking a seat next to each other on the bench. "It's such a beautiful night," she said, gazing up. "I've never gotten over the sight of a sky full of stars, and I hope I never do."

"Me too."

Denavi looked at Eza, and he tensed, worrying that she was going to ask why he was awake. He wasn't about to lie to his friend, but he really didn't want to dwell on *those* thoughts anymore – even though if she hadn't appeared, he'd still be lying there staring at the ceiling with the thoughts happily running circles in his head.

"Am I really your sister?" she asked softly.

That made Eza smile. "I wouldn't have said it if I didn't mean it. You know that. We have the same dad, so that makes us brother and sister. Sure, he's not your *father*, but that doesn't mean anything, does it? He loves you as if you were his own, so you are."

Denavi's eyes drifted back to the stars. "That means everything to me, Eza. Thank you." She laid her head on his shoulder. "Brother."

For a long time they were both quiet, listening to the whispering of the breeze through the longleaf pines around them, watching the upper branches dance against the stars. "You never told me why you were still awake," she reminded him.

"I was hoping not to."

Denavi raised an eyebrow. "Is that an 'I don't want to talk about it so I'm not going to,' or an 'I don't want to talk about it but I will if my sister asks me to'?"

"I don't really want to talk about all this any more. Or feel it. Or – I don't know."

"Ah. Anxiety thoughts."

"Yeah." Eza blew out a deep breath. "Cammie might choose to go home with her father tomorrow."

"But – she can't," Denavi said in confusion.

"I can use my magic," Eza told her. "To disguise Cammie. She could return in secret and have her family back."

"Eza, no..."

"If that's what will make her really happy, then that's what I have to do." Tears came from his eyes as if they'd been squeezed out by the tightness in his chest.

"But –"

"But nothing," Eza said. "I've already thought of all the *buts*. And if I have the power to make Cammie truly happy, if that's the one thing Cammie wants more than anything else, and I refuse to give it to her because I'd rather have her with me, that makes me a really horrible person."

"So you'd use your magic on her and watch her walk away from you forever?"

Eza's bottom lip started to shake as his mind happily

played him a scene of that happening, of Cammie strolling off with her father, bouncing with happiness, not even looking back to say goodbye. "Yeah."

There was a pause, as if Denavi was trying to figure out how to change the subject like Eza and Cammie did. "You sound really worried about something that may not even happen –"

Eza cut in. "You say *worry* like I'm choosing to have these thoughts. I'm not. They just *show up* in my head, and I don't know where they come from, and I can't get rid of them."

The interruption didn't seem to bother Denavi. "What has your doctor told you?"

Eza leaned his head against Denavi's. "She gave me some questions to ask myself when I'm feeling anxious about something happening. The first is, what are the chances of the bad thing actually happening?"

"That makes sense. Sometimes people worry about things that are basically impossible, and that's a waste of energy."

"Yeah. But the chances of Cammie going back...I really don't know. Fifty-fifty, maybe. She keeps telling me how happy I make her, but then she gets jealous of you and my dad and says nothing can replace a father."

"Maybe daddy can do for her what he did for me," Denavi offered.

"Maybe. But you *needed* a dad. I don't think Cammie

could receive that kind of love knowing her own dad was out there."

"Okay, so the bad thing might happen. What's the second question?"

"If the bad thing happens, how bad is it actually going to be?"

Denavi was quiet. "I feel like it'd be pretty bad."

"I don't know what I'd do. I love Cammie so much. To love like that and have it suddenly taken away from me..."

"I bet you could write a great play about it," Denavi joked.

Eza poked her in the side and she squealed. "You're skipping to the third question," he scolded. "But yeah. I'd be devastated. I don't..." He trailed off and couldn't finish.

Denavi seemed to sense his discomfort. "What's the third question, then?"

"If the bad thing happens, what will still be good in your life?"

Neither of them said anything.

"Well?" Denavi asked.

"Lots of stuff," Eza had to admit. "I'd still have you and dad. I'd still be a student at Carnazon." A few moments passed. "I could be a Ranger after all. My life was really good before I met Cammie, and I guess it'd be good afterward."

"Great. You won the three questions game. Do you feel better?"

"No," Eza said. "But I think I'm tired enough to fall asleep."

"With your boots on?" Denavi asked, pointing down at his feet.

"Yeah. Definitely with my boots on."

SEVENTEEN

Walking Barin back to the trading circle was none of Denavi's business, but she'd asked Eza and Cammie if she could come along anyway. Cammie had been so focused on her last few hours with her father that she had passed the question to Eza, who was visibly nervous and trying to hide it. He had agreed, but the more Denavi thought about it, the more she wondered if she'd made a mistake. If Cammie took him up on his offer and went back to Exclaimovia, Eza would probably rather be alone on the return. Just as Denavi was starting to wonder if she should find something to do at home instead, Barin announced that it was time to leave, and the four of them plus Aleiza set out for Tranquility's eastern gate.

Barin was disguised in Introvertian clothes, with his Exclaimovian attire stashed in his pack, and after a brief discourse about the nauseating blandness of Introvertian fashion, he closed his mouth and allowed himself to be walked to the gate. Cammie chattered away at him, but Barin took his vow of silence very seriously, smiling and nodding and patting her on the head while keeping his words inside.

Once they left the city and joined the Forest Road, Eza

and Denavi hung back as Aleiza came to sit on Eza's shoulders. "I haven't seen her do that very much," Denavi observed.

"It's not easy now that she's taller than I am," Eza admitted.

"Why did she do it, then?"

"She knows it makes me feel better when I'm upset."

Denavi looked up. "Aleiza can tell when you're upset?"

"My mind link to her is always open. It's possible to close it; I had to do that once when we were rescuing those dragons from Exclaimovia and all seven hundred of them were trying to talk to me at once. But she sees everything I see, and she always knows what I'm feeling."

"So she knows about your anxiety?"

"She probably knew before I did, but didn't know how to warn me. We're not at the point of being able to talk with words yet; that'll take a few more years of practice." Eza rubbed Aleiza's claws, which were resting gently on his shoulders.

The morning stretched on, and Denavi had to admit it was an extremely pleasant day for a walk. The previous afternoon's thunderstorm – somehow Eza had known there was going to be one, which Denavi found impressive – had blown away and left a warm and welcoming blue sky overhead. It would have been a

225

great day for almost anything outdoors, really: sitting on a boat in a lake, or lounging by the Rapidly Flowing River with her feet in it, or hiking up into those mountains by the road to see if they really were impassable.

Lunch was a typically raucous affair; Barin peppered Eza with questions about the theater tour and the Dragon Academy, interrupting him before he could finish answering any of them. Eza didn't seem to mind too much, and it almost seemed like he was grateful that he didn't have to speak. Cammie didn't know what he was about to suggest to her, Denavi suddenly realized. That's why Cammie was acting like everything was normal while Eza looked like someone had just dropped a mountain on his shoulders.

The tension was almost unbearable for Denavi as they got closer and closer to the trading circle. Last night she'd been sure that Eza was exaggerating things; of course Cammie was going to stay in Introvertia, wasn't she? But the longer they walked today, the less sure Denavi got. She'd never heard Cammie laugh so loudly, screech so passionately, or just seem as thoroughly *at ease*. Maybe Eza should have told Cammie about this plan in advance, given her time to think about it – who knew what she was going to choose if she had to decide suddenly –

They reached the trading circle around four in the

afternoon and Eza tugged Cammie's elbow as the clearing opened up around them. "Go on ahead, daddy," Cammie said. "I'll catch up to you in a minute."

Denavi didn't want to seem like she was eavesdropping, but she *had* to know what was going to happen. She moved behind Cammie, partly so Cammie didn't spot her and partly so she could see Eza's face.

"Cammie," he began, "I know how much you miss Exclaimovia, and I want you to know that I had an idea. I can make it so that you can go back and live with your family again. My Artomancy. I can disguise you just like Gar disguised us when we went into Exclaimovia, only more, so that no one would ever recognize you. You can live there in secret. I'll – I'll do it if you really want me to."

Cammie was silent for so long that Denavi wondered if she'd heard his words. "You're offering," Cammie clarified at last, "to let me go home?"

Eza nodded. "If that's what will really make you happy. I've seen how much you love being around your dad –"

"So now I have to choose between going home or between living in Tranquility with you?"

Eza swallowed hard and nodded.

This was it. Denavi's palms were sweating and she wiped them on her pants. She had to be ready to hug Eza if his shoulders slumped in devastation –

Cammie pushed her glasses up her nose. "That's easy. I choose you."

"I – what? Easy?"

"Yes, Eza. Easy. The opposite of hard. I want to live in Tranquility forever with you, even if it means not being near my family. That's the life I choose. I keep telling you and you keep not believing me."

"But you talk so much about missing your dad that –"

"My people are complainers, Eza. I'm a complainer. I always have been. When we first met, I complained about Introvertia even though I was the one who'd made the decision to come visit, remember?"

"I always did think that was strange," Eza confessed, a smile breaking through the nervousness on his face.

"And on our journey to Exclaimovia, I complained about sleeping on the ground, and about you not making small talk with me, and...honestly, I don't even remember everything I complained about. It just oozes out of me. Anything that bothers me comes out of my mouth. And yeah, not having my family around bothers me. But it bothers me this much –" She pinched her thumb and forefinger together. "And being around you makes me happy this much." Cammie spread her arms wide and wrapped them around Eza, dropping her head onto his shoulder.

Eza cast a relieved glance at Denavi before returning Cammie's embrace. "How am I supposed to know when you're complaining and when there's a real problem?" he asked.

"I'll tell you. I won't make hints and suggestions and expect you to read my mind. I'll be direct with you. Trust me to do that, okay?"

"Sure thing."

Cammie pulled back and looked him in the eyes. "That's way better than *I'll try*, my love."

"It's easy to believe in myself when you believe in me."

"Denavi, write that line down," Cammie said over her shoulder.

Denavi laughed, and so did Eza, and all the tension evaporated into the afternoon warmth.

Barin came over to see what they were all laughing about, as if he couldn't handle the idea of a good time being had without him. "Are you planning to give me a proper farewell, Cammaina, or linger here all day?"

"I would linger all day if I could, daddy," she told him. "I can't wait to see you again."

"Goodbye, General," said Eza, stepping forward.

Barin laughed. "I told you, stop calling me *General* like we don't know each other. I'm going to be your father-in-law one day, after all. Call me Barin."

To Denavi's everlasting surprise, *Eza* was the one who put his arms out to offer a hug, and Barin looked extremely impressed as he stepped forward into it. "Take good care of my firebug, son," said Barin quietly. "I've known Cammie for her entire life, obviously, and she's never talked about anyone the way she talks about you. You bring her incredible delight. I consider it an honor to have you courting her."

Tears came to Eza's eyes and Barin clapped his shoulders with a roaring laugh. "I MADE HIM CRY!" Barin shouted at Cammie. "That was...actually kind of fun."

"DADDY!" Cammie shrieked back at him. "Be nice to Eza!"

"I'm just playing, firebug. I have to get my teasing in now because I don't know when I'll see you again."

The wind seemed to go out of Cammie's sails at that comment. "Be safe, daddy," she said quietly.

"I will, Cammaina. I love you."

"I love you more."

"Not possible."

With that Barin took off at a fast march toward the east, the sunlight on his back. He followed the Forest Road as it bent to the right and then he was gone from their sight.

Cammie watched him go, and even after he'd disappeared she stayed rooted to the spot, leaning backward into Eza as he stood behind her with his arms around her stomach. Denavi tried to imagine how she was feeling – how Denavi herself would feel if something happened and Ezarra had to leave without any idea when he'd see Denavi again. Panic rose up in her and she started breathing hard. No, no. She couldn't lose Ezarra, not her daddy...

Quickly Denavi got a hold of herself, forcing her emotions back down. It was only imagination, she reminded herself. Ezarra wasn't gone; he was waiting at home for her. But if Cammie was feeling what Denavi had just felt...if she was feeling even *half* of that...

"You know," Eza was saying, "if Barin's going to be my father-in-law, that means my dad is going to be your father-in-law."

"True," said Cammie.

"So, you know...it wouldn't kill you to hug him."

Cammie turned around to face him. "Ezalen Skywing of Introvertia is telling me to hug someone?"

"Well, I am your squad captain. I can pull rank if you want me to."

"You would never."

"Cadet Ravenwood, I order you to hug my dad." Eza hesitated. "If you want to."

Cammie exploded into laughter. "I love you so much. Let's go home."

Eza opened a rainbow door in front of them, the portal glowing in every color imaginable. "We can rainbow-jump back and save some time."

Cammie's eyes got huge. "We walked all the way out

to the trading circle when you could have gotten us here in an hour?"

"I figured you'd want more time with your dad, so we took the long way here and the shortcut home."

"You're so thoughtful," Cammie said, putting a hand on the back of his head and moving in for a kiss.

Denavi turned away and pretended to examine the Impassable Mountains. They couldn't really be completely impassable, right? That had to be an exaggeration. Maybe there was a way through them...

She had *a lot* more mountain-related thoughts than she'd ever thought possible before Eza and Cammie were finally finished, and the three of them stepped through the rainbow door.

Night was falling over the courtyard at Carnazon Fortress as Shanna Cazaran and Razan Enara faced off again, wooden scanas in their hands. "We can't use our dragons this time," Razan said.

"Fine," Shanna agreed. "No using our dragons."

As if to punctuate the point, her purple dragon, Evaza, went winging off to the west over the walls of Carnazon. Razan told his own dragon, Oreaza, to stand guard on the outer wall, but Oreaza ignored him as usual, bouncing around the bottom of the courtyard and investigating the cobblestones on the ground. He and Shanna touched swords and the duel began.

Razan kept his weight on his toes, his knees bent, as he probed for weaknesses in Shanna's defenses. She was using a low guard, so Razan launched into the Triepra offense, making her slide backward as he aimed his thrusts at her shoulders. He kept trying to force her onto her left knee, but there was no pain in her eyes, no hesitation or grimacing. "Your movement is looking good," he told her as he finished his attack and stepped back to regroup.

"Thanks. Doctor Deraza kept telling me to take it easy, but... I don't know how to do that." Shanna smiled and pushed a few strands of brown hair out of her eyes. "I missed my squad's first two maneuvers. I'm not going to miss the third."

Shanna leaped forward as the last word came out of her mouth, and Razan didn't have time to think about her attack pattern, shifting backward quickly and setting up in a neutral defensive posture. Shanna's swings were hard, swiping at his head and then his thigh and then his chest, and Razan parried quickly before thrusting at Shanna's stomach. She sidestepped the attack and took a few more steps backward, and the two of them eyed each other again.

"Do you worry about it happening again?" Razan asked. "Hurting it, I mean."

"A lot," Shanna admitted. "I try not to. If I worry, it's like it happens to me all over again every day. I imagine myself being discharged from the army, not able to run or maybe even walk again, not being able to play with my kids. It's like my mind is having a competition with itself to make up the worst possible story, and it acts out those scenes for me over and over again if I let it. So I try not to let it. I may tear my knee again, but if I do, it's a one-time event. Worrying is like having the worst thing happen dozens or hundreds of times, when it may never happen at all."

Razan nodded, suddenly realizing he'd let his guard down, and he brought his sword back up just in case she tried something while he was pondering. "That's a good point," he said. "You should share it with Eza."

"He told you about his anxiety?" Shanna asked, looking surprised.

"I was there when he..." Razan waved his off hand, not knowing exactly what to say. "When he got sent to the infirmary," he finished. "On our last maneuver he told me what what had happened. I'm his second, so if anything were to...happen to him when our squad was on a mission, I'd have to quickly take over."

Shanna's guard was down too, and Razan knew that if he wanted to, he could spring forward and win the duel, but he knew the conversation they were having was more important than winning. *Oh, that's why I'm in Harmony,* he thought in amusement.

"What do you think of all that?" Shanna asked.

"I – haven't thought about it, I guess. I do what I have to do. It's not like Eza can help it. I don't know much about anxiety, but it sounds like something that just *happens* to a person. There's no point in being upset at something that isn't his fault."

"That's exactly what a good second would say. I'm glad we're back to being friends, Razan." Shanna lifted her sword tip. "Now it's time to get impaled."

"You can try!"

Wooden swords clacked together furiously as Shanna attacked in what appeared to be a modified Ariza attack, shifting her weight left and right as she tried to find a hole in Razan's defense. But Razan countered with a strong-side feint, taking back the initiative and sending Shanna scurrying backward to regroup. That made him smile.

And suddenly something massive was crashing into his back, sending him sprawling to the cobblestones. He lost his grip on his scana and heard it clacking to the ground several feet away. "I said no dragons," he protested angrily as he stood.

"No, you didn't," Shanna said with a barely suppressed grin. "You said we couldn't use *our* dragons. This one isn't mine. It's Eza's."

"Wh...how?"

"As soon as you said that, I sent Evaza to his house to talk to Aleiza, and here she is."

Aleiza looked like she had a smile on her face, too, standing over Razan triumphantly. "Okay," Razan admitted, "that was really clever."

"Thank you. I was pretty proud of it." Shanna poked the ground with her scana. "Have you talked to Anneka lately?"

"No. I think she's avoiding me."

"I'm sorry."

Part of Razan really didn't want to be talking about this, but he'd been holding it in ever since that last talk with Anneka, and it would feel good to get it out. Maybe. "I know I should be proud of myself for doing the right thing, but it was *so nice* to have someone who wanted to spend time around me. She'd be waiting in the barracks when I got back from class, and we'd have breakfast together..." The memories tugged at Razan, and he hesitated, not sure if he wanted to keep talking.

"Doing the right thing is lonely sometimes," Shanna told him softly. "But do you remember what I told you, about people attracting others who are like them? If you do the right thing for long enough, you'll end up surrounded by right-thing-doers, and those are the people who you really want to care about you. Being around someone who hurts others, just to cure your own loneliness...that's like treating a paper cut by slicing off your arm."

"If those right-thing-doers could hurry up a bit, that'd

be fantastic."

"And there's the complication," Shanna said, examining the end of her scana as if she was trying not to make eye contact. "Because now you have a reputation as the kind of guy who hangs out with Anneka. That upset a lot of people."

"But I changed," protested Razan. "I apologized to Cammie. Things are supposed to be better now."

"You spent weeks building that reputation for unkindness, Razan. It's going to take time for you to build a new one. You may have said you're sorry, but people always say actions speak louder than words do. People won't change their minds about you until they see for themselves that you're different."

Razan was quiet. "Then I guess that's what I have to do."

"And you will, because you're kind-hearted underneath it all."

He forced a smile he didn't feel.

"You're just really insecure," Shanna added.

"Oh, for the love of loud noises. One deep talk at a time, please." Razan whipped his scana up. "Let's go back to fighting."

Once again the sounds of their duel echoed off Carnazon's courtyard walls.

EIGHTEEN

Excited chatter from the next bedroom, Eza's room, jolted Cammie out of sleep *way* earlier than she wanted to be awake. She was utterly exhausted emotionally, from the overwhelming joy of seeing her father again to the crushing disappointment of having to say goodbye after only two days. The exhaustion was physical, too, from the day-long trek out to the trading circle and the much briefer rainbow-jumps home. What she really wanted was to sleep until noon, but apparently the rest of the house had other plans.

She swung her legs down from the bed and padded out the door and into Eza's room, where he and Denavi were discussing something. "What's so important that it interrupted my beauty sleep?" Cammie demanded.

"No amount of sleep could make you more beautiful than you already are," Eza told her.

"Stop being sweet when I'm complaining," Cammie joked, breaking into a smile.

"Never."

"I cracked the code," Denavi said breathlessly. "It was one of the simpler ciphers, just like I thought. The letters were assigned a value according to – well, it was a lot of math, but I got it!"

Cammie had never seen Denavi quite so proud of herself. It looked good on her. "And?" Cammie asked, the suspense already getting to her.

"It's a set of directions. A map, written in text, basically."

"A map to what?"

"That's where it gets really exciting." Denavi was bouncing up and down on her toes now. "The code says it's directions to a focus crystal in the Impassable Mountains, and instructions on how to handle it."

Cammie looked at Eza, who shrugged. "What's a focus crystal?"

"Okay. So. There are magical nexus lines, which intersect at nexus nodes, right?"

Cammie nodded.

"You told me that when Gar the Artomancer came to you, he thought that Carnazon Fortress used to be a four-line nexus node, one of the most powerful known to exist. But it's not. How is that possible? How can magical nexus lines *move*?"

That had Cammie's attention. All thoughts of sleep vanished. "So...what's the answer?"

"The answer is that nobody knows," Denavi told her.

Cammie blinked. "I – wasn't expecting that."

"I said nobody *knows*," Denavi clarified. "I didn't say nobody has any ideas. There are legends in Claira, and probably in Esteria and Telravia too, about powerful crystals, enchanted by arch-mages long ago, that actually draw magical energy to themselves. In theory, they could create a new nexus node wherever they were powered up, by making the nexus lines flow to that crystal."

"In theory?" Eza asked.

"Well...they may not actually be real. I mean, Telravia probably has a couple, but they wouldn't tell anyone, because a focus crystal would be worth fighting a war over and they wouldn't want their enemies to know. Claira may even have one or two, but if we do, it's not the sort of thing they would have told someone like me. These crystals are supposed to be portable, so you could bring one with you to an important battle, but if you managed to lose and the other side took the focus crystal...that'd be really, really bad."

Eza looked deep in thought. "So you're saying that Carnazon *used* to have one of these crystals, but the crystal was moved and that's why it's not a powerful nexus node anymore?"

"Well...maybe. It's possible that focus crystals are a myth. The history books get things wrong sometimes. It's also possible Gar simply misremembered. But if those crystals are real, and Gar is correct, then that's the only way I know of that a place could stop being a nexus node." Denavi spread her hands. "But we know almost nothing about the way that kind of magic actually works. Maybe the lines move on their own like a river changes course. Maybe they get stronger when people practice magic around them, so the Carnazon node shut down after Introvertia gave up magic."

Silence fell. Cammie didn't know what to say, but Eza looked deep in thought.

Denavi was looking at him too. "Honestly, Eza, with as much as you read, I'm a little surprised you didn't know any of this."

"We didn't have magic for eight hundred years," Eza pointed out. "There aren't a lot of old books about magic left. Believe me, I asked Mr. Cappel a hundred times. If those books or copies of them still existed in Introvertia, he'd find a way to get his hands on them. But we didn't need magic, so the books were useless, and people just kind of got rid of them. *Let's keep this random stuff around in case we need it later* isn't really a thing Introvertians do."

"It's a shame, the way all that knowledge was built up over centuries and then just disappeared."

"Well," Eza said, "let's help get some of it back. We need to tell the king and queen about this. If Claira thinks they've found a focus crystal, and if they've already sent one search party after it, we need to make sure we get there first."

Less than an hour later, Cammie was standing in the throne room next to Eza as Denavi patiently explained all the things she'd said back at the house. King Jazan and Queen Annaya listened with fascinated looks on their faces, trading glances with each other every so often as if they were speaking without words. When Denavi finished, King Jazan stood. "The last time you gave us information, Miss Kiresti, it helped to win the Battle of the Denneval Plain for us. We would be foolish not to trust you this time." He turned to Eza. "Take a small group. You say this Azanna had five people with him. There must be a reason he was not with a larger force, given the importance of these focus crystals. Your group should be about the same size."

"Yes, Your Highness."

"Notify me of your selection before you leave, then go with all haste. Whatever is at this location – whether a focus crystal or something else – we need to know what it is and why it was so important to Claira."

Eza led Cammie and Denavi back out into the front hall. "I need Denavi for sure," Eza said. "She's the only one who can read the code."

"And me too, right?" Cammie asked.

Eza hesitated. "It might be really dangerous..."

"Isn't that a good reason to have the strongest spellcaster you know in your group?" Cammie watched his face change, as if she could see the anxious thoughts moving into his brain in real time. "Look. If I was going into danger, you would want to be there to help me, right? I want the same thing. You can't say no."

Silently Eza nodded. "You're right. So Denavi and

Cammie. And Shanna. She does physical magic, so we'll have four schools represented."

"Sounds like you need one or two more people," Cammie said.

"I want Razan." He looked at Cammie. "If it's okay with you."

"You could pick anyone in Introvertia and you're going with *Razan*?" Cammie asked in disbelief.

"Shanna and I have have trained with him for years. Each of us knows how the others think and move. If we end up in trouble, we need someone like that."

"Your choice," Cammie said doubtfully.

"Five people and three dragons. I think that's about right." Eza looked back into the throne room, and Cammie could see his hand shaking from nervousness.

"You don't have to do this," Cammie said, taking his shoulders. "There are other people the king can send. You can tell him how you feel –"

"I'm not going to let anxiety stop me," Eza interrupted. "I don't want people to treat me differently or start thinking there are things I can't do. I'm going to face my fears, Cammie, even if it's scary."

"Then why did you try to send me home?" Instantly Cammie regretted picking a fight with Eza and wished she could have the words back. She'd been so unguarded around her father that the thought had just slipped out of her mouth. Harassing him about his anxiety was...not a classy move.

"The danger is part of it," Eza admitted. "But think about where we're going. The Impassable Mountains. There's going to be a lot of hiking, and sleeping outdoors, and maybe even mountain climbing, and you know you don't like any of that stuff."

"Do you think I'd be happier sitting on my hands at home?"

Eza had to smile. "No. But I sense a *lot* of complaining in the future."

"Oh, wagonloads of it. You're going to put up with it because you're patient and kind, and even when I drive you crazy, you love me more than you ever thought it was possible to love a person." She tilted her head at him. "Am I right?"

"Absolutely. And if you think about it that way, every time you complain, you're actually complimenting me, because you're saying you want to be by my side even if it means enduring hardship."

"I *compliment* you by *complaining*?!" Cammie asked in shock.

Eza laughed. "That's how I choose to take it."

"Wow. You must be the most complimented man in the entire five kingdoms, then."

With a wink, Eza offered his elbow to Cammie, and she put her hand on it, following him into the throne room to tell King Jazan and Queen Annaya their plan.

Aleiza, Oreaza, and Evaza flew overhead as Eza, Cammie, Razan, Shanna, and Denavi exited Carnazon Fortress and left the city gate heading northeast, a route that would take them around the north side of the Impassable Mountains. Eza still hadn't gotten used to just how massive Aleiza was. She was already a foot and a half taller than the average Introvertian dragon when he'd bonded with her, and she'd been growing another two or three inches a week since then. All the time they spent together was paying off – and all the time Aleiza spent with Denavi while Eza was away, too. Aleiza didn't seem picky about who was feeding her magical energy, as long as she was feeding.

The Impassable Mountains had earned their name fair and square, Eza knew. If this code paper was taking them to a location in the heart of the mountains, there was probably only one route to get to the place. He couldn't help but wonder what was waiting for them. If there was a focus crystal up there, who had put it there, and why, and how had they gotten up it there? For that matter, what did it even look like, and how would they know it when they saw it? Denavi hadn't been joking when she'd said there was a lot about magic that was just plain unknown.

But *somebody* obviously knew it, because Azanna had somehow gotten his hands on a Clairan military code that specifically mentioned focus crystals and directed him to a specific location where one was supposed to be. Who had found that information, and how? Eza didn't know, and didn't have any way of knowing.

After a few hours heading east, Denavi paused to check some landmarks, then looked doubtfully up into the mountains. "We're supposed to turn south here, and go between those two cliffs, but it looks like a dead end."

"The mountains are like that," Eza told her. "The rocks play tricks on you. Something that looks like one big boulder is actually two close together with a path between them."

"It works the other way, too," Shanna put in. "You'll see what you think is a path, but it's just two rocks sitting next to each other, or it turns into a dead-end immediately."

"So how are we supposed to get to wherever it is we're going?" asked Cammie.

Denavi held up the paper. "This thing has what looks like pretty detailed instructions, step by step. As long as we don't miss a step we should be okay."

"And if we do miss one?"

"We backtrack to the last place where we were sure of the instructions and try again," Razan said.

Cammie didn't respond, and Eza put his hands on her shoulders. "Funny thing about that," he said in her ear. "It turns out the people who have trained in survivalship and navigation are pretty good at survivalship and navigation."

"I'm complaining *so hard* on the inside right now," she informed him.

Denavi had told them the paper had about thirty steps in the instructions. The first three were simple enough, and involved crossing a stream, slithering through a certain crevice in a large rock, and climbing over a big boulder into a clearing filled with mountain raspberry.

"Do you remember these plants?" Eza asked Cammie.

Cammie thought about that for a minute. Eza knew she hadn't forgotten, because she didn't forget anything, but he could tell it was taking her a moment to place the memory. "It was when we first met Azanna," she said triumphantly. "I was trying to convince him you were on a botany project, and that was the first flower I pointed to. You said they would be bearing fruit in six weeks, and that was...ten weeks ago." She looked in wonder at the plants. "Are there still berries on them?"

"Let's find out!"

Eza gently lifted the flowers on one plant, revealing fat red fruit underneath. "Here," he said, giving her one and taking another for himself. They were incredibly juicy, nearly exploding in Eza's mouth, and he could tell from the look on Cammie's face that she was enjoying hers too. "Nutrition break," Eza called to the rest of the group.

The five of them plundered all the ripe berries they could find; while they were snacking, Eza sent Aleiza high into the air to scout. All she could see to the south was mountains, and it didn't look like there was anything of interest around. Well, maybe the focus crystal was buried in a cave or something like that. There were still twenty-seven steps left to go on their code sheet, anyway.

But the fourth step was where things got bizarre.

"It says we're supposed to scale this cliff," Denavi said, staring straight up at an eighty-foot sheer wall of granite. "Eza?"

"That's...about ten feet too tall for me to rainbow door someone to the top," he said apologetically. "How long is our longest rope?"

"I've got a hundred feet in my pack," Razan volunteered.

"What if we tie a slipknot down here and let one of the dragons try and find something to secure it on?" asked Shanna. "We can pull the rope tight and climb up it."

"Climb up eighty feet of rope?" Cammie asked. "Cause, uh, this girl doesn't *climb*..."

Eza scowled at the cliff. "Yeah, Cammie has a good point. Even for those of us with calluses on our hands, that's a long climb, and a big fall if something goes wrong."

"We'll belay," Shanna pointed out. "Use a rope as a harness."

Too far to rainbow door...

"I have an idea," Eza said abruptly.

"Is it less dangerous than climbing up an eighty-foot wall?" Cammie asked hopefully.

"Nope."

All four of the others got silent. Eza sent Aleiza up to the top of the cliff to see what was there. It was an open grassy clearing, with plenty of room to land...which was good.

He stepped back from the wall and then took off sprinting toward it, throwing his hand up at the last minute and opening a rainbow door in front of him. The other end yawned in open air, seventy feet up, almost to the top of the cliff but not quite –

Eza leaped into the first portal and immediately emerged in midair far above his astonished friends. Instantly he was falling – directly into a new rainbow door, as he opened the other end on top of the cliff where Aleiza was. He misjudged the distance slightly and fell five feet, landing on his back and gasping as the air was knocked out of his lungs. Faintly he could hear his friends calling from the base of the cliff, but his vision was starting to go black from the pain, and it took all his energy to crawl to the edge and wave down with pretend cheerfulness.

"Who's next?" he tried to shout, but it came out as a faint wheeze.

He'd had the air knocked out of him before and knew he'd be fine in a minute, but the rest of the group was clamoring for him. At last he managed to shout down, in something that resembled a confident voice, "Who wants to be next?"

"Definitely not me!" Cammie shouted.

It ended up being Cammie anyway, and she got a running start toward the cliff wall before leaping into the open rainbow door. The other end was just ten feet from Eza, close enough to see her eyes wide in terror as she fell toward the other open portal. But the exit side of this second portal opened right next to Eza, and vertically, so that Cammie stumbled out of it on her feet instead of plummeting like Eza had. "Nice job," he told her. "You're cute when you're free-falling."

"I will never. Do. That. Again."

"I just want to remind you that you begged to come along."

The light in her eyes meant she knew he was only teasing. "Oh, so we're rubbing things in now? That's fine. Just wait until we stop for the night."

"Ooooh, Cammie's threatening me," Eza said in a pretend-scared voice. "I'm shaking."

"You'll be shaking from laughter when I get done with your ribs."

In a minute the other three were on top of the cliff and Eza was sitting down to stuff himself with flatbread from his pack. It was anyone's guess how many times he'd have to do things like that to get them over or around obstacles, so he had to keep his energy topped up. Overexerting himself out here could mean death – for all of them.

"Next we're supposed to head toward that peak over there," Denavi said, pointing. "And then there's supposed to be a bridge over a ravine."

"Bridge?" asked Cammie, bewildered. "Like...people travel this way a lot?"

"Or at least used to," Eza agreed. "If the bridge is that old, let's hope it's still there."

Fifteen minutes later they were standing in front of a...well, to call it a *ravine* seemed entirely too mild. This was a massive gouge in the earth, two hundred feet across easily and so deep that Eza had gotten dizzy when he'd tried going close to the edge and looking down. "That rainbow-jump routine is *not* going to work here," he said to no one in particular.

"There obviously used to be a bridge," Denavi said, standing next to two rotting wooden poles and pointing to two matching poles on the other side. "But it looks like it was a rope bridge, and..."

251

She didn't have to finish.

"Gar the Artomancer could do that easily," Eza mused. "He can go miles in a single jump."

"Do you know where he lives?" Razan asked. "We could go back and get him."

"Great idea, Razan, but the Prismatic City is at least a day's journey to the east by rainbow door, and that's if he's even at home. We don't know if Claira might already have sent a second group after this focus crystal. If they're as important as Denavi thinks, and if they believe they've finally tracked one down, then we need to beat them to it."

"How much rope do we have?" Eza asked abruptly. "Everyone brought at least a hundred feet, right?"

Everyone had except Cammie, who wasn't carrying a pack.

"Then let's splice these together. If we tie the right knot, Aleiza can take it back and loop it over itself around that tree there. We have enough to run over and back twice, so we'll set one up to walk on and the other at shoulder height to hold onto."

"We have to *walk* across *that?*" Cammie asked, pointing at the ravine. "On *ROPES?!*"

"Hey," Shanna said. "Evaza flew a couple hundred yards that way and said the ravine is only thirty feet across at that point."

An embarrassed silence fell.

"Well," said Eza, "we almost made that a *lot* harder than it needed to be. Let's get across the ravine and then make camp. It gets dark really early here because of the shadows of the mountains. Razan, you'll take first watch. Wake us all up if anything happens."

NINETEEN

Introvertians sure did love their trail food, Cammie thought, munching on a piece of dried meat that she'd sprinkled with the spices her father had brought back for her. It had only been about six in the evening when they'd been forced to make camp due to darkness, but Cammie knew she wouldn't be tired for several more hours. She laid out her sleeping bag right next to Eza's, the way they'd slept way back when they were first traveling to Exclaimovia together.

"This brings back memories," she told him with a smile.

Eza nodded. "Before we loved each other. I don't even remember how it felt not to be in love with you."

Cammie rolled over onto her side, propping her head up on her elbow. "When we started to court, you told me the first moment you knew you loved me. It was when we were spending the night in the Harmony barracks, and Razan sneezed at four in the morning, and you waited outside in the lounge until I woke up, getting really excited every time the door to the girls' dorm opened and then getting really sad every time it wasn't me."

That brought a smile to his face. "That's when I knew

for sure, yeah."

"When was the first time you started to suspect you might love me?"

Eza giggled, then got quiet, as if he didn't want to say. "It's kind of embarrassing."

"Then embarrass yourself."

"Okay. This was about a week after the dragon rescue. We were walking through Tranquility and I was explaining why springtime is my favorite season, and you teased me for talking too much."

Cammie howled with laughter. "*That* was your a-ha moment? Me making fun of you?"

"Close. When you said that, I realized I was doing whatever it took to make you happy – even if it meant making small talk – and I was doing it without realizing. It just *naturally* came out of me because I knew it would bring a smile to your face. That was the a-ha moment. That was when I knew the most important thing to me was making you happy."

"You've succeeded. Beyond your wildest dreams." Cammie looked into his green eyes. "I wish there was some magic that could let you feel what I'm feeling, so you can understand how cherished I feel around you. I don't ever want you to doubt again. Come on. Let's dance."

She offered him her hand, and in the growing darkness they danced together, sometimes slowly, sometimes quicker, sometimes closer and sometimes apart. This wasn't like the last time they'd danced, where Cammie had been sending a message to Eza through her movements. This was just *dance*, feeling the rhythm of each other's bodies and learning to speak without words. Cammie's eyes were on Eza, watching his muscles so she could anticipate his movements, but out of the corner of her vision she could see Denavi watching with a delighted smile, as if being treated to a show on a stage, while Shanna stared with something that might have been jealousy and Razan pretended not to notice.

At last Cammie slowed. "I think I have to stop. I'm really sore from today, and something tells me tomorrow isn't going to be any easier."

"Lie down," Eza told her. "It's magical massage time."

"Oooooh. This is my favorite thing. Well...you're my favorite thing. But this is my favorite thing that you do."

"Good save."

Eza's hands pressed against her calves, and she felt a gentle tingling warmth flow into her. The ache in her muscles instantly began to fade, replaced by relaxation and ease. She knew this scared Eza, because the Artomancy power of heat could feel amazing or could really burn Cammie, which is why he'd only allowed himself to treat her this way a handful of times. But, as Cammie had told him the last time, there was no way to get better except by practicing.

The warmth trickled up to her thighs, then to her lower back, then her shoulders. It felt so good that Cammie couldn't even speak; she just closed her eyes, resting her head on her sleeping bag and letting Eza do what he did. She was so thoroughly relaxed that it was tempting to fall asleep, but if she did that, she'd stop feeling the massage, and that was no good at all.

But then she was waking up the next morning anyway, rolling over and opening one eye to see Eza sitting cross-legged on the ground, with wispy clouds dotting the patch of sky that they could see above the mountain peaks. "Buh..." she said, her mind still recovering from the ecstasy of that massage.

"Buh to you too," Eza laughed. "How do you feel?"

"Perfect, Eza. Thank you so much."

"You should have seen the others after you fell asleep. They were all demanding to know what I was doing to you and wanting me to try it on them."

A pang of jealousy stabbed at Cammie, surprising her. "Did you?" she asked, a little more aggressively than she'd meant.

"No. I..." Eza hesitated, as if he thought the answer would make him look silly. "I feel like that's our thing, and I don't want to share it with anyone else."

"Good. Don't. I mean, you can if you want to. But...it is definitely our thing."

"Then it'll stay our thing."

Cammie smiled widely, throwing off her sleeping bag – no, Eza's sleeping bag; he'd spread it on top of her like a blanket the way he always did – and stretching her arms, then fingers, then legs, then toes, with loud grunts of satisfaction. "So, lots more hiking and climbing today, right?"

"Sure looks like it."

"Oh, darn," Cammie said with pretend disappointment. "What a tragedy. I can feel my muscles getting sore already. I may need another magical massage tonight."

"I love you, you goof."

The group had covered the first five steps on the code sheet the day before, which wasn't bad considering they'd left Tranquility in early afternoon and had only spent a few hours in the mountains before the sun set. With some luck they might even reach their destination later today, and if not then early tomorrow – unless the obstacles waiting for them were even worse than the ones they'd already gotten past.

"What do you think these directions are leading us toward?" Cammie asked Eza.

"I only have one guess. Think of the two things we had the hardest time getting past."

"A cliff and a ravine. So?"

"How would a big group of people get up that cliff?"

"Ropes, I guess. A few people at a time."

"Exactly. And how would a big group of people get across that ravine?"

Cammie thought about that. "Well, if the bridge was still there, then the bridge. But that would be a few people at a time, too. Without the bridge, they'd probably have to make their own way to get across."

Eza smiled proudly. "Great thinking. You noticed the right answer."

"I don't feel like I noticed anything at all."

"Seems to me like we're heading toward some kind of fortress. When you said *a few people at a time*, you described a choke point. The route to this place was intentionally designed so that a small group of defenders could fight off a much larger attacking force through the use of choke points. But that means there must have been a group of defenders. And if there was a group of defenders, there must have been some place for them all to eat and sleep. So...a fortress."

"I have...so many questions," Cammie stammered. "You got all of that just from the fact that we had to climb a cliff?"

"And cross a ravine, but yeah. That's first-year tactics stuff."

"Second...if there's a fortress in these mountains, how in the sun did nobody know it was up here?"

Eza spread his hands. "This all has to do with magic,

remember? It's been hundreds of years since anyone in Introvertia cared about magic, except the people like me who enjoy reading old history books. Unless there was some battle fought at this fortress, or some reason it would be in a book, probably the only records of it are in the government archives in the basement of the palace."

"So even the king and queen might not know what's up here?"

"It sure sounded to me like they didn't. If the only reason to be here was magic, we probably abandoned the place as soon as we renounced magic."

Cammie's eyes drifted up toward the peaks. "But if there was a focus crystal there, wouldn't somebody else have come in and taken it by now? I mean, if that was hundreds of years ago..."

"Maybe. Like Denavi said, the location of these things was not public knowledge, so it's possible nobody outside of Introvertia knew it was here, and when Introvertia forgot about it, the knowledge just disappeared."

"So how did Azanna, and whoever in Claira sent him, find out?"

"You sure do like questions," Eza teased.

"Not as much as I like answers!"

That made him laugh. "Maybe we'll get them all someday. For now, let's move out."

Razan had even more trouble keeping Oreaza's focus on him than ever before. There was just so much to see and smell up here in the mountains. Oreaza was supposed to be scouting, but she kept flying off to investigate new things, only returning when Aleiza chastised her. Razan didn't know how to feel about the fact that his dragon would listen to another dragon, but would completely ignore the man who was supposed to be her companion.

After the excitement of the first five steps on the code paper, the next fourteen were rather mundane, just a matter of following landmarks. Eza pointed out a few choke points to Cammie, who seemed delighted to notice them. "You see that?" he'd asked her at one point.

"Yeah. We had to go single file between those two rocks."

"And you saw all the high ground above us?"

Cammie's eyes had lit up. "Choke point!"

Then they'd had to crawl on their hands and knees through a hole that had obviously been tunneled through an enormous rock. Razan liked open spaces; having a million tons of rock on top of him, in an area so tight he couldn't even look behind him to make sure Shanna was still back there, was definitely *not* his favorite thing. He emerged from the end just in time to see Cammie grab Eza's elbow and shout, "Choke point!"

Oh, he'd seen them dancing together the night before.

He'd just made it a point to ignore them, not out of spite, but out of...longing. He wanted someone to dance with him, and didn't want to be reminded that he didn't have anyone. Shanna had spoken a lot of sense when she'd reminded him that Anneka wasn't right for him – but Anneka had loved him, or said she did.

Maybe it was childish that he didn't want to be alone. Maybe it was the most grown-up thing there was. Being dependent on others was one thing, and being independent was better, but being independent wasn't the final step on the journey. The last step was being *interdependent*, knitting your life together with someone else. Razan had independence. What he wanted was interdependence.

Cammie saw him looking, with what must have been a scowl on his face, and she almost certainly misinterpreted the look. "Everything okay, Razan?"

He nodded. "You and Eza have a beautiful thing together. I was just admiring it."

That clearly caught Cammie by surprise. She wore her emotions on her face, he'd noticed. "Thank you, Razan. That's very kind."

He just nodded again and pretended to examine a tree a few feet away while waiting for Shanna and Denavi to emerge from the mouth of the tunnel.

The next ten landmarks passed fairly quickly as well. There was a winding path up and up and up the side of a mountain, with six switchbacks that left it exposed to what looked like defensive perches on the high ground. "Choke point!" he heard Cammie shouting from the front of the line, her voice echoing off the mountains. After that was a single-file stone staircase, with no handrail, cut into the side of another cliff; like the path, it climbed to the left and then switched back to the right, making it easily guarded by anyone at the top. "Choke point!" called Cammie from the bottom, staring up at the top with her hands on her hips.

They'd had to climb that staircase on their hands and knees, with Eza at the bottom, ready to cast a quick rainbow door and catch anyone who fell off. Thankfully no one did, and Eza had looked calm and confident as he scaled the steps, although he was on his hands and knees too. There was only one landmark to catch: "Left at the fork," Denavi read from the paper. "I guess we'll know the fork when we see it."

A half-mile ahead, the flat ground they were on did indeed fork, continuing forward and wrapping around the far side of a mountain while another path branched off to the left. "Aleiza says it's a fortress, alright," Eza said. "Uh...she also says there's trouble."

"What kind of trouble?" Razan asked.

"She doesn't know how to describe it. People, but not people."

"Well, that's ominous," Cammie said.

"I'm going to have a look," Eza declared. He paused...and then vanished.

Razan couldn't believe his eyes. "What –"

"Eza?" asked Shanna.

"Shhhh," came Eza's voice from right in front of them. "It's Artomancy." Razan could see a faint shimmering as Eza waved his arm. "It works pretty well when I'm standing still, but I have to be careful when I move."

Razan watched as the gentle shimmer walked to the edge of the rock shelf next to them and peeked to the left. "Well," Eza said quietly. "I think Aleiza just about had it right. There are some sort of *somethings* there, roughly as tall as we are, but...their faces are blank."

"Blank?" Cammie asked.

"Like there's nothing inside. They look...kind of like Telravia's battle horrors."

"Telravia was here?" Cammie sounded panicked. "Maybe they took the focus crystal and left these things behind –"

"Only one way to find out," Eza said. "When we go around the corner, these things will probably all see us. Razan, Cammie, hit them with magic. I'll do the same if I can, but I'll be hanging back to help the rest of you. Shanna, look for anything you can do. Denavi, you can close to sword range if you want, otherwise stay with me and hope we don't need you. There's a boulder off to the right where I want Razan to go. Shanna, try and make your way to this trench thing on the left. Send your dragons in hard as soon as I say go." The shimmer turned back toward them. "Be safe."

Eza popped back into view and Cammie vanished from sight instead. Razan knew why. He was protecting his girlfriend. It was understandable, really. She *was* the only one of them who hadn't been trained as a soldier, and had probably never done something like this before except in the two maneuvers she'd been on – and this would be *way* different than a maneuver.

"Go!" Eza ordered, and instantly the dragons were soaring out from behind one of the mountain peaks. Fire burst in the middle of the horror creatures, trailing behind Aleiza as she soared back up into the sapphire sky. Instantly the creatures let fly with giant balls of glowing black energy, which missed Aleiza when she banked to the right and vanished behind another mountain.

That distraction gave Razan time to move to his cover, and he fired off a burst of lightning from both hands, sizzling one of the creatures on the spot. The sight of them took his breath away – their faces weren't *empty* like Eza had said, but there were glowing gray-red eyes in their faces. Even from this distance they radiated... something like hatred and fierce possessiveness, as if this fortress were *theirs*, and they loathed all outsiders. Razan couldn't stand to look at them for more than a moment, but just as he went to duck behind the rock he saw two of those black energy balls hurtling at him. He pressed himself against the ground, trying to get as small as possible, and the top of the rock exploded, sending shards of stone in every direction, including into Razan. A hundred of them pelted his cheek, turning his face's left side into a mess of blood and tiny open wounds.

Now he was *mad*. He whipped around the right side of the rock again, searching for the nearest horror creature. There were five close to him, but facing Shanna, hurtling black balls at the rock near her. Huge pieces fell off the side of the mountain, falling right where Shanna was supposed to be hiding –

Razan screamed in fury and fried three of the horrors with the three strongest lightning charges he could manage. As the other two started to turn toward him, he let loose a fireball, diving back behind cover and not waiting to see if they were counterattacking.

Only then did he think about Oreaza, who was...hiding.

The young dragon was screaming terror into her mind link, the clearest thing he'd ever heard from her. He felt like she was begging him not to send her down there. Through her eyes he could see bursts of fire, black energy, and lightning surging across the battlefield. *So you just want to sit up there while we might die?* he shouted back at her, knowing she wouldn't understand the words, but trying to convey a feeling of desperate need.

Out of nowhere Aleiza climbed over the walls of the fortress, attacking the battle horrors from the rear and strafing six of them in one pass before they even knew what had hit them. Five of them launched energy balls at Aleiza, who was banking up and out of her strafing run. Razan watched in horror through Oreaza's eyes as the balls got close to Aleiza –

And were suddenly swallowed up by a rainbow door that opened directly underneath her, the other end appearing right over the horrors' heads – as their own energy balls slammed back down on them, blasting them to tiny pieces. Razan closed the mind link and peeked over the top of the watch, watching bits of them fly through the air and patter to the ground. Hmm. There was no blood. He didn't know why he'd noticed that, but he had.

Fifty more horrors poured out through the front gate. This could be bad. The battle had gone fine so far, but eventually he and the others would be exhausted from using magic – and how many of these things were inside, anyway?

But there was Aleiza again, with Evaza at her side, dropping low over the fortress walls and roasting dozens of the horrors while they were still bunched together coming out of the gate. A massive fireball came from seemingly nowhere — it must have been Cammie – detonating in the middle of the horrors and sending a wave of flame out along the ground, catching the rest of them in its heat. Just like that the second pack of horrors was down.

Razan waited for a third group to arrive, but silence descended on the mountains. If the fortress had any other secrets, it was keeping them inside.

TWENTY

Denavi was sure she'd watched Razan and Shanna both die, but with all that magic shooting across the battlefield, she couldn't get over to either of them. As soon as the second group of those dark creatures got blasted out of existence, Denavi sprinted toward Shanna...who was uninjured.

"I know physical magic," Shanna reminded them all as Eza and Cammie arrived at her side. "Moving stuff with my powers is what I do. I've never moved something quite as heavy as those rocks before, but they were already falling, so it didn't take much to just nudge them out of the way. I'm fine. Really."

Denavi had learned that the more forcefully people tried to insist they were fine, the more they were extremely not fine. But Shanna had no physical injuries, so Denavi turned to Razan, who was just jogging up to them. The side of his face had been turned into ground onala, probably when that rock exploded.

"Are you okay?" Cammie blurted in shock on seeing him.

Annoyance flashed in Razan's eyes. "I'm injured, but fine. I can fight."

"Hold still," Denavi told him, putting her hand on the

269

right side of his face and holding her hand a few inches from the injury. Skin was the hardest part to get right, because it liked to scar up if it didn't heal properly, and Denavi was sure Razan didn't want a hundred tiny scars all over his face. She breathed out, letting the healing energy bubble up in her, then directing it into Razan. His jaw clenched; Denavi knew it sometimes hurt when the muscles were knitting themselves back together, but Razan said nothing, staring into her eyes as she worked on him, probably trying to distract himself from the unsettling sensations in his cheek. "There," she said at last. "All set. You won't have any scars."

Razan ran his hand over the side of his face. "Thanks."

"Thanks for getting injured so I had something to do," Denavi teased.

The joke landed, and all five of them shared a relieved chuckle.

Shanna looked uneasily over at the fortress gate. "Should we wait here and see if anything else comes out?"

"Or maybe send one person down with that invisibility spell so they can scout?" Razan asked.

Eza shook his head. "We're all going in together. If one person goes alone there's too much risk of something going wrong." He looked at Razan and Shanna. "Post your dragons on a high perch and have them watch the road. If they see anything, have them fight so we can get back out and set up a defense."

There was nothing left to say. The five of them, without their dragons, walked into the courtyard, then through the front doors of the fortress and into a massive marble chamber with a ceiling thirty feet high. The walls were gray, but the floor and ceiling were white, coated with eight centuries worth of dust. Every footstep echoed in the cavernous room, so that it sounded like a hundred people were marching. As soon as they came through the front doors, Denavi felt a tingling all over her body. The looks on her friends' faces said they felt it too.

"That's how you know we're on a nexus node," Eza told them. "All your magic is going to be stronger here."

"Fascinating," Cammie murmured. "Only the fortress itself is a node. The defenders would benefit from its power, and the attackers wouldn't." She looked over at Eza. "Choke point?"

He chuckled. "Not exactly, but good thinking."

At the opposite end of the room were two staircases, one going up and one going down. Denavi had seen the enormous spire on top of the fortress, and hadn't considered that the whole complex might extend *down*, too. "Which way?" Cammie was asking Eza.

Eza stared at the staircases, as if the answer might be there. "Where would you put a focus crystal?" he asked himself. "Does magical energy flow through the air or the ground?"

"The ground, I think," said Denavi. "That's why most nexus nodes are in the mountains."

"So...down?" Eza asked her.

"Your choice," Denavi answered, not wanting any part of the decision. "You're the leader."

"Don't remind me. I think you're right, though. Let's go."

The air smelled musty as the group started down the staircase, which was wide enough that all of them could walk side by side. Eza used his Artomancy to cast a light spell on his sword, holding it out in front of him. In its bright white glow they could see a large hall at the bottom of the stairs, with pillars every few feet to keep the ceiling up. *That's...not a comforting thought,* Denavi thought, allowing herself a tiny smile. The room looked like it might have been a dining hall, or perhaps a meeting room; three long tables with benches stretched the length of the room. Another staircase down awaited the group at the opposite end of the room, and Eza led them slowly through the room, checking the side entrances for any sign of a trap or ambush.

A sneeze burst from Cammie's mouth, echoing a thousand times off the walls and pillars. "Sorry," she said faintly, sounding as if her nose was clogged. "It's all the dust."

But the sound was answered by furious yelping and

howling from behind them, and in the next moment ten enormous wolves poured out from one of the side doors, between the group and the staircase back to the first level. The first wolf howled again, lightning forming in its mouth and then blasting out at Eza, who barely dived out of the way in time.

"Magical creatures!" he shouted unnecessarily. "Hit them hard!"

Denavi had absolutely no spells that could help here, and she hoped none of the others would need her healing magic by the end of the fight. She drew her scana, but she wasn't eager to use it; it was shorter and lighter than the Clairan longsword she'd trained with, and she didn't know how to –

But a wolf was sprinting toward her, its mouth wide open, and Denavi rolled to her left, swiping up with the sword as she did. The scana buried itself in the animal's belly, nearly yanking itself out of Denavi's hand as the wolf blew past her. But Denavi kept her hold, watching the wolf stagger and drop to the ground. On instinct she leaped forward and stabbed it one more time in the neck, just to make sure, then whipped around in time to see Cammie lighting one on fire with a beam of flame that Denavi had never seen her use before.

The burning wolf screamed, a horrible sound, and ran around the room, crashing into two other wolves and setting them on fire as well. Denavi nearly gagged from the smell of charred fur; her eyes started watering.

A fierce arc of lightning smashed the pillar right next to her, sending pieces flying. Denavi took a few steps sideways on instinct, nearly blinded from the acid tears in her eyes. Suddenly from right in front of her she heard a wolf howl, and her sight cleared just in time to see the biggest wolf, the one who could use magic, rearing up just a few feet away. Denavi leaped forward, stabbing it in the stomach with her scana and trying to roll away. She was too slow, and claws raked her back, opening long slices that instantly burned with pain. The wolf fell back to all fours, stumbling. Denavi's breath caught in her lungs as she saw lightning beginning to glimmer inside its mouth.

Then suddenly Cammie was sprinting in between Denavi and the wolf, holding out a giant circle of crackling electrical energy, like a shield. The wolf's lightning glanced off it and blasted against the ceiling, sending dust and bits of rock down, and then Cammie hurled the lightning shield at the wolf. The shield wrapped itself all the way around the animal, which went down, writhing and screaming. Where had Cammie learned to do *that*?

There was no time to think. Only four wolves were left, but they snarled softly, and suddenly a red glow appeared in all four mouths. "Scatter!" Eza shouted, and fireballs hurtled across the room, exploding on the far wall. Razan and Cammie returned fire, and then the dead body of one wolf rose into the air – Shanna was lifting it with her magic – and smashed into two of the others, knocking them off their feet.

"Close your eyes!" Eza ordered, and Denavi did. Through her eyelids she could see the room turn brilliantly bright – Eza must have blinded the wolves – but the animals flung themselves forward anyway, swiping with paws and snapping with their teeth even though they couldn't see what was going on. Denavi circled around behind them, staying well out of range, but not knowing what else she was supposed to be doing. Her back was really starting to hurt and she was sure her shirt was bloody – she didn't have time to think about that –

One wolf must have smelled the blood, because it was turning toward her, blinking as its sight began to come back. It squatted on its haunches and pounced at her –

And then something huge smashed it, knocking it to the ground. It was Shanna hurling one of the other wolf bodies. Denavi sprinted back toward Shanna, not sure where she was supposed to be or what she was supposed to be doing. This was like a knife fight in a closet. She hadn't trained for this kind of combat.

Cammie launched a fireball at one of the wolves, but just then another one leaped at her back – directly into a rainbow door, which dumped it out from the ceiling. The bewildered wolf landed on its nose, letting out a quiet whimper before Razan hit it with lightning and it flopped to the ground motionless.

That left only two, which fled back through the door they'd come from, leaving behind the bodies of eight wolves and the smell of charred fur.

Pain was roaring its way through Denavi now, and she sat, grimacing. Getting her hands to the injured part of her back was going to be a tough task, but she put all her concentration into drawing the healing energy up from inside her and knitting her muscles and skin back together. She didn't want a scar on her back to go with the one on her stomach.

"Do we go after them?" she overheard Cammie asking Eza.

"We have to. We can't leave enemy forces behind us. They could pop up again at the worst time."

"Maybe we should go back and tell the king to send a bigger force," Shanna suggested. "We've already gotten into two big fights, and someone's been injured in each of them."

"I just don't think there's time," Eza insisted. "Especially now that we've cleared out all the enemies in the courtyard and down here. We made things a lot easier for anyone who might be coming behind us. If we get really overwhelmed, sure, we'll retreat. But as long as we stand a chance, we have to fight. We have to get to that focus crystal before anyone else does." He looked down at Denavi. "Are you okay?"

She nodded, finishing up with her back and touching the skin to make sure it was smooth. "Better than the wolves, anyway."

"True story," Cammie said, pointing at the body of the one that had injured Denavi. Its fur was still smoking.

"Eat something, and then let's go," declared Eza.

With food in hand, Eza wandered over toward the door where the wolves had retreated, standing very still as if listening. There could be dozens more down there, Denavi realized. But Eza was right. They couldn't leave their flank unguarded like that. The last thing they needed was to be neck-deep in another fight and have those wolves show up out of nowhere.

It only took a couple of minutes for the group to stuff their faces, and then they followed Eza and his glowing scana through that door and down the corridor, which was narrow. Only two of them could go shoulder to shoulder: Eza and Razan in the front, Cammie and Shanna in the second row, and Denavi bringing up the rear. The hallway stretched on, and on; it would be a horrible place to get ambushed, Denavi thought, with no cover and nowhere to hide.

Thankfully the hallway ended thirty yards later in

what looked like a storage room. Sacks were arranged around the edges of the room and on shelves, but the wolves were nowhere to be found. Two more doors led off this room, and Shanna and Eza knelt together in front of one, then the other. "Surely you're not looking for tracks," Cammie said.

"Checking the dust," Eza answered. "But there's no buildup. Both of these doors have been used in the past – well, at least two or three days." He got to his feet and gave a long sigh, leaning on one of the ancient shelves and letting his eyes drift up toward the ceiling. Denavi had seen that he didn't like being the one who had to make tough choices when leading a group. Maybe that's why he'd wanted to be a Ranger, so that he could operate by himself. "I don't want to leave those wolves behind us, but I also don't want to spend hours going down both of these hallways, and the ones that split off of them, and the ones that split off of those."

"Maybe I could sneeze again and see if they come running back?" joked Cammie. It was funny, but this time no one laughed.

Eza chewed on his lip. "Shanna, is there any way you can use your physical magic to make a giant pile of stuff in front of the door we came in through, as a barricade?"

"Easy," she said.

The rest of the group backtracked into the hallway, and Shanna spent the next ten minutes stuffing the doorway with benches and sacks and whatever else she could find in the room. The barricade looked pretty solid to Denavi, and if it wasn't, there was nothing they could do. Back they went to the mess hall where they'd fought the wolves – Denavi couldn't help thinking that it smelled like cooked meat for the first time in centuries – and then down the staircase at the other end of the room.

Thankfully there was nothing waiting to murder them when they reached the bottom of the steps. This looked like the soldiers' barracks; they were standing in a wide hallway with a door on the other end, and smaller rooms off both sides. Denavi poked her head inside one of them; it held rusting metal bunk beds and floor chests. The next room looked like the armory and training ground. Racks of weapons sat along the wall, with training dummies in a line nearby.

"Those swords are glowing," Eza said suddenly, pointing at them.

"Yours is glowing," Cammie reminded him.

"Only because I'm keeping the spell going. The moment I stop –" The room went dark except for the glimmer off the other weapons, and Denavi heard Cammie gasp. "The spell stops too." The room reappeared around them as Eza's sword began shining once more.

"But these are...powering themselves?" Cammie wondered.

"All I know is we're taking them with us," Eza told her. "Find some way to secure all these, either in your packs or between your pack and your body. Use rope if you have to." He looked at Denavi. "Are magical weapons common in Claira?"

"Ladri Arkian, the kingdom's founder, was supposed to have used one, but I always thought that was a myth. I never imagined..." She reached out and took one from the rack, a long scana more like what she was used to. It was exquisitely balanced, and the blade glowed a faint emerald green. "I wonder if it cuts harder than a regular sword," she mused. Even if it didn't, though, the sword would still make a perfect fighting weapon. Nearby was a short bow, which Denavi also took. If she couldn't attack with magic, at least she could learn how to shoot a bow so she wouldn't be totally useless in the future.

But that was the future. In the here and now, Eza and Razan and Shanna were strapping as many weapons as possible to their packs, testing the weight to make sure they could still move. Denavi was the only one who'd opted to actually use one; perhaps the others were wary of whatever enchantments might be on them, or perhaps they were used to the weight and balance of their own scanas and didn't want to quickly adjust to a new weapon.

A set of double doors sat at the end of the training room, closed at the moment, but Eza was looking at them with an expression that said they wouldn't be that way for long. "Shanna?" he asked, and her hands began to glow with magical energy. After a few seconds, she thrust her hands forward and both doors blew off their hinges. Past them was a stone staircase down, cut into the walls, running across the left side and far side of the room. Denavi couldn't tell how far it went down, but she couldn't see the floor.

And something began laughing maniacally.

TWENTY-ONE

"I smell your blood..." The crazed voice was drifting up from below. "Your life. I've nearly forgotten the taste. But come, if you dare. You shall be my next meal."

Cammie grabbed Eza's arm. "Can we go back for help now?"

His heart thudding in his chest, Eza stepped closer to the staircase, following it with his eyes as it ran along the left wall, then the far wall, then the right wall and stopped on the floor. He couldn't see whatever had taunted them, but he could see, in the center of the room, a glowing hundred-sided crystal on a pedestal. "That has to be it," he murmured to himself. At least, he *hoped* it was.

He scanned the top of the room. The ceiling rose another ten feet above his head, and around the rim were long, thin windows through which blue sky was visible. They were just below ground level, then.

"Why do you linger?" the voice purred smoothly. It sounded like a man, but Eza couldn't tell for sure. "Do not hesitate to embrace death. It is merely the next path that we all must walk."

"You first!" shouted Cammie.

The laugh came again.

Eza stepped back from the brink. "I think I see the focus crystal, but I'm guessing that guy, or thing, isn't just going to let us walk out of here with it. We'll probably have to fight."

"We could just tell him we're here for the crystal and see if he lets us take it," suggested Razan.

"Worth a shot," agreed Eza. He scooted closer to the edge. "We don't want to hurt you!" he called. "We don't want to take your home away from you. We only want the glowing thing that's down there with you. If you let us take it, we'll leave immediately and never come back."

An unholy screeching greeted these words. "Take my magic, the gift which has sustained my life these centuries?" the voice wailed. "Now you *deserve* death! Come and receive the agony that is rightfully yours!"

"Worth a try," Eza sighed. "Same plan as before. Leave your packs and the magical weapons here. Go fast and go hard. The stairs are..." He pointed at Cammie.

"A choke point?" she guessed.

"You got it. But this time we're the attackers. We hit the stairs as soon as I try to blind him. Got it?"

Heads nodded.

"Be safe," he told them all.

It was odd, he thought. He'd expected anxiety to be screaming at him this whole time, but it had vanished. When he was by himself, his mind would spin itself in circles, happily dreaming up horrible things that might happen, but now that he was in an actual life-and-death situation, all those thoughts had gone into hiding. He was nervous, scared halfway to death, but the mind-blinding anxiety wasn't there – which was a huge relief.

Creeping to the edge of the stairs once more, he cast his most intense light spell on the focus crystal and instantly pulled back. The room exploded in white light and a howling came from below. "Go!" Eza shouted, sprinting down the stairs as fast as he could. *Should have used a rainbow door*, he realized halfway down, but it was too late –

He nearly stopped when he saw the person-creature-thing and had to force himself to keep bounding down the stairs. It was ten feet tall, and looked vaguely like a man except that its skin was ashen and cracked all over. Gray-red eyes, like the horrors from the courtyard, glowed on his face, and his mouth was pulled back in a sneer. Eza hit the floor and sprinted away, taking cover behind the focus crystal. The creature wouldn't dare shoot at that.

Razan reached the ground next and blasted off a fireball, which the monster deflected upward with what looked like the same magic energy shield Cammie sometimes used. An even bigger fireball burst from its hands and Razan flung himself to the side, barely escaping the blast. Eza reached out with heat magic, trying to set the thing's skin on fire, but no matter how hard he pushed, it felt like the monster was pushing back and Eza was unable to get through.

There was nowhere to hide, no cover in this room, except being out of sight on the far side of the focus crystal. "Scatter!" Eza shouted. There was no time to say more. He sprinted toward Cammie, to help her run away, just as the monster sent a massive ball of glowing black energy hurtling toward her. Instantly Eza opened a rainbow door in front of her, with the other end on top of the monster's head. *Boom* it thundered as it exploded on the monster's skull, and the thing roared, the sound shaking dust loose from the walls and ceiling.

Razan was behind the monster now, firing lightning bolt after lightning bolt at it, but the monster looked utterly unharmed. Suddenly the whole room shook and Cammie fell on top of Eza as the monster tore part of the stone stairs off the wall and hurled them at Razan. Again Razan narrowly escaped as the stone burst into hundreds of pieces from the impact, splinters and shards of rock hurtling all over the room. Shanna immediately grabbed a big piece of the debris with her magic and flung it at the monster, but it stopped in midair, rotating, before being sent straight back at her.

Cammie had used the distraction to send a fireball at the monster's head, but that magic shield appeared again and the fireball went nowhere. It was like the thing had eyes all over, Eza thought. And then it was shooting back, electricity arcing from its fingers, searching for victims. Cammie dived behind the focus crystal; Shanna and Razan took cover behind the rubble of the stairs – but Denavi was caught in the open with nowhere to go, holding her glowing magical sword up as if it would help –

Five bolts of lightning converged on her and Eza watched in horror. The monster was distracted – maybe he could set it on fire now –

But in the next moment he noticed Denavi was standing her ground. Her sword was shining so brightly it hurt Eza's eyes in this dark underground room, and it seemed to be absorbing the lightning, crackling with blue-white energy. Of course a *magical* sword would absorb *magic*, his mind thought distantly before he yanked himself back into the moment. They could use that – if they hadn't left all the magical weapons up at the top of the stairs...

The monster seemed as shocked as Denavi was by this, taking two giant steps toward her and swinging its arm with a fierceness that didn't seem possible. Denavi sidestepped and thrust her sword into its calf, opening a massive wound that spewed – not blood, but something thick that scorched the ground where it landed and began smoking.

"Target the wound!" Eza shouted, and in the next moment one of Razan's lightning bolts smashed the monster's calf. The thing screamed, its back arching, and it flailed its arms wildly, catching Denavi in the ribs and spinning her across the room. She skidded to a halt and quickly got back to her feet, grimacing in pain but still moving. "I'm going to recharge your sword!" Eza shouted, funneling magical energy toward it the way he did when feeding Aleiza. The sword quickly began to glow again –

But the monster was pounding off toward the rubble of the stairs, forcing Shanna and Razan to scurry away like insects. The thing grabbed a piece of rock and hurled it – but not at Shanna like Eza had thought. At Eza himself.

Panicking, he tried to stop charging Denavi's sword so he could throw up a rainbow door – there was no time – he put his right arm up to protect his face and he *felt* the bones snapping as the rock smashed into him. Pain lanced up his entire body and he tried not scream. Denavi could heal him –

But even as he watched, the monster picked up Shanna with its magic, heaving her toward the opposite wall. Eza caught her with a rainbow door just in time, depositing her neatly on the ground. Cammie – it must have been Cammie but Eza couldn't see her – hit the beast right on its open wound with a beam of fire and it screamed again.

Eza's lower arm was dangling loosely and his breath

was speeding up from the pain that stabbed his mind every time he moved – which was almost nonstop. They just weren't hurting the monster fast enough, he thought. Two of them were injured already and Shanna would have been if he hadn't caught her. They needed a miracle.

The windows...

"Cammie, make a hole in the ceiling!" he shouted.

She didn't ask any questions. A surge of earth magic shot upward, pounding the ceiling and bringing down a huge chunk of it, opening a hole...

Aleiza came screaming down out of the brilliant sky, with Evaza right behind her. The monster seemed so shocked to see dragons that it didn't react in time to keep Aleiza from strafing it, a tight burst of fire from her mouth hitting it square in the eyes as it looked up. Aleiza banked, staying in the room, giving the monster two new targets to worry about.

Denavi saw an opening and jumped forward, jamming her blade into the monster's lower back. The thick acid-blood spewed out again, and the monster shrieked as it turned toward Denavi, who was completely exposed on open floor. There was nowhere for her to go.

Razan leaped out from behind the focus crystal and let out a ferocious scream as lightning poured out from his hands and into the monster's new wound. The monster jerked and spasmed for a full second, then roared in pain. Suddenly a sharp-looking rock was in the air –

And before Eza could even blink it was buried in Razan's chest.

Razan staggered backward, blood pouring out, and collapsed onto the ground.

"RAZAN!" Cammie yelled, and Eza knew what was coming. She shrieked again, wordlessly, so loudly that it echoed off the walls and hurt Eza's ears. The monster turned toward her, but Aleiza chose that moment to blast it in the face with fire again, distracting the monster for just long enough – it turned its back, and its open wound, toward Cammie –

A knife-sharp beam of ice surged out of Cammie's hands, stabbing the monster straight through the heart just like it had done to Razan. In the next instant another beam of ice pierced the back of its head and burst out of its face. Cammie's fury and fear had supercharged her magic!

Acid-blood poured from the monster's chest and head. Cammie leaped forward again, electricity crackling from her hands into the monster's face as she continued shrieking. The monster's head exploded, splashing acid all over the ground.

"Make sure it's dead," Eza shouted, as he and Denavi converged on Razan. Eza's broken arm hurt like it had been submerged in flame, but he couldn't care about that right now.

"His heartbeat is weak," Denavi said, feeling Razan's neck.

"Heal him!"

Denavi's palms lit up and she passed them over Razan's chest. A few moments later, she shook her head. "He's too badly injured. If we take the rock out, he'll die."

"Let me," Eza said. He hadn't used his Artomancy healing power since Aleiza had been wounded at Denneval, hadn't needed to. Now, with panic in his chest and tears coming to his eyes, he tried to concentrate harder than he ever had before. The magic welled up within him and then he could *see* inside Razan, just like he had with Aleiza, and he started to knit the torn muscles together –

But even as he did, he could tell Razan's heart was slowing. The rock had pierced the entire left side and blood was everywhere. "No," Eza insisted. "No, Razan. You can't..."

Razan's heart took one more beat. Then another. Then it stopped.

"RAZAN!" Eza shouted, just like Cammie had, yanking the rock out of Razan's chest and furiously trying to seal the open wounds in his friend's heart. Denavi had said pulling the rock out might kill him, but if he was already dead – maybe it was the only chance –

The muscle just wasn't knitting together fast enough. "Why won't you heal?" Eza asked quietly. "Just – heal!" Denavi joined him, and together they tried to close the holes, but Eza could see how much blood had leaked out, and the holes were so huge...

Eza could sense Cammie and Shanna standing behind him, watching him and Denavi work. Eza didn't want to give up on his friend, couldn't give up. But his magic was starting to falter; it had taken a lot out of him to catch that energy ball and fireball, and his arm was still an ocean of pain, and he just didn't have any energy left. Denavi's breath caught in her chest; Eza had forgotten that she'd been knocked across the floor, too. Between the two of them, they just didn't have anything left to give.

He looked down at his friend's body, feeling too shattered to even cry.

Razan was dead.

TWENTY-TWO

There was no time to grieve, Eza knew. Aleiza had said the road to the fortress was empty as far as she could see, but now that Eza and the others had dispatched the horrors in the courtyard, the wolves in the basement, and this...*thing* guarding the focus crystal, the next people to arrive would just be able to stroll in and lay hands on the thing. Eza looked around the room while Denavi magically pieced his arm back together, flexing it and turning it around when she was finished. There was still pain, but it was much better than it had been. "Thanks," he told her.

She nodded wordlessly.

Suddenly the focus crystal began to rattle, and Eza dropped into a defensive stance.

"Sorry!" Shanna said. "Sorry. That was me. I wanted to see how heavy this thing is so we can figure out how to move it."

"And?"

"I think it's light enough for me to push with my physical magic. It feels like it's about fifty pounds. Must be hollow inside, or made of some kind of honeycomb."

Eza's eyes wandered up to the top of the staircase. A rainbow door opened there, with the other end below the focus crystal's stand. "Give it a good shove," he told Shanna.

The crystal teetered and fell off the stand, into the rainbow door, reappearing at the double doors where they'd entered the room. "We can move it that way," Eza said. "Gonna be a long trip, but we can do it."

It felt *wrong* to eat at a time like this, casually munching on flatbread and dried onala while Razan's body lay on the ground next to them. But the food wasn't for fun; it was to get them all back to Tranquility, with the focus crystal, or else what happened to Razan might happen to all of them. Even if it didn't happen now – even if there wasn't a force like Azanna's coming up behind them right at the moment – it would definitely happen later, if Claira or Esteria got their hands on the focus crystal and trained an army of powerful sorcerers to invade Introvertia.

And if Telravia got their hands on it, Eza didn't even want to *think* about what would happen.

That alone was enough to spur him into action. He led his three friends up the staircase, rainbow dooring past the missing piece the monster had torn away from the wall, and retrieving their packs and magic weapons on the way to the top where the focus crystal was waiting for them. He hadn't noticed during the fight, but here, this close to the crystal, the magical energy was so strong that the hair on the back of his neck was standing up. What was it made of? How –

Questions later. Work now.

The crystal rolled through a rainbow door, emerging at the top of the staircase to the upper level. Up the steps it went next, then through the entry chamber and outside into the courtyard, one set of rainbow doors at a time. Going back the way they came would be *tedious*, Eza thought. A crazy idea occurred to him.

Aleiza had left the monster's chamber almost as soon as the thing had died; she liked wide open spaces and didn't want to be underground. She was circling above the fortress now, and Eza took a peek through her eyes. The monster's chamber had been at the back end of the fortress; Eza could see the scar in the earth where Cammie had torn the roof open to let the dragons in.

And in the distance he could see Tranquility.

How was that even possible? But there was the Rapidly Flowing River, and the Forest Road, maybe two miles away, and another mile down. Tranquility was seven or eight miles past that, clearly visible from this high in the air. But – if he could see the Forest Road from here, shouldn't that mean the fortress was visible from the road, too?

"Eza?" Shanna asked, bringing him back to the present.

"We're not going back the way we came," he told her. "We're going straight down the mountains toward the

Forest Road."

"*What?*"

Eza didn't answer with words; they just kept rolling the crystal around to the back of the plateau the fortress was on. Below them the mountains dropped away in steep cliffs and ravines. On a sheer cliff face a few hundred yards away, some mountain goats sat, side-eyeing them skeptically. Eza and Cammie's last encounter with mountain goats hadn't gone well, and he hoped there wouldn't be a repeat.

However...if the goats could find ledges, surely Eza could, too...

"You're going to take us *down* that way?" Shanna prodded. "Eza, we barely managed to come up the way that Denavi's map led us, and that was man-made on purpose to be safe to travel. This...is suicidal. You can only rainbow door us, what, seventy feet in one shot?"

"It's either that or go back the long way, and I think this is the better choice. Two of us will go first, so they can catch the crystal if it's rolling too fast. Then the crystal, then the third and fourth. I'll go in the first group. That way if the crystal falls, I can catch it."

"I'll have to be third or fourth so I can push it through," Shanna reasoned.

"Cammie, you're with me, then," said Eza. "Denavi, you're with Shanna. Let's go."

Cammie had been quiet for far too long, Eza realized.

She would have a lot of words to say when she got the chance to speak, but for now there was still work to do. She'd probably only seen people die twice before, in the fight where Denavi was captured and again at Denneval. But those were battlefields, and the people were strangers. This was different – Razan was a friend and he'd been injured fifteen feet from her, and she'd been standing over him when he took his last breath...

She and Eza would both cry, when they could, but that time wasn't now.

A promising ledge jutted out from the rock fifty feet below them, and Eza popped himself and Cammie onto it. The crystal rolled slowly through a moment later; Eza stopped it easily. Denavi and Shanna came through at the end. "See?" Eza said. "Simple enough."

"You shouldn't have said anything," joked Denavi.

Over and over and over again, for hours, the four of them and the focus crystal tensely jumped from one narrow ledge to another. Eza's legs were starting to shake from the exertion – he'd never moved *four* people plus another object before, and that was after three intense magical battles and a long walk the day before. He couldn't let his strength fail; his friends needed him –

But he had spotted a landmark far below him, a particular cleft between two mountains that he always noted when he was walking the Forest Road because it meant that he was about two hours from home. More than once he'd stopped at the cleft and gazed up, into those white peaks, and wondered what was up there. Now he knew. Being that close to home gave him new strength, and he forced himself to push on.

Then disaster struck just before they made it down to ground level. Their current ledge was the last one Eza could see. Below them was a drop of about a hundred and fifty feet, about twice as far as Eza could rainbow door. He hunted around above and beside them; maybe they could move sideways to another ledge and then down from there, but it truly seemed as if there was just nothing below them. They'd come so far. This couldn't possibly be the end. His entire body was aching now from all the magical energy he'd used, but he had to keep pressing, couldn't give up just yet. If only there was a way...

"Rope," he murmured. They had plenty in their packs, but nothing nearby to anchor it to. Aleiza and Evaza were still soaring overhead, though there was nothing they could do, either; they were too light to support the weight of someone hanging off them.

"Earth magic," Cammie said. "Watch." She looked over the side of the ledge, to a spot just about at the absolute limit of Eza's rainbow door range, and her hands began to glow. A new outcropping began to appear, sticking to the rock of the mountain. It looked solid enough to Eza...

"Are you sure that thing will hold?" Shanna asked doubtfully.

"I'll go first," Eza said. "Good job, Cammie. You helped a lot."

Cammie smiled nervously. She was definitely going to break down the *moment* she could, Eza knew. He opened a rainbow door on the edge of their current platform, then stepped through as slowly as he could.

The earth ledge seemed solidly attached to the mountainside, at least. Cammie had done a good job building it. Eza hoped it would support the weight of four people plus a globe of crystal, but it was a little too late for second thoughts. The focus crystal came through, just as slowly, and Eza stopped it with one hand. Cammie, Shanna, and Denavi followed through, moving slowly and keeping their weight above their feet. No sudden movements and they'd all be fine.

But Eza had misjudged the distance, by about ten feet. His furthest rainbow door would only get them about that far above the ground. He and the others could survive a fall from that height, but would the focus crystal? Eza had no idea what it was made of or how resilient it was – they might have already broken it from rolling it around like a giant ringball –

Cammie could make a new ledge like the one they were on, but the rock sloped differently down there; it was almost vertical, in a way that made Eza unsure whether the earth magic would stick to it as well. Maybe – but maybe not –

He lay on the edge of the platform for so long that Denavi finally broke the silence. "Do we know how long this ledge is going to hold us?"

"We can't make it to the ground from here," he announced, then explained to them what he'd just been thinking.

"Okay," Denavi said. "You go through first. Shanna second so she can catch the crystal when it comes through."

"But she has to stay behind to send it through with her physical magic," Eza reminded her.

"I've felt the ball, Eza. It weighs about fifty pounds. I can roll it with my hands, if I push hard enough."

"We're on a ledge made of *dirt*," he protested. "You could slide off and fall."

"Then you'll catch me with a rainbow door."

"Then the crystal will be up on that earth ledge by itself!"

"Sorry, up on what?" Denavi had a smile on her face that Eza didn't understand.

"The earth ledge..."

"And earth does what when you hit it with Cammie's water magic?"

"It turns into mud." Eza finally saw where she was going. "So even if the crystal does end up stranded on the ledge, we can just melt the ledge and I can bring it to the ground with a rainbow door!"

Denavi winked at him. "You did good, brother."

"Brother?" asked Shanna, who hadn't been present for that conversation.

"Long story. I'll tell you when we get back."

Shanna smiled. "Maybe not right away. I might need to sleep for a few days."

With that plan in place, Eza opened a rainbow door, pushing it as far as he could. He managed a few extra feet, but still fell out of the exit seven feet above the ground. He absorbed the impact with his knees and rolled to the ground, his joints jarring from the blow, his arms holding the magical weapons flat against his legs so they didn't slice him open. The landing *hurt*. Cammie wasn't going to enjoy that.

Shanna came second, drop-rolling just like Eza had done. They'd practiced the skill together in the Harmony barracks after learning it in their first year, leaping off beds and rolling as they landed, making an almighty racket and laughing so hard they thought they'd get in trouble. Cammie came third, crashing to the ground in a heap of knees and elbows since she'd never learned how to fall properly. Eza could tell she'd be sore the next day. "I'm definitely giving you a magical massage back at the house," he promised.

That got a genuine smile out of her.

Eza was on the ragged edge of exhaustion at this point; he'd pushed a lot of things through rainbow doors today, not to mention three all-out battles against horrors and wolves and that guardian. Now that they were on flatter ground, with a downhill walk and maybe one or two more rainbow doors until they reached the Forest Road, he was already looking forward to his bed at home. But that was later. At the moment all that existed was the focus crystal, and Denavi gently pushing it through the rainbow door.

Shanna caught it with her magic as soon as it fell out the other end, guiding it smoothly to the ground. Denavi came behind, landing even more smoothly than Eza and Shanna had.

The end was in sight, the Forest Road barely a mile in front of them, with only one or two steep rises in the way, and then it was seven miles of easy walking to Tranquility.

That walk took Eza two hours when he was by himself, but it ended up being three when moving slowly, nursing injuries, and pushing a giant crystal sphere. The city guards saw them coming a mile away, as the Forest Road rounded the last spur of the mountains, and came sprinting to help.

"Send for the king and queen," Eza said, abruptly realizing he could have sent Aleiza to relay the message several hours before. "We have something they'll be...very interested in."

Within twenty minutes a wagon had shown up to take the focus crystal off to wherever the king and queen wanted it to be, with a second wagon behind it that Eza and the others could climb into.

Eza had never been more glad to see his house – not after arriving back from Exclaimovia, not after the Battle of Denneval Plain. He leaped off the wagon almost before it had stopped moving, helping Cammie to the ground as Denavi hopped down next to her. Shanna stayed on; Eza had thought she might come into his house, but she probably wanted her own bed, and Eza couldn't blame her. They dropped their packs and magic weapons just inside the front door; Eza had completely forgotten to mention those swords to the guards, so that would be a separate conversation later. Cammie collapsed onto one couch and Eza onto the floor next to her, and Denavi's boots and socks were flying through the air a moment later as she plopped onto the other couch.

Cammie was lying on her stomach, her head turned toward Eza so that he could see the tears welling in her eyes. "It's okay to cry," he told her, with a lump in his throat. "I'll start that massage –"

"No," Cammie said immediately. "No. I don't want to feel good right now."

Then she was crying, and Eza was crying too. A

burning ache, acidic like that monster's blood, churned inside Eza's heart. His friend Razan...gone forever...

They'd done the impossible, honestly. They'd found their way to a fortress that had been abandoned for centuries, killed dozens of magical horrors and spellcasting wolves and then that guardian thing, whatever it was – and returned with a focus crystal that could turn Carnazon Fortress back into a nexus node, maybe changing the course of Introvertian history forever. If Introvertia won the war – *when* Introvertia won the war – their names would be in the history books.

But Razan wouldn't be there to see it. Eza thought of happier times, of celebration after winning ringball at the Company Games, of the two of them and Shanna hiking in the mountains as wide-eyed twelve-year-olds in their first year at the Academy, and the tears kept coming.

TWENTY-THREE

Cammie sat, in her full Academy dress uniform, next to Eza and Denavi and Shanna on a podium in Carnazon's courtyard, in almost the exact location where General Leazan had stood all those weeks ago and announced that magic was coming back to Introvertia. An empty casket in front of them represented Razan; a squad of soldiers was being dispatched to retrieve his body, but they wouldn't be back for a week or more, and King Jazan and Queen Annaya had wanted a hero's funeral for Razan the next day, as well as decorations for the four who had returned. King Jazan had made some suitable remarks about Razan's faithful service to the crown and his noble sacrifice; Cammie had only half-listened, gripping Eza's hand the whole time. Insomnia had wrecked her the night before, and she'd jolted awake half a dozen times. Each time it happened, Eza's eyes had come open at the sudden movement, and he'd gently held her hand and whispered to her until she fell back asleep.

But what if it had been *him*? Suddenly she saw where all his anxiety thoughts had been coming from, his crippling fear of somehow losing her. She kept seeing in her mind those final seconds of the fight, except it was

Eza taking the rock to the chest, Eza lying on the ground as the life drained out of him, Eza forcing a smile while his eyes faded...

A lump climbed into her throat just thinking about it. Then she had to let go because it was Eza's turn to speak. He took no notes with him to the podium. "Razan Enara," he began, "wasn't perfect, but then, none of us are. That should comfort us, because it tells us that even imperfect people can be great heroes if they act with bravery and do what they know is right."

He gripped the edge of the podium, looking out at the nearly two thousand assembled students, professors, and military staff. "One thing I know about Razan is that he believed in Introvertia. He believed in who we are and what we stand for, as much as any person standing here. His love for this kingdom was unsurpassed. And I believe..." Eza looked down and swallowed hard; Cammie could tell he was fighting not to burst into tears in front of everyone. "And I believe that if Razan had been told before we left that he would give up his life so that Introvertia could be safe from harm, that by his death he would guarantee that others would live...he would have gone willingly. Not just willingly – joyfully." Eza took a deep breath. "And if Razan could put others before himself even to the point of death, I hope beyond hope that we can find it in our hearts to put others before ourselves in life as well. Go out of your way to say kind

305

words. Find those who are hurting and be their healing. Comfort the lonely and bring joy to people who are discouraged. You do not have to fight and die in order to make Introvertia a better place. You can do that right now, today, everywhere you happen to be. Honor Razan's legacy by going and doing it."

Thunderous applause followed Eza as he sat back down next to Cammie, his legs shaking from adrenaline, and she took his hand. "Perfectly said, my love," she told him.

King Jazan and Queen Annaya were retaking the stage, holding boxes. "And now," the king said, "we bestow upon these four, these heroes of Introvertia, the Order of Valor."

Queen Annaya continued. "Two Introvertians, an Exclaimovian, and a Clairan. Their success on this journey proves that our people can overcome our differences to live together in peace. On the day when all kings and queens everywhere truly believe that, the world will be a brighter place."

Eza stepped forward and King Jazan pinned a large silver-and-blue medal to his chest. Eza bowed and moved away. Shanna stepped forward next to receive a medal from Queen Annaya, then Denavi. At last Cammie stepped up, bowing in thanks as the queen pinned her medal and then sitting back down.

This was supposed to feel a lot more like a

celebration, wasn't it?

"We have one final surprise in store for you all," said the king. "Many of you may not be aware that, many centuries ago, this fortress was itself a nexus node. The focus crystal brought back by our four heroes will permit it to become one again. For a very long time, the official maps of Carnazon have included a reference to a basement hall called the Focus Room. We never understood the name or its purpose. Now that we have a focus crystal, however...all has become clear."

The king gave a signal, and someone standing on the far end of the courtyard disappeared through a door. There was just enough time for the people in the courtyard to start murmuring among themselves and suddenly an incredible buzzing teased Cammie's ears.

She clearly wasn't the only one. All over the courtyard people looked at each other in shock. The murmurs got louder before Queen Annaya motioned for silence. Cammie knew what that sensation meant. It was –

"For those who have never felt it, which is most of you, you are experiencing the effects of a magical nexus node," she announced. "I'm told you'll acclimate to the buzzing quickly and not notice it afterward. While you're in proximity to the node, you'll find that your magical powers are heightened, and your acquisition of magical skill will be much easier. In short, the students who train here will become the most powerful spellcasters in the kingdom, and quickly. This is Carnazon Fortress as it was meant to be!"

A cheer exploded from everyone, especially the students. Eza rushed to say something to the king, who leaned down to listen to him and then nodded before motioning for silence.

"At the request of Cadet Skywing, we have bestowed a name on this nexus node. Carnazon Fortress is now the home of the Enara Node."

That brought even more celebration, and Cammie put her mouth close to Eza's ear. "That was thoughtful."

"The crystal's here because of him. He deserves it."

A few people came up to shake hands with Cammie and the others, but most of the students seemed to be trying out their magical powers, delighted at how much stronger everything was while on the node. "I wonder how far I can rainbow door us," Eza mused.

"Out of the courtyard in one shot?" Cammie asked.

"Bet on it."

Fwoosh went the rainbow door, and Cammie, Denavi, and Eza were stepping out onto the street outside the fortress a moment later.

Eza clearly didn't feel like walking home, because he rainbow-jumped them the whole way back, stepping in the house's front door and crashing headlong into Gar the Artomancer, who was standing in the living room.

"For the love of beets, you're a hard man to track down," Gar greeted him.

Cammie grunted her disgust and moved around Gar, sitting on the couch and staring at the opposite wall as if she wasn't curious what he had to say. Denavi slipped past and disappeared up the stairs.

"I've been away," Eza said vaguely.

"I got that much. Your dad said the same thing when I came by two days ago asking for you: *he's away*. Your people aren't normally evasive, so that smelled like excitement to me. I was around yesterday when you kids came back, and I heard everyone going nuts about a focus crystal. Could hardly believe my ears. I didn't think any still existed." Gar strolled to the window in Cammie's line of sight, checking out the garden. "I was there in the courtyard a minute ago, too. Good speech."

"Did Gar the Artomancer just say a kind word?" Cammie needled him.

Gar turned to her, a sad smile on his face. "I'm not here to puff myself up," he told her. "This time, anyway. I'm here because I need your help."

Cammie silently mouthed the words "need your help," sure that she'd heard the Artomancer wrong.

"I can't tell you exactly what just yet," Gar continued. "I'm sorry, Ezalen. But I don't think I've given you any reason to distrust me. Dislike me, maybe." He cracked a smile. "Don't want too many people liking me, after all.

Then you start to get folks asking for favors and you can't get anything accomplished cause of all the people wanting you to do stuff for them. It's miserable. But I trained you in Artomancy, and I helped you in Exclaimovia after telling you I wouldn't. I think I've proven myself to you. And now I may need you to return the favor."

Cammie didn't like the sound of this *at all*. It sounded like more danger and she'd had her fill of danger.

"I need you to keep training," Gar said. "Use that node you just opened. Become the strongest Artomancer west of the mountains. I'm the strongest on the east side, obviously..."

"Aaaaaand there it is," Cammie declared.

"But things are happening. I'll – I promise I'll tell you more when I can, okay? Just trust me."

Cammie didn't want to admit it, but Gar actually did look...maybe *scared* wasn't the right word, but definitely uneasy or tense. He might not have been the *best* Artomancer east of the mountains, but Cammie had no reason to doubt that he was in the top two or three. Anything that got him upset was probably a big deal.

"I'll memorize that textbook you gave me, Gar," Eza promised. "The next time you show up, I'll be ready."

"It might not be me who shows up looking for you," Gar said. "Lots of powerful people are about to be *very* upset that the Carnazon node is reactivated. A fight may be coming to you sooner rather than later."

"I'll tell the king, then. We'll make sure people are training at Carnazon every hour of the day and night."

"I have some strings to pull on my end, too. We'll be ready for this when it happens, okay?"

"You bet we will."

Gar turned to Cammie. "You ever wonder how your people managed to straight-up steal seven hundred Introvertian dragons?"

"Uh, yeah," she admitted. "It should have been impossible."

"I'm pretty sure I know. It's related to all the stuff I was just talking about. Once I'm certain, I'll tell you, too. Take care of yourselves, okay? I try not to get fond of people. Feelings are messy and I don't like them. But I'm fond of you two." He looked over at Denavi, who'd been silently lurking in the corner this whole time. "Probably you, too. If these two put up with you then you must be decent. Till next time." *Fwoosh* went a rainbow door and he was gone.

Eza sighed. "I think we should tell the king and queen about all this as soon as possible."

"No," Cammie said immediately, tugging on his arm. "Stay with me. Just...be with me."

Eza slipped out of his black formal jacket, revealing a green undershirt beneath; Cammie did the same, except her undershirt was sleeveless. He sat down on the couch next to her and she slid up to him, putting both arms around his stomach and resting her cheek on his shoulder. His arm strayed to her back and began gently scratching.

Her eyes closed; she was still exhausted from waking up so many times during the night, and from not sleeping well on the hard ground for days before that. But she didn't fall asleep. She wanted to enjoy every moment of Eza's presence.

Just like the night she'd gotten the magical massage, she wasn't even aware of falling asleep, only of awakening. Eza had somehow gone to sleep sitting up, his head cocked down and to the side, and Cammie was lying on her side on top of his thighs. They must have been absolutely drained to sleep so long in such a crazy position.

Now that she was awake, her body was screaming at her to move, to stretch, but she knew Eza was a light sleeper and his eyes would snap open the second she did. Maybe if she just straightened her leg a little...

Nope. Eza was already alert, looking down at her with a giant smile. "That was a nice nap."

"It was," Cammie said, stretching out but not moving off his lap. "I think we both needed it."

Eza began to run his fingers through her hair, massaging her scalp as he went. "This is why we go to battle, by the way."

Cammie blinked up at him. "So we can sit on a couch while you play with my hair?"

"Not just us. People. All over Introvertia right now there are fathers kissing their wives, sisters playing with their brothers. People are making dinner, and reading, and staring at the sunset. All of that beauty, all of that love...that's why we fight, even when it hurts to lose people like Razan. His death is going to hurt for a long time. Maybe for the rest of our lives. But every time you walk down the road and you see a couple with their arms around each other, or you see a boy playing with a toy in front of his house, or you see people enjoying their favorite food at a restaurant, you can stand up a little straighter, because you helped that to happen. You helped keep them safe."

"That was good," Cammie said admiringly, holding up her arm so Eza could see the goosebumps. "You should make speeches more often."

"That was a quote from a book, actually. The bit about Razan I added, but the rest is from *Heroes of Introvertia*."

Cammie laughed, feeling fatigue and grief drain out of her body and relaxation flow in. "You're the most incredible person I've ever met."

"You should look in a mirror, then."

Denavi reappeared at the bottom of the stairs, three books in her hands, wearing one of Eza's Ranger cloaks.

313

"Can I borrow this?" she asked, pointing at the cloak.

"Go ahead, sis."

Denavi tried to keep from smiling at the word *sis*, but failed. "That feels good."

"Are you on your way to the children's hospital?"

"Yeah. Mr. Cappel told me I was good at telling stories, so I'm going to read to the kids if I can't heal them. Wish me luck!"

"You won't need it. You're going to do great."

She smiled again and whooshed her way out of the house, the cloak trailing behind her.

"That's what we should all be," Eza told Cammie. "All Introvertians, but not only us. All people everywhere. Denavi's been through some horrible things in her life, things nobody should ever have to experience, but there she goes, with a smile on her face, to make someone else's life better. That's what all of this is about. You and I...we're doing the same thing."

"You're sentimental today," Cammie teased.

"I'm sentimental all the time. You know that. But I finally figured out the cure."

"Oh?" asked Cammie, suddenly interested.

"Yeah. It's one of these." Eza bent down and kissed her on the lips.

"Mmmmm," Cammie said as he straightened back up. "Cadet Skywing, I'm afraid your case of the Sentimentals is much worse than we originally thought.

It will take a great deal more *cure* to bring you back to full health."

A huge grin lit up Eza's face and he immediately played along. "Well, doctor, if that's what I have to do to be healthy…"

Cammie pulled him down toward her as the sky grew darker outside.

TWENTY-FOUR

It was about half an hour before dawn when Eza stepped out into the garden, taking a seat on the bench and gazing up at the stars that twinkled overhead. He didn't know how he'd managed to sleep even that long, to be honest, given the nap he'd taken with Cammie earlier in the day. Tranquility itself was more tranquil than usual. The pine trees were completely still, with no breeze rustling their branches. The silence was like its own noise, Eza thought, one that was comforting to his ears. In the total calmness, he felt himself relax, closing his eyes and taking a deep breath.

Solitude and silence. This was nice. As long as his mind didn't go crazy and start imagining the worst things that could happen to all the people he loved, this was nice.

After long minutes, a warm glow began to light the eastern horizon, over the jagged peaks of the Impassable Mountains. Eza watched the colors as they changed, nature's very own sky art on display for everyone to see. Sunlight began to catch the underside of the scattered clouds, turning them a fiery orange against the deep purple of the final moments of night, and on a whim Eza turned his shirt into those same colors, trying to replicate the sunrise on cloth. It looked pretty good, he thought. Maybe he'd give the shirt to Cammie, or maybe he'd keep it, or maybe he'd turn it back to its normal colors...

Eza didn't *jump*, exactly, but he jolted a little bit when the house's back door opened again, not expecting to have company. Denavi came outside, wearing boots, which immediately got Eza's attention. "Cammie's not going to be awake for a couple of hours," she said by way of greeting. "What do you say you and I take a walk?"

A few minutes later, with Eza in a new shirt and a note left by Cammie's bed in case she woke up early, he and Denavi were strolling down toward the Music Square, which was quiet this early. A few people played gentle, hopeful melodies that seemed appropriate for welcoming the dawn to a new day. Denavi slowed, smiling her appreciation for the music. "I've always wanted to learn how to play an instrument," she mused.

"I can play the ballaina. A little bit, anyway. I'll show you if you want."

Denavi turned her smile on Eza. "I'd love that, brother. Speaking of which...I realized something a few days ago."

"What's that, sis?"

"If I'm really your sister...then that makes me your older sister."

Eza thought about that, and then exploded into

laughter. "You're right," he agreed. "I look forward to you blessing me with your older-sister wisdom."

Denavi's face turned serious. "I was hoping you'd say that."

"What do you mean?" Eza asked as they left the Music Square, heading toward the palace.

"I want you to know I'm proud of you."

The compliment sank deep into Eza's heart and he found himself smiling so hard he thought he might burst. Compliments always made him happy – this one more than most, although he couldn't exactly say why.

"I'm proud of you for facing your anxiety head-on instead of 'putting boots on your feelings,' as Cammie likes to say, and trying to run away."

Eza cocked his head. "Boots-on-feelings is an odd thing for Cammie to have told you about me. I didn't know the two of you were close enough to talk about things like that."

"I don't know if we're *close*, exactly, but she sure does love to talk, and sometimes interesting things come out if you just let her go for a while."

That drew a laugh from Eza. "Don't I know it."

"Anyway, I'm really proud of you for that. I know you felt the pressure of being in charge, and I know it tore you up to see Razan die, especially after you were the one who asked him to come on the mission. But I think you also know we had to be the ones to go. You and Cammie are two of the strongest spellcasters in all of Introvertia. I am, as far as I know, the only healer. Shanna and Razan were the right choices, too. I could tell, especially in that last fight, the way you could almost read each other's minds. Yeah, the king and queen could have sent a different group of people. But if it hadn't been you, if it hadn't been Cammie and me and Shanna and Razan, a lot more people would have died. How do you think they would have killed that guardian thing without Cammie's magic? How do you think they would have gotten past those horrors on the surface without Cammie and Aleiza? How do you think they would have gotten the crystal back without your Artomancy?"

Eza found himself nodding along. Denavi's words *felt* true in a way that left Eza no doubt.

"Anyway," she finished, "I'm proud of you for all that. I've fought with a lot of brave men and women, and you and Cammie are two of the bravest. And I hope I never have to fight again, but if I do in order to protect my new home, and I get to be beside the two of you, that's an honor I'm happy to have."

"It's a good thing the sun isn't all the way up or everyone could see me blushing," Eza joked, feeling heat rise into his cheeks. "Thanks, Denavi. You're a good older sister."

The two of them hugged in the middle of Broad Avenue, with the rushing burble of the Rapidly Flowing

River as background music. The sky was getting lighter now, though there were more clouds down toward the horizon than Eza had realized. The spring equinox was two months in the past now; summer was going to arrive soon, and the rainy season with it. There might not be rain today, but before long it would be coming.

"Can I ask you a question?" Eza asked.

"Anything. I don't like keeping secrets."

"I know what I want in the future, which is to be happy with Cammie. I know what Cammie wants, which is to spend her life doing theater. I don't really know what you want. Right now it seems like all you want is...I dunno, to be a Skywing, I guess. To hang out with my dad and me and Cammie and enjoy life."

"That's it," Denavi agreed, brushing black hair out of her face. "I just want to be a kid. I know seventeen makes me an adult in Introvertia, but I feel like I never got to be a child. Kids are supposed to be carefree and innocent, you know? And that was stolen from me when my dad died. I grew up sooner than I wanted to, sooner than any child should have to. Now that I have daddy, and you, and a place to belong and a family who loves me...all I want is to enjoy that for a while. I want to do other things too, like help kids the way I wish someone could have helped me, but I don't know what I want to do with the rest of my life yet. I don't think I need to know right now. I just want to be loved."

"You're in the right place for that," Eza told her. The two of them sat down at the edge of Broad Avenue, the river babbling ten feet away. A breeze finally came out of the mountains, bringing the scent of pine needles and dogwood blossoms along with it. "I love Cammie a lot," Eza said. "But it's also nice to be here with someone who can just appreciate silence." Denavi responded to that comment with a lopsided smile, and more silence.

They'd been there for about half an hour, the sun steadily growing warmer on their faces, before Eza stretched. "I have one place I want to go before we head home. If we hurry, we might be back in time to make dad some breakfast."

Delight leaped onto Denavi's face. "Let's go!"

Eza and Denavi finished breakfast about half an hour before Ezarra finally made his way down the stairs, still stretching. Denavi shot Eza a mischievous glance, and instantly he knew what she was planning. "Hey, kiddos," Ezarra started to say, but Eza and Denavi crashed into him halfway through, wrapping him up in a hug so hard it knocked him backward. His foot hit the bottom step and he took a hard seat on the staircase, with four arms still around him. "That's a really nice way to wake up," he said, smiling up at his son and his adopted daughter.

"I read an Introvertian proverb that says it's good to wake up with a smile on your face," Denavi teased him. "So you're welcome!"

"That's one of the many things that makes you the best daughter I could ever ask for."

Denavi grinned and her face turned bright red, but she made no attempt to hide the blushing. "Thanks, daddy," she said, helping him to his feet.

Cammie was apparently roused from the depths of slumber by all the noise, staggering down to the bottom of the stairs a few moments later with one eye still half shut. "Where's the stampede?" she joked.

"If you tasted this fried onala hash, you'd be stampeding too," Eza told her. "We saved you a plate."

"Thanks!"

Cammie joined them, and instantly the table got louder with the sounds of laughter and stories. This had to be the strangest family anywhere in the five kingdoms, Eza thought happily. He loved every minute of it.

It took Cammie quite a while to finish her breakfast because she kept telling tale after tale, slapping Eza's hand away the first three times he tried to sneak some of the hash off her plate, and finally just holding his hand so he couldn't try anything again. At last her food was gone, though, and as Ezarra cleared the dishes off the table, Eza steered Cammie to the couch. "I want to ask you on a date," he told her.

"A date," she repeated, perking up. "And what is this date?"

"Queen Annaya's old theater company is located here in Tranquility, and they're performing a play called *Hope in the Wilderness* for the next few weeks. I want to take you tonight."

"Have you ever been to a play before?" Cammie asked.

"Oh, wagonloads. Seven at least. I was acting in all of them, but..."

Cammie giggled. "So you've never seen one as a spectator?"

"Nope. Tonight's the night."

"You'll have to dress up, you know."

Eza blinked a few times. "I –"

"Let me guess, you don't own formal clothes."

"You've seen my closet."

"Wait, the Academy has a formal dance every year, right?"

"That's right. It's coming up next month, actually."

One of Cammie's eyebrows drifted upward. "So what did you wear last year and the year before?"

"I've never been," confessed Eza. "Shanna and Razan and I always went camping that weekend instead."

"But you're going this year...right?"

Eza grinned and held out his hand. "Cammie

Ravenwood, will you be my date to the Dragon Academy formal dance?"

"Well...I have to think about it..."

Eza pounced on Cammie and slipped his fingers into his armpits before she could react. "Think quickly," he teased her as he tickled.

Cammie tried to say something but all that came out was a squeak. Eza couldn't even pull his hands out if he'd wanted to because Cammie's arms were clenched so tightly at her sides. "Sorry, what was that?" he asked innocently. "I couldn't hear you."

"YES!" Cammie shouted through her laughter, so loudly that Eza's ears rang.

"Yes you want me to keep tickling?"

"EZA!" she squealed.

Chuckling to himself, Eza relented, and Cammie caught her breath. "I will get you back," she swore. "Somehow."

"Oh, probably. For now, though, we have a play to prepare for. Do you want me to do anything with your hair before we go?"

Cammie thought about that. "I...need a few minutes with the scissors. Do you have any pine sap around?"

"What, I'm not sappy enough for you?" Eza teased. "You need extra sap now?"

A mischievous grin came to her face. "You'll see."

Cammie went upstairs, scissors in one hand and glass

jar of pine sap in the other, while Eza sat on the couch for ten minutes, impatiently bouncing his leg, curious what Cammie was doing.

The breath left his lungs when she hit the bottom of the stairs. Her hair had been cut short, up to her ears, and she'd used the tree sap to make the top stick up like short porcupine quills. "You look stunning," he managed at last.

"You look stunned," Cammie agreed. "Can you make it silver?"

"Sparkly silver?"

"Sparkly silver," Cammie nodded, delight all over her face. She ran to the kitchen as soon as he was done, checking her reflection in a metal frying pan. "This is perfect."

"The people at the theater will be floored."

Cammie winked at him, the brightness of her hair making her split-colored eyes stand out even more. "I'm counting on it."

It had been a long time since any day had passed as slowly for Eza as that day did. He and Cammie went for a long walk around Tranquility, had lunch at the Cherry Blossom Restaurant, and spent some time in a dress shop that they happened to pass. Cammie was in her element, showing Eza all the delicate stitching, the accent colors, the different types of cuts. "Your people really know their way around a needle," she said admiringly.

"Ooooooh...I want this one."

She pointed to a sky blue dress with silver accents that nearly matched the color of her hair. "I'll buy it for you," Eza offered.

"Well...if you really want to, then I suppose I'll let you," Cammie joked. "I'll need new shoes to go with it, though."

"What, you can't wear scuffed-up boots with a new dress?"

Cammie pretended to gag. "I know you weren't serious, Eza, but wow. All of fashion just screamed in agony at that thought."

"But the boots are brown and brown matches light blue..."

That made Cammie howl with laughter inside the store. "STOP. PLEASE."

Eza smiled to himself. "My job is done."

They visited three different shoe stores before they found a pair that Cammie reluctantly accepted. It seemed that in Exclaimovia, women normally wore shoes that doubled as torture devices, and that's what Cammie was looking for. "Why would anyone wear shoes that are so uncomfortable?" Eza marveled.

"Because they *look good*," Cammie explained as if it were the most obvious thing in the world.

"But...they hurt..."

Introvertians obviously had no patience for

something so impractical, so in the absence of any proper torture-shoes, Cammie had to settle for a simple pair of black flats. "You can make them match the dress, right?" she asked as they walked out of the store.

Eza drew in the air, and the flats rippled into the same sky blue as the dress. "Perfect," Cammie said admiringly. "Now the only question is what you're going to wear."

"Just my Academy dress uniform, I think." He could see Cammie's eyebrow raise again, and he added quickly, "You can get me something fancier for the formal dance, though."

"Mmmmm. I promise I will."

At last evening finally came. Eza had gotten into his Academy formalwear, and he'd even let Cammie use a little of the pine sap to style his hair. The play was due to start in an hour, so Eza escorted Cammie out of his house and onto the street. Their timing could not have been more perfect; the golden hour was just ending.

Brilliant sunlight caught Cammie's silver hair and blue dress, making her shine like a sapphire ring. Eza slowed without meaning to; the sight totally captivated him. Cammie turned to face him, her brown and blue eyes brighter than usual. "You're the most beautiful woman in the whole world," he told her breathlessly.

Cammie's eyes wrinkled at the corners as she smiled. "Thank you," she whispered, taking the back of his neck and pulling him toward her. They kissed in the sun's warm glow, and in the time it took them to finish, the light began to fade. The golden hour was over.

Eza held out his elbow to Cammie, and she slipped her hand inside it as they strolled through the streets. It was hard to tell whether people were staring in admiration of Eza's Dragon Academy uniform (he'd taken the hero medal off it just because he didn't want the extra attention) or in admiration of Cammie's dress and hair. Personally, he thought it was Cammie.

The third-row tickets cost nearly everything he had left over from the theater tour, but it was worth it to him to watch Cammie's eyes get wide as they entered the theater. It was tall like a cylinder, with four levels of box seats on top of each other, looking down on the main stage. "Look," Cammie told Eza. "The room is perfectly shaped so the sound carries. If I got on stage and spoke just like I'm talking now, it would spread out to every single seat."

"That's really incredible," Eza said, looking around. Polished stone gleamed on the sides of the theater, and the seats were covered with rich gray fabric. He led Cammie to their seats, where she immediately kicked off her flats and folded her bare feet underneath her. "What was the point of getting shoes if you're not going to wear them?" he prodded her.

"I *told* you. Shoes are for *looks*. They're not to *wear*."

"They're – that's –"

"Sit down and hug me."

Eza wrapped his arm around her, and she leaned her head on his shoulder. This was perfect. The curtain went up, the play began, and there was nowhere else Eza wanted to be. Even if a war was looming outside, Cammie's presence next to him made everything okay for a little while.

TWENTY-FIVE

Around nine the next morning, as tended to happen, a thumping sounded on Eza's front door. Eza was already awake, of course, and was fully immersed in rereading *Heroes of Introvertia*, which he reluctantly set down in order to answer the knock. "The king and queen need you immediately," said a breathless messenger. "*Immediately.*"

Whoosh came Eza's anxiety, wondering what he'd done wrong and whether they were about to kick him out of the kingdom. Maybe Razan's parents were mad at him and wanted him expelled from the Academy. Maybe...

Those aren't reasonable thoughts, he gently told himself. That was one of the techniques Dr. Deraza had taught him. *The king and queen have never said they're displeased with you and aren't suddenly going to change their minds, and they would defend you if Razan's parents were upset with you. After all, they said you're a hero. Cling to that. Don't create your own doubts. Trust them to tell you if something is wrong.*

That helped a little, but Eza still felt shaky as he leaped up the stairs three at a time to wake Cammie. "What?" she asked blearily as he shook her shoulder.

"The king and queen want to see us right now."

"Define right now."

Eza pulled the covers off Cammie, who whined in protest. "Right now."

Cammie must have heard the urgency in his voice, because she sat up. "Give me the pine sap."

Eza handed her the jar, which was on the table next to her bed. Cammie got some on her fingers, ran them through her hair so it porcupined, and smiled at Eza. "That's the great thing about having my hair like this."

"That and it looks incredible," Eza told her.

"Now get out so I can change my clothes."

But Eza had hardly finished closing the door before Cammie opened it again, wearing a different shirt and pair of pants. "What –" Eza began.

"Theater. Sometimes you only have fifteen seconds to change clothes between scenes."

"It came in handy. Let's go!"

They hustled through the streets, arriving at the palace less than fifteen minutes after they'd been summoned and immediately being ushered into the throne room. Eza stopped in his tracks as soon as he entered, recognizing a face he didn't expect to see. Why was –

"Colonel Ennazar," Cammie blurted, saying what Eza was thinking. "Or – Councilman Ennazar, now."

"Aric will do just fine," Ennazar said with a smile. "Hello, Cammaina. How are your studies coming along?"

"Very well, thank you. Why are you here?"

Eza stifled a laugh. Cammie was extra blurty this morning, it seemed.

Ennazar smiled as well. "Straight to business, I see. Very well. I wanted the two of you in the room because you meant a lot to me as students, but also because this proposition directly affects you. Suffice to say that the two of you made quite an impression on the Council, Cammaina with her barbecueing of that skeletal dragon and Ezalen with the way he used his Artomancy to avoid the effects of Arianna's death mist."

That made Eza even more uneasy than he already was. He didn't want to be the kind of person who impressed Telravia.

"So," Ennazar continued, "I've been sent here by Telravia in order to make a military proposition. We want to use your new nexus node to train some of our soldiers, perhaps a few thousand at a time. The Council feels this is a reasonable request to make of our ally, and that the only correct response would be for you to agree."

But there was something strange on his face, Eza thought, as if he was trying to hide his disgust at the words. Had he been sent to carry a message he didn't want to be sending?

"In exchange," finished Ennazar, "we will give our

finest magical training to Cammaina and Ezalen. We're aware of how valuable they have been to your kingdom, and we know that you would like nothing more than to see them at the peak of their abilities."

"The Council is requesting to station Telravian troops on our soil in order to train at Carnazon?"

"That is, in essence, the request, yes."

"Then I'm afraid it's out of the question," King Jazan said, in a tone that said he thought Ennazar must be crazy to even ask. "Our kingdom is closed to outsiders. We have a military alliance with Telravia, nothing more. I'm not even sure why you want access to our node in the first place, since Telravia already has at least one four-line nexus node that I'm aware of, which is at Desolation Peak. Your troops would have to pass directly through there in order to travel several more days to Carnazon."

That was something Eza hadn't even considered. Why *did* Telravia care about coming to Carnazon? Eza could only think of one reason they might want to be close to that focus crystal...which was to steal it.

Ennazar looked as if he'd just swallowed salt. "The Council has instructed me to inform you that, in the event of our request being refused, our military alliance with Introvertia is to be terminated, with immediate effect."

Eza and Cammie looked at each other in horror. No more alliance? Claira and Esteria and Exclaimovia versus

Introvertia and Telravia would be one thing - but now Claira and Esteria and Exclaimovia against Introvertia alone? And what if Telravia decided to switch sides entirely, and the fight became four against one...?

"Does that change your answer to our request?" Ennazar asked weakly.

King Jazan looked to Queen Annaya for confirmation, and she nodded. "It does not, and it cannot," the king said with determination in his voice. "We will not accept foreign troops on our soil, not even for training purposes."

Ennazar looked at the ground, then at Cammie. When he finally spoke, his voice was very quiet. "I want you to know I opposed this, but I'm only one vote. The other six were unanimous. Once Arianna has made up her mind, it's rarely possible to sway her, and it's rarely possible to sway anyone against her. I think my presence there amuses them, to be honest, since I'm the only one with the courage to speak my mind. It's astonishing to me how the most powerful sorcerers in the five kingdoms could be so weak and cowardly in the face of someone like Arianna – " He stopped suddenly, seeming to realize he was babbling. "For what it's worth, I'm sorry, and I'll continue doing what I can for you."

"It's very gracious of you to apologize, and we receive it," King Jazan told him. "Please convey our sincere regrets to Arianna and the rest of the Council."

"It looks like you're having second thoughts about your decision to leave," Cammie told Ennazar.

Yep. She was *extra* blurty today.

That got a dry laugh from Ennazar. "No one can undo the past, Cammaina. But each choice presents us with new opportunities that we could only have had by making that choice. I intend to find those opportunities and make the most of them."

"You take our best wishes with you," said King Jazan. "The next time we meet, I hope it will be on more favorable terms."

Ennazar nodded at the king and queen, then at Cammie and Eza, and then he was gone.

King Jazan sighed. "And just like that, we're alone against the storm. Our only hope is that Claira and Esteria don't find out about this immediately. As long as they think Telravia is still with us, they'll be tentative. Once they find out what's happened..." He paused, as if gathering his thoughts. "We have to send out diplomats immediately. We'll offer peace to Claira. Perhaps Cammaina can contact her father and request that he redouble his efforts."

Eza waited until he was sure King Jazan was done. "Your Highness, if I may..."

King Jazan held out his hand for Eza to continue.

Eza told him about Gar's visits, and what Gar had said about knowing who stole the dragons. "He made it sound like he was going to show up again and expect me to come help him. If he does that...what should I do?"

"Help him," King Jazan said instantly. "Go with him and help him. If he can tell you how our dragons were stolen, that is a significant victory. If you can persuade him to get the Artomancers on our side...that may just make up for the loss of Telravia."

Cammie snorted a laugh. "Gar? Help someone other than himself? Good one."

"Gar is...rather self-absorbed," Eza added helpfully.

King Jazan was trying to hide a smile, clearly amused by Cammie's outburst. "Then use that if you must. Appeal to his vanity. Or tell him you doubt he can help us; he may take it personally and want to prove you wrong."

"Ooh! I get to be the one who insults Gar!" Cammie said excitedly.

Queen Annaya laughed openly. "You are a ray of sunshine, Cammaina, and your presence here is a gift."

Cammie gave a curtsy. "Thank you."

King Jazan rose. "Dismissed. Go to Carnazon and train. Either we or Gar will have need of you very soon."

Eza suddenly remembered something he'd almost forgotten. "Your Highness, we brought back some weapons from the abandoned fortress. They appear to be...magical weapons. What should we do with them?"

"Are they with you at the moment?"

"No, Your Highness. They're at my house."

"Don't move them. I'll send someone by for them. The royal scholars will study them and see if they truly are magical weapons. If they are, and if we can make more...that would be quite the advantage."

Cammie tilted her head. "You know about magical weapons?"

King Jazan laughed. "Never heard of them, honestly." He looked at Queen Annaya, who also shook her head. "But they sound important, so we'll take them seriously. Thank you, Ezalen. Dismissed."

Cammie and Eza entered the south gate of Carnazon with textbooks under their arms – Cammie with *Victory Through Elemental Magic* and Eza with the Artomancy book Gar had given him. Denavi was right behind the two of them, but no one had found a healing-magic textbook for her, so she was there to figure things out on her own. The tangible buzz of magical energy teased Cammie's ears; it felt strange, as if an insect were flying close to her head. She knew she'd get used to it in time, but for now it was still strange.

The whole courtyard was full of students practicing magic or working with dragons. Target dummies had been set up along one wall and pillars made of stone by another wall so the elemental spellcasters could practice fireballs and lightning without setting a target dummy ablaze. Another corner of the courtyard was full of people sitting and reading, which was exactly where Eza and Cammie went...at least at first.

"I don't want to read anymore," Cammie said after about ten minutes. "I want to do magic."

Eza smiled at her. "You're really Exclaimovian this morning, aren't you?"

Cammie giggled. "That's me. Some days it hits hard, and today's one of them."

"Fine." Eza got to his feet. "Let's practice."

Cammie's first fireball nearly melted one of the stone pillars. "Whew!" she said excitedly. "I didn't realize it was going to be so easy on a node like this."

"Let me fix that for you," said Shanna from behind them.

"Shanna!" Eza said happily, hugging her. "It's great to see you again."

Shanna quickly put the pillar back together just in time for Cammie to unleash a vicious lightning cascade on it. "What about that lightning shield thing you did to the bears last month and the wolves this time?" Eza asked.

"Oh, this?" Cammie asked, whipping her hands out to create a glowing, crackling disc of lightning in front of her. With a thrust of her hands she sent it out to the stone pillar, where it wrapped around, sizzling and flickering as the rock absorbed the energy. "Yeah, that's fun."

"Do another fireball," Eza told her.

Cammie drew up energy from inside her, *feeling* the tingle within. Her muscles began to shake and her toes curled as she pushed the energy out into her hands and it left her palms in a fireball so intense the heat made her turn her face away –

But the ball had no sooner left her hands than it disappeared into a rainbow door, reappearing inches from the stone pillar, which melted into slag instantly.

"What'd you do?" Cammie screeched at Eza.

"I helped your fireball along. That may be useful in battle. I can rainbow door your fireball anywhere I want. I can hit people from the back, drop it on their heads..."

"Niiiiiice."

Shanna was staring at the gooey pile of rock, which was only now starting to solidify. "I don't know if I can fix that," she confessed.

"I want to try something else," Cammie told them. "Something I read in *Victory Through Elemental Magic*. Instead of one big fireball...I'm going to try a bunch of little ones."

Back when she'd first started reading from the textbook, she'd been surprised at how *intuitive* it was. She'd been expecting precise hand movements, or specific magic words, or something like that, but the book just kept telling her what she was supposed to *feel*, and sometimes it took a few tries before she could feel it the way the book described. For this spell, the book said it would help for her to visualize the magical energy inside her churning in circles, with small balls bouncing around inside it. Cammie was supposed to count the balls – however many she thought she saw in her imagination – and then guide them out of her hands until all of them had been launched.

It sounded simple enough.

So Cammie closed her eyes and envisioned a churning in her stomach, where ten – no, twelve – balls were bouncing around. She pushed her arms out and the fireballs burst from her – pop pop pop pop – smashing into what was left of that stone pillar and instantly turning to smoke.

"That was AMAZING!" she shouted, hardly believing she'd just done it. "Wow!"

"Oh, so we're doing a bunch of something now?" Eza asked.

"Why do you sound like you're going to try and top what I just did?"

"Because I am," he said with a smirk – and then there were eight of him.

"WHAT?!" she shrieked. "WHAT DID YOU JUST DO?!"

"It's a trick of the light," Eza's voice sounded as all eight Ezas moved their mouths. "It's kind of like the opposite of that invisibility spell I can do. Instead of seeing none of me, now you see a bunch of me."

"It works better than the invisibility spell," Cammie told him, examining all the copies. "That one doesn't quite work when you move, but I can't tell which of these is the real one."

"None of them," eight Ezas said with a chuckle. "I'm invisible in the middle of them." He blinked into sight at the center of the group.

"Do it to me!" Cammie demanded, bouncing up and down and clapping. Suddenly there were nine of her, eight copies and the real thing. "I'M GOING TO TICKLE YOU!" she shouted at Eza, and all the Cammies rushed toward him.

"Wait!" he shouted, and then he was collapsing to the ground, writhing in laughter, trying to defend himself but unable to tell which hands were the real ones.

"I told you I'd get you back," Cammie goaded him, poking him in the armpits and ribs and tummy.

But suddenly the other eight Cammies disappeared and she was the only one left, and Eza was bouncing up with revenge in his eyes.

"Truce?" Cammie said desperately, holding out her hand.

"For now," Eza answered, narrowing his eyes and smiling. "That was pretty clever. I really admire the way you think."

"Thank you," she told him. "I was pretty pleased

with myself, too."

Eza stretched his arms. "That's one really weird thing about Artomancy. Making myself invisible is easy; making you or Aleiza invisible takes a lot more energy. I could have kept those copies of myself going all day long, but when I did it to you, I was already feeling the strain after just a couple of seconds."

"That could have been the tickling," Cammie pointed out.

"Maybe. It just seems like it's easier when I do magic on myself than when I do it on someone else."

"I bet Gar can show you how to fix that." Cammie covered her mouth in pretend shock. "I just said something nice about Gar."

Eza let his eyes go wide, faking surprise as well. "The king did say we could appeal to his vanity. Maybe you were just practicing."

"You can do that part. I'm going to do the insulting."

"He'll be expecting that, though. It would really confuse him if you were doing the flattery and I was the one heaping doubts on him."

Cammie really didn't want to admit it, but Eza was right. Besides, it would be an *incredible* test of her acting ability for her to be kind to Gar. "I'll think about it," she said at last. "That's surprisingly sneaky for an Introvertian."

They stared at each other.

"Rub back off!" Eza laughed, chasing Cammie down and wiping his sleeve on her. "Rub! Back! Off!"

"Never!" she cackled. "I'm a part of you now."

"You definitely are. And I wouldn't have it any other way."

Cammie shook her head. "Stop being sweet when I'm trying to gloat. It takes all the fun out."

"Stop trying to gloat when I'm being sweet."

"But you're sweet all the time..."

Eza spread his hands. "Then I guess you can never gloat!"

"B – wh – NOT FAIR!"

"Who said anything about fair?"

A small cluster of other students had been watching the two of them from a distance, and now that it seemed like Cammie and Eza had reached a lull in their conversation, one of the girls approached. "Hi. You're Cammie Ravenwood, right?"

Cammie recognized Lizia Renan from her elemental magic class; she'd heard the girl's name once, and Cammie didn't forget things. "Hi, Lizia. I don't think we've been introduced, but yes, I'm Cammie."

"It's wonderful to meet you," Lizia said. "I watched some of your recitations during the Company Games and I thought you did a great job. I especially liked the group performance you did with Eza."

Cammie had been expecting her mind to reflexively

pull back from the compliments, but her normal skepticism and guardedness simply weren't there. "Thank you," she said. "That's very kind."

"I was wondering if you could show us how to do some of the magic spells you were just doing."

"I'd be honored," Cammie told her. "Bring your friends over. We'll work on it together."

The rest of Lizia's friends came over and Cammie quickly memorized their names. One other thing caught her eye, though. A little further away stood Anneka Azoana, who Cammie hadn't seen since before leaving for the fortress. Anneka had her arms crossed, but the look on her face wasn't the usual sneer of disgust that she wore around Cammie. It was...emptiness, like a person who was so sad that they couldn't even feel sadness anymore. Cammie wanted to go over and say something, but she knew she was the last person in the world that Anneka would ever talk to. Maybe Eza – no, she didn't like Eza either. Maybe she'd talk to Shanna? Or Lizia?

But in the time it took Cammie to make up her mind, Anneka had dropped her head and departed at a fast walk for the Harmony barracks.

Cammie trained Lizia and the others all afternoon, until it was nearly dark out. She didn't feel drained the way she often did when casting spells in combat, thanks to the crackling energy of the nexus node. Every so often she peeked over at Eza to see what he was accomplishing, and it looked like he was working very hard on the multiple copies spell. Aleiza was banking back and forth over the courtyard, doing pretend strafing runs, and Eza kept making more copies of her appear – eight at first, then an hour later nine, and by the end of the afternoon eleven.

He wasn't the only one who was pushing his boundaries. Cammie had figured out how to cast a different spell with each hand, launching a ball of water with her left just before a blast of lightning with her right, soaking the target so the lightning fried it even more perfectly. The next step after that was casting the lightning shield in front of her, then leaning around it to fire off an ice beam or a searing fireball – and then launching the lightning shield like she usually did. Excitement coursed through her as she watched spell after spell smash into the stone pillars, which Shanna kept reshaping into statues of birds and Clairan soldiers and trees. This felt incredible.

Only when she took a break did she glance up at the upper level of the fortress. Aleiza was perched on the roof of the east side guard tower, but hundreds of other dragons, maybe more than a thousand of them, lined the ramparts, feeding off the magical energy from the nexus node and the students casting spells in the courtyard. The sight gave Cammie goosebumps. She jumped as Eza came up behind her and slipped his hands around her waist.

"What are we looking at?" he asked.

"That," she said, pointing. A few dragons were playfully fighting in the air, zipping back and forth and roaring at each other. "This truly is a Dragon Academy now."

Eza nodded. "You've seen what Aleiza can do by herself. If these others keep growing, if every dragon-companion in the kingdom commands a dragon as big as she is, and if our magic keeps getting stronger...I mean, I know Gar said powerful people would be coming for the crystal, but on a night like tonight, maybe, just maybe, I can make myself believe we have a chance."

Cammie slid beside him, taking his hand. "Are you scared?"

"Yeah."

"Me too. But I'd rather be scared and next to you than not scared and anywhere else without you."

A slight smile teased Eza's face as he nodded. "Thanks." His fingers reached up, brushing Cammie's cheek. "I love you."

"I love you, too."

Hand in hand, they walked out through the south gate, strolling slowly, in no hurry to be anywhere. The purple sky turned black overhead and stars began to sparkle. "Want to help me write a new play when we get back?" Cammie asked.

"Always. What's this one going to be about?"

Cammie squeezed his hand. "We can figure it out together."

Dragon Academy Duty Assignment Survey

Greetings Cadet,

In just a few years, you will graduate from the Dragon Academy and receive the first duty assignment of your career as a dragon-companion. Whichever track you've declared for – and I will be having a followup conversation with each of you in several weeks regarding your choice of track – there are numerous opportunities for you to serve all around the kingdom of Introvertia.

Tranquility

The vast majority of all dragon-companions are stationed here in the capital city, whether soldiers or office workers. Mazaren Fortress and the outlying bases are home to around half of our standing army during peacetime – although nearly the entire army is here for the duration of the war. Many Rangers also operate out of Tranquility or the farming villages just to the north, scouting the eastern plains for wild animals or for signs of approaching enemy armies. The dragon program's main offices are located in Tranquility as well, along Broad Avenue just west of the Music Square.

As the largest city in the kingdom, with more than 300,000 residents, Tranquility is a hub for arts and culture. Six theater companies are based out of the capital; two art museums, a history museum, and several art academies are located here as well. For those who enjoy city life, and the option of having things to do when they don't want to be at home, Tranquility is the ideal choice. It does not, however, offer much in the way of outdoor recreation. With the exception of the Impassable Mountains to the east – which are not considered appropriate for recreational climbing – there are very few options for hiking, hunting, fishing, or canoeing within an easy walk from the city.

Tranquility's houses are primarily two stories tall and made of gray stone from the Impassable Mountains. Residential lots are typically large, with room in the back for a vegetable garden. It is common, in any given block of houses, for one lot to be left open so that evergreen trees and bushes can grow there.

Dawnrise City
Although generally thought of as merely a western suburb of Tranquility, Dawnrise is a full city in its own right, containing over 150,000 people. The dragon-companions here are based out of Ozion Fortress, on the

south side of the city, and are responsible for patrolling the Nether Reach, the strip of land south of the Rapidly Flowing River that separates Introvertia from the Great Sea. This strip has been left intentionally empty; although Introvertia could have settled it and established a trading port on the Great Sea, the fact is that we are happier *not* to have contact with other kingdoms. We patrol the Nether Reach regularly to ensure that no other kingdoms have set up outposts there; we have yet to find any evidence of this happening, thanks to a particularly vicious barrier shoal located off the coast, which prevents any ships from approaching.

Because of its position in the middle of the south-central part of the kingdom, there are not many opportunities for Rangers, nor are there many jobs for those on the political track, since the program offices are headquartered in Tranquility. The primary duty assignments are for combat soldiers. However, Dawnrise boasts a number of lakes and forested hiking trails north of the city, which are perfect for outdoor recreation, and the spring cherry blossoms must be seen to be believed, so it is widely considered an excellent duty station.

Homes in Dawnrise tend to be smaller than in Tranquility, typically one story and two to three bedrooms. On a dragon-companion's salary, you can certainly afford Tranquility, but if you wish to live below your means in order to save money for other hobbies, such as opening an art gallery or raising horses, Dawnrise's lower cost of living is perfect for you.

Rushwind

Tucked away in the extreme southwest of the kingdom, Rushwind is the second largest city in the kingdom, with nearly 250,000 people. There are a number of duty assignments available for all different tracks. Combat soldiers maintain a constant presence in the city, occasionally crossing the Rapidly Flowing River and traveling west to ensure that the land on the other side remains uninhabited, as well as doing their best to keep the Cloudscraper Mountains, which come very near to the town, free from wild predators such as wolves and bears. Rangers roam the mountain passes that separate Introvertia from no-man's-land to the west and from Telravia to the north. Rushwind is also the headquarters for the dragon trainers, those who work with very young dragons to teach them basic commands and behaviors before those dragons are paired off with Academy students who have completed their Year of Silence; many opportunities in that office are available to students on the political track.

Rushwind arguably has the greatest natural beauty of anywhere in the kingdom. With the Cloudscraper Mountains against the northwestern sky, dazzling sunsets on the other side of the Rapidly Flowing River, rolling hills and countryside, and tranquil lakes. It's also said that the citizens of Rushwind are the most open Introvertians in the kingdom: more likely to know their neighbors' names, a little more eager to smile at passersby instead of minding their own business, a little quicker with compliments. Not all Introvertians are alike, as we well know, so you may find yourself appreciating that openness – or not. If you prefer keeping to yourself, you will probably want to select a different duty assignment.

One-story homes in the city tend to be made with thick walls constructed from baked clay blocks, giving them a reddish color. Two-story homes are made from stone, or from a mixture of crushed stone with local clay. If there is one drawback to living in Rushwind, it would be that its position in the far southwest means that travel to the other cities can take a considerable time. Those with close family in Tranquility will want to think twice before requesting this duty assignment.

Resolve

Located in the far northeastern corner of the kingdom, fifty miles north of Tranquility and more than seventy miles northeast of Rushwind, Resolve is the city closest to both Telravia and Claira. That makes it a crucial pillar in the defense of Introvertia. About a third of the standing army is based out of Resolve during peacetime, along with the majority of the Rangers. In fact, Resolve is almost certainly the most interesting duty station for Rangers; on any given day they may be required to go up into the mountains, or to spy on the passes from Telravia, or to scout the Telravian border, or to ensure the safety of trade convoys heading toward the neutral towns in between the three kingdoms.

With a population of fifty thousand civilians – not counting the soldiers who happen to be stationed there at any given time – Resolve is the among the smallest duty stations. The options for arts and music and culture may be rather less than in Tranquility, but for those companions who like a quieter life in a smaller town, Resolve is a perfect choice.

The local architecture is almost exclusively stone, mostly due to convenience since the city butts up against the Cloudscraper Mountains, but also out of necessity so that the city could not be burned if it were ever attacked by Telravia or Claira. Resolve also sits on some of the most fertile farming land in the entire kingdom; the fields outside the city are bursting with ripe produce, so dragon-companions stationed here will get the freshest tomatoes, peaches, and strawberries in the whole kingdom.

As-needed

For those who prefer an even quieter place than Resolve, Ranger duty stations are available in small towns across the kingdom. On the eastern border, Rangers base out of approximately twelve farming villages, patrolling the eastern plains for predators and bandits; in the northwest, they keep station in the Cloudscraper Mountains, basing from one of the mining towns in the foothills. The Rangers at these stations tend to form very close, life-long bonds with each other, so if you're looking for deep friendships with a small number of Introvertians, in a place where life moves a little more slowly, consider taking a duty assignment at one of the as-needed locations.

As you can see, Cadet, your life is full of possibilities! You do not need to finalize your choice until just before your graduation, and you will be eligible for transfer after five years at your first duty assignment if you decide you'd like to see a different part of the kingdom. I would encourage you to spend some of your term breaks visiting these locations and seeing them with your own eyes so that you can make an informed decision.

As always, I appreciate your service to the kingdom. Our dragons are growing stronger every day as our cadets improve their magical ability. Your continued dedication to your studies is vital to the defense of Introvertia, and I am pleased to see every cadet doing his or her part to make the kingdom safe.

> General Anra Leazan
> Director, Dragon Academy
> Carnazon Fortress
> Tranquility, Introvertia

Dragon Academy Squad Duty Letter

Greetings Cadet,

I'm Colonel Naraza, the liaison between the army and the Dragon Academy. As you are no doubt aware, all third-year students are divided into squads for the purpose of advanced training. You will be in the same squad, with the same squadmates, from now until graduation – and quite possibly beyond, depending what duty assignments you and your squadmates receive.

Each squad is made up of twelve students, performing various different roles, just as in a real military unit. Here is a synopsis of each role:

Commanding Officer – this student's job is to lead the squad, as well as to determine battle strategy and tactics. One of the most important qualities of a good commanding officer is the ability to identify his soldiers' strengths in order to maximize them on the battlefield, so a good commanding officer will be observant and flexible. Many cadets want to be commanding officers, but I must warn you: this role is not for everybody. It requires exceptional humility; every success belongs to your people and every failure belongs to you, so you must be willing to take no credit when things go right and to shoulder all the blame when things go wrong. If all of this intrigues rather than frightens you, if you feel a strong pull to prove you're capable of that responsibility, you may request the role of commanding officer, subject to the directorate's approval.

Executive Officer (Second) – this student's job is to form a bridge between the commanding officer and the rest of the squad, as well as to assist the commanding officer as much as possible. If you are the sort of person who wants to help lead, but who does not want all the pressure of leadership as described in the previous paragraph, you may request the role of second.

Scout – there are typically two scouts within each squad, although the number may be three or even four at the commanding officer's discretion. Scouts must be comfortable functioning alone for extended periods of time, capable of maintaining their own focus – and keeping their dragons focused – through long watch shifts or in physically uncomfortable conditions. The scout's job is to feed useful information to the commanding officer and executive officer, whether about terrain, an enemy army's position or numbers, weather, or anything else you feel may be relevant. This is a crucial job; many battles throughout history have been won or lost based on the quality of an army's scouting.

Quartermaster – this student consults with the executive officer regarding the commanding officer's plan for a given maneuver or exercise and obtains any additional equipment or supplies that may be necessary. If the squad needs a wagon, or extra food, or some money to buy goods upon their arrival in a distant place, it is the quartermaster's task to requisition those things from the Academy and ensure that they are returned afterward. It may not sound like the most exciting assignment, but you will see the value of it the first time the squad shows up and all their equipment is already waiting for them so that they can move out immediately.

Soldier – five roles have been previously described, and the remaining seven members of the squad are the soldiers. I must be straightforward with you, Cadet. Often you will hear, from well-meaning people, that everyone should be eager to step up into leadership. But I ask you: if everyone was a leader, who would they lead? The kingdom needs followers, and we must not consider that word "follower" to be an insult, because soldiers who follow orders are the backbone of the army and of each squad. As such, the task of a soldier is to execute the commanding officer's instructions, and to work together with each other to ensure the success of the squad's operations. If you want no part of leadership, if you want to simply show up and do your duty, the soldier role is exactly what you're looking for.

If you have a preference regarding your role, please indicate that on the interest form available in my office. All role assignments will be ultimately decided by myself and the other officers on the directorate, according to the cadet's track record in his or her Academy classes and personality attributes as indicated on his or her intake test.

Good luck, Cadet. For many students, squad duty will be one of their most cherished memories of their time at the Academy. I hope you will say the same.

Colonel Kirian Naraza
Army Liaison, Dragon Academy
Carnazon Fortress
Tranquility, Introvertia

A Fury Like Thunder

The Adventure Continues!

Dragons of Introvertia Book Four
Tranquility Storm

With Carnazon Fortress restored to its former glory as a four-line nexus node, Cammie and Eza are improving at magic every day. But Gar the Artomancer has warned them that the other kingdoms will not simply stand back and allow Introvertia to become so powerful...

Yet Exclaimovia has still not entered the fighting. Can a desperate Esterian deception convince them to attack, or will they remain on the outside – for reasons that only they know?

And what will happen when the biggest battle in centuries comes to Introvertian soil?

Made in the USA
Coppell, TX
27 December 2024

43529660R10203